THE COMPLETE CASES
OF INSPECTOR ALLHOFF, VOLUME 2

THE COMPLETE CASES OF

INSPECTOR ALLHOFF™

VOLUME 2

D.L. CHAMPION

ILLUSTRATIONS BY
JOHN FLEMING GOULD

ALTUS
PRESS

BOSTON • 2018

TABLE OF CONTENTS

THE 10:30 TO SING SING

BIG JOE PETRONI HAD A SUNK-HINGED, GILT-EDGED, STEEL-BARRED, TIME-LOCKED AND CRACK-PROOF ALIBI FOR THE THIRD MURDER IN THAT AMAZING KILL-SEQUENCE—THE LEGLESS COFFEE-DRUNKARD OF CENTRE STREET HIMSELF—PLUS BATTERSLY AND SIMMONDS TO CORROBORATE IT. BUT THAT DIDN'T STOP ALLHOFF FROM PUTTING HIM ON THE 10:30 TRAIN FOR THE CHAIR UP THE HUDSON.

CHAPTER ONE
JOE ALIBI

THE BLIZZARD had raged two days and for the first time in my departmental career I found myself grateful for the fact that I sat warmly in Allhoff's tenement apartment instead of pounding a snow-driven beat.

Outside the window, down on Centre Street, a snow plow was stalled like a disabled tank. The boys from the sanitation department, red-faced, with heads bowed against the storm, struggled to get it going again. A copper, muffled up like a Russian general with a head-cold, plodded wearily around the corner and disappeared in the haze that fell white and silent from the clouds.

I turned from the window, sighed with vast satisfaction and lighted my pipe. I stretched out my legs and toasted my feet before the electric heater on the floor, reflecting comfortably that half the uniformed force was out in the cold combing the town for Big Joe Petroni. The sense of well-being that pervaded me was so rare in Allhoff's slum that I enjoyed it to the full.

Allhoff, himself, sat across the room, crouched over his desk, his little eyes riveted upon the coffee pot before him. He awaited with all the serene patience of a lustful rabbit, the brewing of his morning cup of coffee. Following his most rigid rule no word had yet been spoken, no police business had been transacted. Allhoff needed at least three

cups of coffee in the morning before either his tongue or brain cells began to function.

Around me the room was in its customary condition of disarray. Soiled linen was piled carelessly in one corner.

The dishes stood stacked and unwashed in the sink.
Through the open door of Allhoff's bedroom, the unmade
bed was visible, the sheets colored a dispirited gray.

The coffee pot began to gurgle and Allhoff pulled his thick chipped cup toward him. Outside I heard footsteps upon the rickety stairs. I heard voices, one of which I recognized as Battersly's. A few moments later Battersly entered the room alone.

He nodded to me behind Allhoff's back and took his seat at his desk, disturbing in no wise the episcopal silence of the apartment. Allhoff's hand shot suddenly out, snatched the coffee pot off its electric base and poured viscous fluid from its spout into his cup.

He shoveled sugar in with a prodigal hand, raised the cup to his lips and ingested the liquid with the sound of a cow delicately sipping a bowl of soup. He repeated this procedure three times in as many minutes. Then he uttered a bass melodic belch, pushed the chipped cup away, swung his head around and regarded Battersly and myself with obvious distaste.

"Well," he said with the air of a man making the best of his company, "what's new this morning?"

I put down the onion skin reports I had been reading. "Nothing," I told him. "Apparently the entire force is too busy looking for Big Joe Petroni to bother about anything else."

Allhoff grunted. It was a deep grunt and an eloquent one. It meant, I was well aware, that the police department in general and Battersly and myself in particular were unutterable idiots, that Inspector Allhoff was the only departmental brain in the whole city. It meant, moreover, that he calculated the chances of the force finding Big Joe were something in the neighborhood of twenty to one, while he, Allhoff, could have done it on his left ear if the commissioner had thought to ask him.

He grunted again and looked at the coffee pot speculatively as if considering whether his membranes could absorb another beaker of the black brew.

He decided in the affirmative, poured his cup full and remarked over his shoulder: "You'd think they'd work up a case first. From the reports they've got nothing on Big Joe. What do they want to pick him up for? Big Joe Petroni won't talk even if they borrow the rubber hose from the fire department."

I raised my eyebrows at that. "No case?" I said. "What do you want? A signed confession? There were two murders, weren't there? Buggsy Davis and Wally Rugene. They were both deadly enemies and competitors of Joe Petroni's. Joe had publicly threatened Buggsy for chiseling in on his Shylock racket, promised he wouldn't live a month. Wally Rugene was Buggsy's right-hand man. It was his testimony for the state that sent up Big Joe's kid brother only last year."

Allhoff turned a belligerent profile in my direction. "So what? Is that evidence?"

"It'll do until they turn up something else," I told him. "Who else had a motive for the murders?"

"You can't burn a guy, my thick-witted friend, by going around demonstrating no one else had any reason to commit the crime so it must have been him. The whole damned department's searching for Big Joe. All right, what are they going to do with him when they get him? Always provided they do find him. Joe's no dope. I bet he's not even in town. I bet—"

Battersly interrupted him by leaping to his feet and snapping his fingers. "Gee," he said, "I forgot."

Allhoff glared at him balefully. He didn't care much for *my* company, but his emotional attitude toward young Battersly was that of an enraged bull toward a matador.

"Forgot what?" he snarled. "Your corn plaster?"

Battersly flushed at that inference and I became alarmed myself. Allhoff was directing the conversation toward a channel that was deep, treacherous and conducive to headaches.

"No," said Battersly hastily as he strode toward the door. "The guy outside. He came in with me. I met him downstairs. He wanted to see you but I wouldn't let him. I told him to wait outside."

"Why?" snapped Allhoff.

The question was unnecessary. He knew the answer quite well. No one was permitted to speak to Allhoff before he had gulped a quart of his morning coffee. No stranger was permitted to enter his august and disheveled presence until he had steeled himself with caffeine.

Battersly tactfully let the question go. He went through the door to the hallway beyond. I heard the rumble of voices down the stairwell and a moment later Battersly reentered followed by a short wide Italian whose shoulders looked as if they had been constructed by a master bricklayer.

ALLHOFF STARED at the visitor with amazed and blinking eyes. I stood up myself, surprised. Allhoff's gaze moved suddenly to Battersly. His mouth contorted savagely. He took a deep breath and his voice pitched through the room, battered itself against our ears and the walls like an angry wave.

"You fool!" he roared. "Every copper on the force is combing the town for Big Joe Petroni and you—you won't let him in the house. You keep him waiting in the hall. Suppose he'd changed his mind and taken a powder. I'd've been the laughing stock of the whole damned city. You did it deliberately! You tried to make a fool out of me. My God, is there no end to the injury you do me? Wasn't it enough that—"

Apprehensive, I threw myself into the middle of his sentence in an effort to stem the tide.

"Allhoff," I said sharply. "Battersly didn't recognize Big Joe. He'd never seen him before. He—"

"Shut up," yelled Allhoff, his voice rising to a squeak. "You dumb, interfering louse. You—"

Big Joe Petroni cleared his throat. "It is a very bad thing for mor-morale," he said primly, "for flatfeet to fight among themselves, particularly in front of civilians."

This was a rather surprising maxim from Big Joe Petroni, but I was grateful for it. It took Allhoff's attention from Battersly. He turned his hot little eyes on Big Joe Petroni.

"That was a very beautiful thought, Joe," said Allhoff bitingly. "If you've any more of them you better talk fast because in ten minutes you'll be locked in a cell alone. With no audience."

"I don't want to go to the can, Inspector."

"Well, well," said Allhoff with a politician's phoney heartiness. "He doesn't want to go to the can. Neither did Mulenbroich. Neither did Capone. But they went, didn't they? And who the hell's going to keep you out of the can, Petroni?"

Big Joe Petroni took a thin cigar from his pocket and lighted it. It seemed to me that there was a flicker of nervousness in his eyes, yet his manner was assured enough as he spoke.

"I was hoping you would, Inspector. Seeing as how you got such a reputation for fair play and honest dealing, I come direct to you."

I exchanged a swift glance with Battersly. Big Joe was certainly laying it on with a trowel. If Allhoff had a reputation for fair play and honest dealing it had never reached my ears. However, at the moment, Allhoff nodded sagely and accepted the tribute as something rather too obvious to comment upon.

"So," went on Big Joe, "I come direct to you figuring I could get a fair shake."

Allhoff's lips twisted into what he firmly believed was a benignant smile. The one hole in his armor was flattery and it was apparent that Big Joe Petroni knew that as well as I.

"You'll get a fair shake," said Allhoff. "But headquarters wants you for questioning. There's nothing I can do about that."

"Sure there is," said Big Joe. "I didn't kill them two guys, Inspector. I'm clean."

"Why not tell that to the guys who're looking for you? I'm not on the case."

"I'll be honest with you," said Big Joe slowly. "I don't want to get smacked around by those dumb flatfeet who use nightsticks instead of brains like you, Inspector. I don't want to sit in a cell while my lawyer cuts the red tape. Besides, I don't want to be stuck for a big, legal fee, if I don't have to."

In all probability, I reflected, Big Joe was being honest. Though undoubtedly for reasons of expediency.

"Well," said Allhoff. "Where do I come in?"

"I didn't kill them guys," said Petroni. "And I can prove it. But if them flatfeet take me in they'll hold me for forty-eight hours. They'll smack me around a little just for the hell of it, whether I prove I'm innocent or not. So I figured if I give myself up to you, Inspector, if I prove to you that I'm clean, you'd fix things up so's I don't have to stand for the pinch."

AN UNHOLY light came in Allhoff's eyes. I knew what he was thinking. If, while the entire department was hunting for Big Joe, assuming he was implicated in two murders, Allhoff could produce him and also prove him innocent, it would once again be a great victory for Allhoff over the rest of the force.

He swung around in his swivel chair and faced me. "Simmonds, give me that first murder. Buggsy Davis. What've you got on it?"

I thumbed through the old reports.

"Davis," I read, "Robert Eugene, twenty-seven. Previous record—"

"The hell with the previous record," snapped Allhoff. "What about the actual killing."

"Found dead," I told him. "A bullet through his conniving skull, on February fourth. In his own home. The copper on the beat heard the shot at precisely two forty-three. He entered the house, found the body. The killer undoubtedly exited through the open rear window."

Allhoff nodded curtly. He turned to Big Joe Petroni. "All right," he said. "Now what have you got to say?"

"February the fourth," said Big Joe slowly. "Two forty-three. I got an alibi."

Allhoff snorted. "Don't expect me to take the word of stoolpigeons, punks, or that assorted mob of racketeers you keep on your payroll."

"Why, of course not," said Big Joe as if such a thing would never occur to him. "You'd take the word of the Federal Life Insurance Company, wouldn't you?"

"Go on," snapped Allhoff. "Give me the details?"

"On February fourth from twelve thirty until some time after three I was in the offices of Federal Life applying for insurance. I filled out the papers, went to their doctor, waiting for a half-hour till he was ready for me, then took my physical examination. I didn't leave there until at least half past three."

"Check that," said Allhoff to me. "Right away."

THE ROOM was silent as I picked up the phone. Battersly watched Big Joe and Allhoff like a child enjoying his first play. Big Joe chewed blandly at his cigar, apparently quite calm beneath Allhoff's searching gaze. I talked over the telephone for some ten minutes and then hung up.

"Click," I said. "Joe has his alibi."

Allhoff grunted. "All right," he said. "Give me that other case."

"Wally Rugene," I read. "Shot through the heart, found in a Brooklyn alley. February twelfth. Time of death uncertain. The M.E. estimated he'd been dead anywhere from twelve to twenty hours when a street cleaner found him."

"Go ahead, Joe," said Allhoff. "Alibi that."

"Cruise," said Big Joe.

"Cruise?"

"Bermuda. Left on the tenth. Got back six days later. Atlas Steamship Company."

"Check that," said Allhoff to me.

I checked it telephonically. Big Joe Petroni was so serene during the call that I knew the answer before I got it.

"Right," I told Allhoff. "Joe was in Bermuda."

"See, Inspector," said Big Joe. "I'm clean, see. I come to you for a fair shake. I want you to take the heat off of me."

Allhoff expelled his breath thoughtfully and reached for the coffee pot. I considered the situation and decided that for once Big Joe was telling the truth. If the coppers picked him up, he would probably sit in a cell all night, he would undoubtedly get stuck for a fat legal fee and it was not beyond the realm of possibility that some Irish sergeant who didn't like crooks would take a poke at him.

To avoid these things Big Joe had shrewdly played on the fact that Allhoff loved to show up the uniformed force, to demonstrate how perennially wrong they were while Allhoff, by his own admission, had never made a mistake in his life.

Allhoff emptied his coffee cup, put it down and grinned. "Well, Joe," he said.

The telephone ringing on my desk interrupted him. I picked it up and listened to the voice on the other end. I hung up and announced to the room in general: "Paul Wexler was killed fifteen minutes ago. Headquarters thought we'd like to know."

I met Big Joe's eye and I thought I saw a flicker of amusement there.

"Paul Wexler," said Allhoff. "Policy guy, wasn't he? He'd been chiseling in on your district, hadn't he, Joe?"

Big Joe Petroni lied with his face. He looked blank and thoughtful as he said: "Wexler? Wexler? I don't believe I know the name, Inspector."

"Joe," I said, "you're a Sicilian liar. You know Wexler as well as you know your own name. There's been stoolpigeon talk that you were going to get him, take over his policy game."

Big Joe took his cigar from his mouth. "I'm clean, Inspector," he said. "I got an alibi."

"Sure," I said bitterly. "And we're it. Besides, headquarters said that they got the guy that killed him. Nailed him running away from Wexler's car, a gun in his hand."

Big Joe sighed gently. "Well, will you take the heat off of me, Inspector."

Allhoff lifted his coffee cup and spoke over its chipped rim.

"Joe," he said with suspicious softness, "I'll take the heat off you. But it strikes me that maybe you've overplayed the hand. It occurs to me that there's more to this case than meets the eye. I'm looking for it."

Big Joe Petroni shrugged. "Go ahead, Inspector," he said. "I'm clean. All I was asking was a fair shake. I knew you'd give it to me. I'm at the Royal Hotel if you want me." He turned around and went out the door.

ALLHOFF STARED after him for a long time, until the sound of his footsteps died out down the stairway.

"Gee," said Battersly, who could appreciate the obvious as well as any man. "Petroni had foolproof alibis. The department would've looked pretty silly if they'd put him in jail."

Neither Allhoff nor myself paid any attention to this profundity. Battersly, who possessed the tact of a Japanese diplomat, continued: "Anyway, by letting him go, the inspector didn't put his foot in it."

I got to my feet, drew an involuntary breath of horror. Battersly looked at me and, as the significance of his ill-chosen phrase dawned upon him, his face turned white. Allhoff's coffee cup struck the desk-top like a falling bomb.

He swung around in his chair pushing it away from the desk.

As his body came clear, two wriggling stumps revealed themselves at the point where his thighs should have begun. He hammered his clenched fist on the wooden arm of his chair. His eyes blazed with furious fire. His face was a twisted mask of evil. His lips contorted as if he were on the verge of a sudden epilepsy. Then his voice roared through the room like a diving plane.

"You dare say that to me!" he shouted. "Put my foot in it, eh? Damn you, my foot is buried six feet in the ground. Thanks to you and your lousy yellow belly manners! You filthy—"

He groped down in the sewers of his vocabulary and came up with a group of nouns whose vileness was equaled only by the adjectives.

Young Battersly's face was deadly pale. His lips were tightly compressed and there was a misery in his eyes that made my stomach turn over.

"Allhoff," I said shortly. "Allhoff, listen to me."

He took his eyes from Battersly and turned them on me. I could almost feel their heat.

"Keep out of this. You hate me as much as he does. Sometimes I think that if he hadn't robbed me of my legs you would have done it. You're the same yellow type. The same—"

The deeper pools of his vocabulary, I learned, were by no means plumbed yet. He hurled invective at me until he was exhausted. I took it calmly enough. I was used to it and I preferred to have the storm of his wrath gather about my head than about Battersly's.

At last, out of breath, Allhoff abruptly turned back to his desk, filled his cup with coffee and, still breathing hard, buried his corvine nose in its murky depths.

I went back to the papers on my desk. Battersly stared savagely out the window into the snow-driven depths of Centre Street below. I had dwelt in the middle of this situation for some five years now without learning to relish it.

IT HAD its genesis some time back when Battersly was a raw recruit and Allhoff, legs and all, an Inspector on active duty. A raid on a gangster's hideout on upper West End Avenue had been scheduled with Allhoff as leader of the raiding party. Battersly's assignment had been to effect a rear entrance, disable the Tommy-gun operator, who, our stoolie had informed us, was guarding the stairway facing the door.

Battersly obeyed the first part of his orders, all right. That is, he gained entrance to the house. Then he developed a quite understandable attack of buck fever. Instead of closing with the thug at the machine gun he fled up the stairway at the precise moment that Allhoff, at the head of his squad, axed in the front door.

The first burst from the machine gun riddled twenty holes in Allhoff's legs. A week later gangrene set in and amputation was necessary to save his life. There were many times when I found myself wishing it hadn't.

Of course, all of us in the department had figured that this was the end of Allhoff's career. But the commissioner was of no mind to lose his best man so easily. Since a police inspector minus his legs was a Civil Service impossibility, the commissioner had arranged things so that

Allhoff, through devious bookkeeping, still drew his former salary and still did a full day's work for it.

Officially unattached to the force, Allhoff had rented this slum tenement because of its proximity to headquarters. There, well in the commissioner's graces because of his undoubted ability, he wielded as much influence as ever before. Which was far too much for my liking.

With a nice sense of ironic justice the commissioner had granted Allhoff's Machiavellian request that Battersly be assigned to him as assistant. I, as an old-timer who had come up with Allhoff, had also been detailed to his office, ostensibly to take care of the paperwork, actually to step in when Allhoff became too hysterically angry at the younger man.

For that amputation had cost Allhoff more than his legs. It had cost him some of his reason, too. He had become a bitter, brooding old man who at times teetered over the balance line which divides sanity from madness.

Anyway, here we were, the three of us, for better or worse. Each day's routine was a hell that had to be lived through. Though, had it not been for my family and the pension which was due me in a few years I would have quit long ago. Battersly, with a martyr's sense of expiation, resolutely stuck to his job no matter what indignity Allhoff heaped on his head.

CHAPTER TWO

PROTECTION

FOR A KILLER

I ARRIVED at Allhoff's apartment the following morning some forty minutes late. Battersly was already there and Allhoff had consumed his matutinal gallon of coffee. He looked up as I entered and surprisingly enough, grinned.

"We've got a case," he said. "And they're sore at me."

"Who's sore at you?"

"Those uniformed morons across the street. They're sore because I sprung Big Joe."

He grinned happily as I regarded him curiously. The single thing that seemed to give him any measure at all of enjoyment was the fact that someone was sore at him.

"Yeah," he went on. "They say they might've got some information out of Big Joe if they'd got their hands on him. Those three killings have got 'em licked. Especially the last one. You know, Wexler."

"Wexler," I said, taking off my coat. "I thought they caught the killer red-handed. That's what the morning paper said. A guy named Muller."

"That's what they thought," said Allhoff. "But they can't figure it. They're sending him over here to me."

I sat down and scratched my head. "But the beat copper heard the shot, caught the guy with the gun in his hand."

"No motive," said Allhoff.

"There must be a motive. Or else the guy is nuts. What the hell do they mean no motive?"

"For once you're right," said Allhoff. "Of course there's a motive. They're just too dumb to figure it. That's all. They claim this guy Muller is a thirty-dollar-a-week book-keeper. They claim he never knew Wexler at all. That there was absolutely no connection between him and Wexler. This Muller, they say, is an ordinary clerk. No underworld connections at all."

"Well," I said, "Someone's wrong."

"Naturally. *They* are. That's why they're sending him over to me."

At that moment I heard heavy footfalls on the stairs. Battersly stood up and opened the door. A heavy Irish copper named Reardon came in. Handcuffed to him was a thin insignificant-looking guy whose pinched face was pale, whose blond mustache was twisted upward with what seemed pathetic bravado.

Reardon saluted and in response to Allhoff's gestured invitation sat down. Muller, perforce, sat down in the chair next to him. Allhoff reached for the coffee pot, filled his cup and stared at little Muller with his evil eyes.

Muller looked more frightened than ever. Allhoff lifted his coffee cup and drained it without removing his gaze from the prisoner. He banged the cup back on the desk and said: "So this is the killer, eh, Reardon? And he won't talk?"

"He'll talk," said Reardon, "but what he says don't make no sense. He says he held a grudge against Wexler. We checked and checked and there ain't no tie-up between them. None of Wexler's guys ever seen him. He was never in none of Wexler's hang-outs neither."

Allhoff eyed Muller unpleasantly as if he had one hell of a nerve coming along and confusing the police department. Muller, without waiting for Allhoff's question, said suddenly: "It's a lie. I knew Wexler. Saw a lot of him around the night clubs."

"So," said Allhoff. "You run around to nightclubs."

Muller nodded. "Sure. Every dime of my salary goes on liquor and women. Money's only made to spend. I was on a lot of parties with Wexler."

I looked at Muller and got the impression of an anemic Flatbush Don Juan.

Allhoff said: "And how much is your salary?"

"A little under forty dollars a week."

"And it all goes on nightclubs and women, eh? What's your wife have to say about that?"

"She's dead," said Muller. "I'm a widower."

"No family?"

"One daughter."

Allhoff refilled his coffee cup and picked it up. "Where's she? Does she live with you?"

"Yes, but—but—she's not home now."

Allhoff put down the cup and looked at Muller as if he had something. "Where is she?"

"Upstate. Visiting an aunt. Now look here, Inspector. I admit shooting Wexler. Isn't that enough? Isn't that the end of the matter?"

"I hardly think so," said Allhoff slowly. "As a matter of fact, I think it's only the beginning. Reardon, take him away."

Reardon took him away and as their footsteps vanished down the stairs Allhoff turned to us. "You, two. Go out to Muller's apartment. Look around. Test your powers of observation. And for once in your lives bring me back some evidence voluntarily without my having to drag it out of you."

Battersly and I donned our hats and coats and went out, none too happily, into the blinding snow storm.

A LITTLE more than an hour later, Battersly and I returned to Allhoff's apartment with a collection of varied, and as I saw it, thoroughly futile information. He tore the coffee cup away from his lips as we came in and proceeded to fire questions at us.

"Well, what did you find? Papers? Letters? Any tie-up with Wexler that the dumb coppers overlooked? There must've been something there."

He stared at us eagerly. I reflected that Allhoff's interest in justice was nothing compared to his desire to show the lads in blue across the street that he was their master.

"Take it easy," I told him, "and prepare yourself for a disappointment. We found nothing. Absolutely nothing."

He scowled at me and said insultingly: "How would you know? Battersly, tell me what you saw in Muller's apartment. Never mind how trivial you think it is. Tell me everything."

"Well," said Battersly uncomfortably, "it was a pretty ordinary apartment, Inspector. Maple furniture. Neat and clean but cheap. You know."

"The sort of a place," I broke in, "where the average thirty-five-dollar-a-week clerk would live if he had a child to support."

Allhoff sipped his coffee sibilantly. He lifted his head from the cup and said suddenly: "Papers? Any papers in the place?"

"The usual papers," I told him. "Gas bills, rent receipts, a time-payment book, old circulars—"

"Payment for what?" snapped Allhoff, turning on me.

I shrugged my shoulders. "I don't know. I just happened to notice the book. You don't think he bought the gun he shot Wexler with on time, do you?"

His angry gaze hit me with almost physical impact. "Damn you!" he yelled. "I get no cooperation in this office. You two deliberately try to hinder me. Back from that day when—"

He glared balefully at Battersly who temporarily stemmed the tide of his wrath by murmuring: "Them time payments was on the radio, Inspector. I happened to notice that."

Allhoff grunted, somewhat mollified. "Radio, eh? What sort of radio? Did either of you happen to notice?"

"There were two radios in the house," I told him. "Which one would you like described?"

"Both of them."

I sighed. The conversation was fruitless and pointless. Allhoff was gathering not a single bit of evidence from our facts. But, by God, he was going to pretend he saw significance in each tiny item merely to show us what a subtle gigantic brain functioned beneath his uncombed hair.

"There was a small radio, a ten-dollar one in the room which I figured belonged to Muller's daughter. There was a big one in the living-room. Undoubtedly it was the big one that he was making the installment payments on. Now that you have that fact, I suppose you can easily tell us why Muller killed Wexler."

To my surprise he let that crack go.

"What was it worth, do you figure? The big radio?"

"Oh, I don't know. Possibly a couple of hundred dollars. Eh, Battersly?"

Battersly agreed it was worth a couple of hundred dollars.

"Ah," said Allhoff with vast satisfaction. "That's the first thing I've had to work on since they dropped this damned case in my lap."

I was too tactful to obey my immediate impulse to call him a liar. Allhoff didn't have a thing. I was certain. His pretense that he did was calculated to impress Battersly and myself.

Grateful silence filled the room. Battersly turned to his favorite intellectual pastime—a scrutiny of the comic pages in the evening paper. I lit my pipe and attended to some routine, while Allhoff sipped coffee with horrible sounds and glared at the wall thoughtfully.

THE STEPS came up the stairway outside swiftly, noisily, and with staccato panic. The door pushed open and Frankie Hadderman burst into the room. He stood near the door for a moment, his twisting lips almost as white as his sagging cheeks. His hands moved nervously at his sides. His eyes were wide open, gray, and filled with terror.

"Inspector," he said and his voice quavered. "You got to help me, Inspector. You got to save my life. The coppers laughed at me. Wouldn't give me no help. They can't do that, Inspector. It ain't right. You got to help me. Got to give me protection."

Allhoff eyed him with distaste. Frankie Hadderman was the sort of crook that every copper regards with hatred and contempt. Frankie had dipped into every sordid crime in the book. White slavery and dope peddling were two of his more elevating avocations. Headquarters knew damned well that he had killed at least a dozen men. Time and again the D.A. had tried to convict him. Time and again he had failed. The witnesses had strange ways of dying, disappearing, or changing their testimony every time Frankie Hadderman stood in the dock.

"Protection?" said Allhoff. "Give you protection? Hell, I'd clean the gun of the guy who killed you. Get out of here!"

Hadderman shook his head like a feverish aspen leaf. His chin trembled and he clasped his hands before his chest. He rushed into the room and threw himself on his knees at the side of Allhoff's desk.

"No," he shrieked and his voice hit the ceiling, crescendo. "No. You can't do this to me. He got the other guys, didn't he? He killed the other guys. Now he's trying to get me. I gotta have police protection, Inspector. You can't turn me down."

Disgusted, I turned my head from Hadderman. Allhoff, for the first time, evinced some interest.

"Who killed three guys? Get up, you rat. Get up and tell me who killed three guys?"

Hadderman stood up on trembling knees. "Joe Petroni," he said in a rustling whisper. "He killed them other guys, didn't he? He knocked off Buggsy, Rugene and Wexler, didn't he? The finger's on me next. He's going to get me unless I got protection."

"Petroni had cast-iron alibis on those three killings," said Allhoff. "And the guy who killed Wexler's in the can right now."

Hadderman shook his head stubbornly. "I don't care who's in the can. I don't care what alibis Joe's got. Lookit. Three guys—all guys Joe was sore at—got theirs. Joe was sore at me, too. And a guy just blasted at me. No, sir. It's Joe Petroni. And he's going to get me, too. For God's sake, Inspector—"

"Shut up," said Allhoff blandly. "Shut up and tell me just what happened."

Frankie Hadderman pulled himself together with almost a physical effort. He spoke rapidly and jerkily as he strove to keep the fear out of his voice.

"I come out of the house today, see. I go down to the saloon where I hang out. I'm being extra careful, too, because I don't like the way them three other guys got theirs. Still I ain't really sure Joe done it. Not then. A guy comes up in a car just as I'm going in the saloon. He fires two shots at me and scrams. He misses twice. But I'm scared, see."

"Wait a minute," snapped Allhoff. "Who was this guy? Did you see him?"

"Sure, I seen him. But it ain't no guy I ever seen before. He don't look like a hired gunman, either. He's a little guy. A little guy in a gray suit. Looked like a clerk or something."

"So," said Allhoff, "like a good solid citizen and tax-payer you went to the police, eh?"

"Sure," said Hadderman slightly relieved as he took Allhoff's irony for commendation. "Sure, that's what I done, Inspector. I went to the precinct house. I asked the sergeant for protection. He laughs at me."

"What'd he say?"

"He told me to go to hell. Said he was in favor of someone knocking me off. Said the city'd be better off without me. Told me to see you, Inspector. Said the coppers weren't on the case any more, that you took it away from them. He was sore at you, too. He called you a name."

Allhoff beamed. He relished being called a name by the uniformed squad.

I SAW the sergeant's point quite well. In the first place I understood why he wasn't at all interested in the sudden demise of a rat like Hadderman. Second, he was nettled at the fact of Allhoff's fluking Petroni's capture and springing him before the boys could ask him some pointed questions. So, since Hadderman wanted protection from Petroni, he had been sent to Allhoff.

Allhoff spilled coffee into his cup. "I'm beginning to like this case," he said to me. "I think I'll solve those three killings."

"Two," I said. "You can't get around the fact of Muller."

"Maybe I can," said Allhoff thoughtfully. "Call Big Joe at his hotel."

I picked up the phone. "What'll I tell him when I get him?"

"Oh," said Allhoff, "he probably won't be in. I just want to see if I'm right."

I looked up the number and dialed it. "If you're so damned omniscient," I said, "where is Big Joe?"

"Well," said Allhoff, considering, "he may be calling on a big-shot lawyer on business. He may be down at the license bureau getting a driver's or a hunting license. He may even be in church."

That sounded like gibberish to me until I got the call through and spoke to the hotel operator. I hung up the receiver, looking at Allhoff in bewilderment. He met my eye mockingly.

"Well?"

"Mr. Petroni," I told him, repeating verbatim what the hotel had reported, "has gone over to Saint Malachi's chapel to discuss a personal matter with Father O'Brien."

"I thought so," said Allhoff with a touch of grimness. He turned to Hadderman. "Frankie, I've decided to give you protection." He shut off Hadderman's thanks with a gesture. "Simmonds, you and Battersly accompany Hadderman to his home. Tail him down the street at a discreet distance. Keep out of the way when you get to his house.

I don't want it to look too obvious that he's traveling with a bodyguard."

Frankie Hadderman shook his head again.

"That ain't no good, Inspector. They got to keep up close to me. That guy's liable to try to get me again. He's crazy as a—"

"Shut up," said Allhoff again. "I don't give a damn about you, Frankie. I want to see the guy who's shooting at you. If he thinks you've got a couple of coppers with you he might lay off. I want him to try again. When he does, Simmonds, grab him. Bring him in to me. Bring Hadderman back, too. Now get going, the three of you."

Battersly and I stood up and walked toward the door. Frankie, looking like a guy at his own funeral, stood still, stretching his hands out in appeal.

"No, Inspector. You can't do that. Suppose he shoots me. I gotta have—"

Allhoff glared at him over the rim of his coffee cup. "Get out!" he yelled. "Get out, or by God, I'll shoot you myself."

He made a movement to open the upper desk drawer. There was scurrying movement in the room as Frankie Hadderman hastened toward the door. He beat Battersly and myself into the street by a good twenty seconds.

CHAPTER THREE

LITTLE MAN WITH A GUN

FRANKIE HADDERMAN lived in a three-room flat on West 54th Street. The living-room, in the rear, opened on a typical New York garden, small, square, floored with dispirited grass, a flourishing ailanthus tree in its center.

Hadderman, as calm as a hurricane, paced up and down the living-room floor. From time to time he would deliver his profane opinion of a police department that refused to protect the life of a taxpayer. Battersly smoked cigarettes glumly while I looked at my watch and wondered how long I was supposed to sit here. Allhoff had set no time limit so I was looking forward to no dinner and an all-night vigil.

A little after six o'clock Battersly got up and wandered into the bathroom. I suddenly became struck with an idea and asked Frankie if there was such a thing as a drink in the house. Without marked hospitality he directed me to the kitchen. I went in there and proceeded to pour myself a slug of dubious blended whiskey.

I stood frozen with the bottle in my hand as I heard Frankie's sudden yell of terror.

He cried out: "Don't shoot me, pal. Don't shoot. I ain't done nothing to you. I don't even know you. I—"

A voice, tense and almost as fearful as Hadderman's answered.

"Why should I care about you? Why? There are those to whom I owe protection. Others—"

There seemed to me to be a sob in his voice as the word broke off in his throat.

Battersly, gun drawn, charged past me from the bathroom. I followed on his heels. We burst into the living-room to find Frankie Hadderman cowering in a corner. His face was the color of desert sand. His jaws worked convulsively and his eyes were the eyes of a man already dead.

Facing him, an automatic in his hand, was a man of middle height and medium build. His cheeks were pale and the hand that held the automatic trembled. All in all he appeared almost as afraid as Frankie Hadderman.

He took his eyes from Hadderman as we came into the room. He stared for a moment at the Police Specials Battersly and I had drawn. His fingers slowly relaxed and his own weapon thudded to the carpeted floor.

Then just as Battersly and I were upon him he did a peculiar thing. He buried his face in his hands and wept, frightfully and horribly, his shoulders moving convulsively as the sobs wracked his body.

I took his arm as Battersly snatched the automatic from the floor. Hadderman, observing his assailant disarmed, found fresh courage. He stood up straight and walked across the floor with his fists clenched.

"You yellow rat," he said. "I'll knock all your teeth out. I'll—"

He grabbed the other by the hair and jerked his head up. I moved forward and slapped Hadderman hard in the face. He looked at me in astonishment.

"He tried to knock me off, didn't he? Leave me take a poke at him. Just one poke. I-"

"There ought to be a reward for knocking you off," I told him. "Grab him, Battersly. We're all going back to Allhoff's."

By the time we reached Allhoff's slum, Frankie Hadderman had thoroughly convinced himself that he was the outraged citizen. No sinless bank president could have been more indignant, more resentful at police conditions which allowed such things to happen.

I told Allhoff what had happened at Frankie's house while Hadderman stood before Allhoff's desk and pointed a trembling forefinger at the man who had entered his apartment with the gun.

"I never did nothing to him," he declaimed. "I never even seen him before. And the rat tried to knock me off.

Sneaked in over the back fence wearing crepe soles. I never even heard him till he was in the room. And them two coppers was outside drinking."

Allhoff put down his coffee cup. He looked at Battersly and myself as if he were about to deliver a diatribe on the evils of drinking in uniform. Then he thought better of it. He told Hadderman to shut up once again and turned to the other prisoner.

"Name?" he roared. "What's your name?"

The man lifted a frightened face. He spoke in a low dull tone as if he were beyond all caring. "Weldon," he said. "Wallace Weldon."

"Occupation?"

"Junior accountant."

ALLHOFF SLOSHED coffee in his cup and ladled in sugar as if national rationing was imminent. He lifted the cup to his lips and closed his eyes registering deep and profound thought. He put the cup down again and said very slowly: "Of course, you're married, Weldon."

Weldon nodded dispiritedly. "Yes, I'm married."

I scratched my head and exchanged a glance with young Battersly. It was obvious Allhoff, completely baffled, was merely asking questions for the sake of asking them. I decided to needle him a little.

"Why don't you ask him how many kids he's got? That ought to clear things up."

Allhoff lifted his lids slightly. "It probably will," he said without losing his temper. "I'm going to ask that question in a very little while. Now, Weldon, why did you try to kill Hadderman here? Did he ever do anything to you?"

"I never even seen him before," screamed Frankie. "How could I do anything to him? How could I—"

Allhoff picked a ruler up from his desk. He swung it through the air like a sword and slapped Hadderman's face with the flat side, leaving a swathe of red an inch wide across his cheek.

"Now," he said sweetly, "will you shut up?"

Weldon spoke in a dispirited monotone. "He's right," he said. "He's never done anything to me."

"Well," I said, "why did you try to kill him?"

Weldon shook his head. He reminded me very much of a Belgian peasant sitting in the middle of the German invasion. He just didn't care about anything any more.

"All right," said Allhoff. "Now, Weldon. Let's get back to the question propounded by my brilliant colleague. Have you any children?"

"Yes," said Weldon in a low frightened voice. "Two children. A boy and a girl."

"Where are they?"

Weldon lifted his eyes to meet Allhoff's for the first time since he had been in the room.

"Home, I suppose," he said scarcely audibly.

"Really?" said Allhoff. His manner was casual but I knew him well enough to realize that his mind was working at top speed, that there was hidden significance to what he said. "Are you sure, Weldon? Stop and think. Perhaps one of them is away? Visiting some relative, perhaps?"

Weldon clutched at the suggestion like a drowning man at a straw. "Sure," he said. "That's right. I forgot. Yes, my boy, Arthur. Visiting his cousin in Maine."

"What's the cousin's address?"

Weldon licked his lips. "I don't exactly know," he said. "I undoubtedly have it at home. I—"

"Never mind," said Allhoff. "Battersly, take them both across the street."

Frankie Hadderman drew himself up like an indignant society dowager.

"You mean to the can?" he demanded. "You can't put me in the can. I didn't do nothing. I was shot at. You can't put a guy in the can for being shot at."

Allhoff looked at him. That look boded no immediate joy for Frankie Hadderman.

"You're not going to the can for being shot at," said Allhoff gently. "I can dig up a better reason than that."

He turned to me. "Simmonds, book both these guys for assaulting an officer. I don't want Weldon charged with attempted murder—yet, anyway. The story is that Battersly was walking down the street and these two guys jumped him. Fix it so they don't get a hearing. I don't want them bailed. Now get them out of here."

Weldon, maintaining his air of utter dejection and indifference, stood up without protest. Hadderman opened his mouth and objected loudly.

"You can't do it!" he yelled. "I'm clean. I'm a citizen. I know my rights. I—"

Allhoff's brows lowered and he picked up his ruler. Hadderman backed away and shut his mouth abruptly.

"One more thing," said Allhoff. "I want to see that guy, Muller, right away. You and Battersly may go home to dinner. I've kept you late enough. Have a copper bring Muller over here as soon as possible."

We took Weldon and Hadderman from the room, went across the street and booked them. I hadn't the slightest idea what was going on in Allhoff's head, but his sudden solicitude about keeping Battersly and myself overtime, had made me very, very suspicious.

CHAPTER FOUR
THE 10:30 TO SING SING

WE SAT in silence the next morning as Allhoff poured coffee down his blasphemous gullet. As soon as the third pint had been emptied into his stomach, he swung around abruptly in his chair and snapped: "Battersly, get me Hadderman. Spring him. Get his name off the blotter. Have them give him back his property."

Battersly got up and strode out of the room. I watched Allhoff curiously. There was something assured about his manner. From whatever evidence I had noted about this damned case, there was nothing resembling a final conclusion, but Allhoff acted for all the world as if he had the whole thing wrapped up, in the bag, and ready for delivery.

I tried to draw him out. "Well," I said, "and what do you expect to find out from your pal, Hadderman."

He snorted. "My pal," he said heavily. "That rat. Frankly, I'd rather put that guy away than Big Joe. Joe's a crook and a bum. But he's not the complete rat Hadderman is."

I agreed with him on that point, and said so. "If I had the choice," I told him. "I'd sooner see Hadderman burn than Joe, too."

He swung around in his chair and regarded me oddly. "You wouldn't care just how he died, would you? You wouldn't insist on his burning?"

"No, I wouldn't. But since you're not quite God yet, you don't control deaths, or means of dying."

His lips twisted into an odd ironic smile. "Maybe, I do," he said slowly. "Maybe I do."

I didn't know what he meant but considering his tone, I was glad it wasn't my demise he was discussing.

Battersly came back holding Hadderman's wrist. Frankie was still scared but still indignant.

"I want a lawyer," he shrilled as soon as he came in. "I insist on my rights. I—"

Allhoff ignored him. He spoke to Battersly. "You saw to it that he was properly released—received his property back?"

"Yes, sir. Even the rod that he had a permit for."

"Ah," said Allhoff, "I thought as much. Take him into my bedroom there. Take his gun away and put it in the bureau drawer. Then handcuff him to the steam-pipe in the bathroom. Give him a chair to sit in. He may be there for some time."

Frankie Hadderman lifted his voice in loud and bitter protest. I raised my eyebrows. What Allhoff had up his sinister sleeve, I didn't know. However, it was clear that he was knocking a large and jagged hole in the Bill of Rights. Unless he pinned something on Hadderman, there would be a repercussion from headquarters on the extra-legal treatment he was handing out. He had as much right to hold Frankie in his bedroom as Hitler had to invade the Netherlands.

Battersly, who had learned better than to question an order, dragged the protesting Hadderman off into Allhoff's bathroom. A moment later he emerged again, closing the door behind him.

Allhoff busied himself with the percolator and kept his mouth shut. That silence endured until a few moments before twelve. Then he looked up suddenly and said: "You two guys go to lunch. I want to be alone for a few moments. I have to think. Oh, and while you're out give Big Joe a ring at his hotel. Tell him I want to see him about two o'clock. Have Muller and Weldon here then, too."

He was so damned matter-of-fact that, for a moment, I believed he had the case all figured out. Then, considering all angles, I decided he was bluffing. On the face of things he didn't have enough evidence for a traffic rap on Big Joe and Hadderman. Besides, it was impossible to disregard the fact that Muller was nailed dead to rights, and Weldon, too.

I decided to eat an expensive steak for lunch and forget the whole thing.

BY TWO thirty we were all assembled. Big Joe Petroni's bulk sprawled itself in one of Allhoff's uncomfortable kitchen chairs. He looked around the room through heavy-lidded eyes. He wore, in addition to a very loud suit, an air of complete assurance. At his side Wallace Weldon provided complete contrast. He perched on the end of his seat. His attitude of beaten futility had vanished and seemed replaced by a very positive fear. His face was white and his lips twitched constantly. Muller with his pathetic blond mustache looked nervous, but far more reassured than Weldon. He was on the far side of Allhoff's desk watching Allhoff emptying his coffee cup with an incredulous expression. Whether or not Frankie Hadderman was still ensconced in Allhoff's bathroom, I hadn't any idea.

Allhoff, completing his slaking rites, slammed his chipped cup down on the desk and looked around the room. His wandering, bitter gaze came to rest on Big Joe Petroni.

"Ah," he said softly, "I understand you were in church yesterday, Joe."

Big Joe nodded gravely. "That's right, Inspector. There are sometimes things that happen in my life I like to talk over with the priest. It eases my conscience."

"I can well imagine that," said Allhoff. "Four times, during the past five months, there were certain guys, all of whom were your enemies, Joe, who had pot shots taken at them. On one occasion you were in the office of a life insurance company. On another, you were in Bermuda. The third time you were sitting in this office and the last time you were in a church."

Big Joe Petroni smiled the smile of a guy who has just been acquitted by a blue-ribbon jury.

"Coincidental, Inspector, ain't it?"

"Too coincidental, Joe. That's what made me think you guilty."

"There ain't no one," said Joe Petroni, with a yawn, "that can be in two places at the same time. Besides, didn't you catch this monkey here right in the act." He indicated Muller with a nod.

"Sure," said Allhoff, maintaining his affable tone, which aroused all my suspicions. "Sure we did, Joe. It occurred to me that he and the other killers might have been working for you."

Big Joe laughed. "My rods are tough. I never seen that guy in my life before. You can ask him."

"What sort of copper, do you think I am?" said Allhoff. "I have asked him."

Big Joe shrugged. "So?"

"So," said Allhoff, "I found out he was working for you. So was Weldon."

Weldon shot up from the seat of his chair as if he had been given an invisible hot foot. "No!" he yelled. "No! I wasn't working for this man. I wasn't working for anyone. I—"

Allhoff interrupted him with a roar. "Sit down! Sit down and shut up! Enough lies have been told in this case!"

Weldon swallowed something in his throat and sat down. Allhoff turned back to Big Joe.

"Just as you said, Joe, I figured the people in this case weren't typical hoods. In fact, investigation proved they weren't. But it still looked as if you were behind it all. So the question became—why do these little middle-class guys do the dirty work for Joe Petroni?"

Big Joe smiled faintly. "Why, indeed?" he echoed. "I guess there ain't no answer to a question like that, Inspector."

"There's not only an answer," snapped Allhoff. "But I know what it is."

SOME OF Big Joe's lethargy dropped from him. But it seemed to me that Muller in a minor way, and Weldon in a major, were far more apprehensive than Big Joe at that moment.

"Go ahead," I told Allhoff. "You've even got me interested now."

He looked over at me and achieved a magnificent sneer. "You!" he said and the contempt he put into the pronoun was worthy of a great actor. "A fine copper you are. The prime clue in the whole affair was that radio of Muller's and you missed it completely."

"Radio?" I puzzled. "Clue?"

"Clue," said Allhoff. "Radio. You'll recall when I questioned Muller here he seemed desperately anxious to provide himself with a motive for killing Wexler. He said he was a night-club habitue, said he drank and threw away his salary on women. Painted a picture of himself as a cross between Lucius Beebe and Mike Romanoff. Well, I suppose you could do those things on his salary, if you neglected your home and did a lot of chiseling."

"So," I said. "I still don't know what you're talking about."

"Of course you don't! You're too damn dumb! Now get this. Here's a guy who's supposed to be a great stay-out feller. A guy who never goes home at night. And on a salary of about forty bucks a week, he spends over two hundred buying a radio! Now do you get it?"

"No," I said.

He made a gesture of complete disgust.

"All right," he said, "I'll make it clear even to you. Any guy who makes as little salary as Muller and spends two hundred bucks on a radio is a home-lover. He's a radio fan. He's spending five weeks' pay on the damned instrument. If Muller was the nightclub cruiser he said he was what would he want a radio for? And if he did want one a ten-dollar box'd be good enough for him. The expensive radio obviously wasn't for his child as the girl had one of her own in her room. It was for Muller. Two hundred bucks' worth. Two hundred bucks he'd much rather spend for liquor and women if he'd been telling the truth, but he wasn't."

I rolled that over in my mind and decided with some reluctance that there was something to it. Big Joe Petroni moved in his chair and said: "So what does that prove? Only that Muller lied. I wish you'd hurry up with all this, Inspector. I got to catch a train."

"Ah," said Allhoff. "A train. I have a very nice train for you to catch, Joe. The ten-thirty. A.M."

"The ten-thirty? Where does that go?"

"To the chair, Joe. Not directly—true. You change at Ossining, Joe. For the chair."

Big Joe appealed to me. "Is he nuts, Sergeant? He ain't got anything on me."

"Look here," said Weldon. "You fellows have me dead to rights. Why all this investigation?"

Muller said nothing. His eyes were focused wonderingly on Allhoff.

Allhoff said to the room at large: "Now, not only do I suspect that these guys are working for Joe, but I find out one of them at least is lying like hell to provide a motive for his murder. Why should that be? How can Joe control these guys that much? How can he make them throw their lives away for him?"

"Maybe," I put in, nettled at his circuitous methods, "maybe he gave them radios."

Allhoff shot me a venomous glance, then continued. "The striking thing Weldon and Muller had in common was parenthood. Each of them had children. And Muller's kid was away visiting an aunt. That got me to thinking."

I EXCHANGED a glance with Battersly. True, Allhoff had made a point with his radio theory, but I was eternally damned if I could see how the fact of a child's visit to a relative had any bearing on what Allhoff was trying to prove.

"And," went on Allhoff, "I went on thinking. Especially since I was told that Weldon had said, while in Hadderman's apartment, 'Why should I care about you? There are those to whom I owe protection—' I discovered afterwards, that Weldon had two children. I almost had the answer then. I asked him if one of them was away somewhere visiting a relative. He jumped at it and told me yes. Then I was sure I was right."

Big Joe was watching Allhoff keenly now and with more interest than he had evinced before.

"So?" I asked.

"So," said Allhoff, "it suddenly became very plain. Big Joe had certain enemies he wanted to get rid of. He couldn't do the job himself because the entire department would have put the finger on Joe immediately. It was well known that Davis, Rugene, Wexler and Hadderman were Joe's enemies. So Joe conceived the bright idea of having four unknowns, four little middle-class guys who'd never committed a crime in their lives do his dirty work."

"But why?" I asked. "How could he make them do it?"

"My God," said Allhoff. "Here's a blue-print. He selected men who were fathers, men who were particularly attached to their children. Then he kidnaped the children. He furnished the fathers with guns, told them where to find their victim and told them to go ahead and shoot if they ever wanted to see their children again."

I considered that a moment and decided it was one hell of a good idea—from Joe's point of view.

"And," I said, "of course the fathers couldn't talk. If they ever squawked about Joe's snatching, they left themselves open to a murder rap. They *had* to keep their mouths shut."

"Right," said Allhoff. "That's why Muller was so eager to demonstrate he had a motive. He was far more worried about his daughter than about himself. That's why Weldon has tried to shut me up this afternoon."

"And the other two guys," I asked. "The guys who killed Davis and Rugene?"

Allhoff shrugged. "What's it matter? I assume they've got their kids back by now. I'm not too upset because Davis and Rugene are lying in pine boxes."

The more I thought of it the more I admired—professionally, of course—Big Joe's fool-proof scheme. While the killings were being perpetrated, Joe, of course, went out and fixed himself unbreakable alibis.

Allhoff turned to Big Joe. "You see," he said, "I don't mind you killing those guys at all. It's your method I object to. As a matter of fact, I'd rather have Hadderman dead than you, Joe."

Big Joe stood up. His eyes were bright and his jaw was set.

"You're still going to have trouble with your case, Inspector. Maybe you're right but you'll have a hell of a time proving it in court. I don't think your witnesses will be very willing to testify. Because, just in case you *are* right, maybe I still have their kids."

Allhoff looked at him oddly and there was a peculiar smile on his face which I couldn't interpret.

"Joe," said Allhoff, looking for all the world like a Nazi aviator waiting for a dropped bomb to explode, "I don't need those witnesses. I've got another piece of evidence that makes you eligible for that train I spoke of."

"Train?" said Big Joe, puzzled.

"The ten-thirty, remember?" said Allhoff. "The Death House Special. The evidence, Joe, is in my bedroom. I'm asking you to get it for me."

Joe regarded him suspiciously. "In your bedroom? Whereabouts?"

"Go right in," said Allhoff. "You can't miss it."

BIG JOE stood still for a moment, then shrugging his shoulders, he spun around on his heel and strode toward the closed bedroom door. Allhoff whipped open the top drawer of his desk and withdrew his Police Special. Battersly and I, watching him, dropped our hands instinctively to our own weapons.

Big Joe opened the door, stepped across the threshold. He disappeared into the room. Then I heard three sharp epithets, only one of which was uttered in Joe's voice. There was the sound of a shot, followed by two more reports.

I sprang across the room, gun drawn, Battersly on my heels. Allhoff was grinning like an illegitimate son of Machiavelli and Satan.

Big Joe stood against the wall, his gun in his hand and blood staining the shoulder of his coat. Before him Frankie Hadderman lay on a filthy scatter rug. There were two holes in his head from which poured two tiny rivers across the dust of the bedroom floor. Battersly closed with Big Joe and wrenched the gun from him. Then, leaving Hadderman there, the three of us returned to the other room.

Muller stared at us with eyes as wide as the Grand Canyon. Weldon was white and trembling. Allhoff sat with his gun in one hand and a raised coffee cup in the other. His grin was the epitome of all the evil gloating that has been done since the Garden of Eden.

Big Joe sank heavily into a chair. His breath came fast and blood dripped from his wound.

"That punk," he said. "I got him, though. I got him. I knew—"

"You've bought your ticket, Joe," said Allhoff.

"Ticket?"

"The ten-thirty to Sing Sing, Joe. Murder of Hadderman. Three police witnesses. You haven't a chance, Joe."

Big Joe Petroni's face contorted. "Damn you!" he yelled. "It was a frame. You can't do this, Allhoff. What about those kids? You want them innocent kids to suffer? You want—"

"Take him out," said Allhoff to Battersly. "Take 'em all out. Back across the street. I'll attend to the details later."

Weldon stood up. He glared at Allhoff and his rage seemed more intense than Joe's. "You interfering fool!" he screamed. "What about my son? What did you have to butt into this for? I'll never see him again now. I'll never—"

"Simmonds," said Allhoff wearily, "will you get them out of here? You know how I hate emotionalism."

I got up seething with anger. Two kids were in danger of their lives and he talked about emotionalism. However, I kept my mouth shut until we'd taken the trio across the street to headquarters.

When I got back to the flat I opened up. "It would be damned difficult," I told him, "to lower my opinion of you, but you've done it. As long as you break your lousy case, as long as you put a guy in the can, what the hell do you care for anyone else? You know what Big Joe's like. God knows what his thugs'll do to those kids to get even. You're a low, crawling, arrogant—"

His fist pounded on the desk like an anvil. "Shut up!" he howled. "You dare talk to me like that! I'm no dumb flatfoot. When I fix a case, I cover all angles. Do you think I'm a superannuated sergeant like yourself—a stupid, half-witted nincompoop—"

"Never mind what I think you are. What about those kids?"

He glared at me. "They've been home for the past three hours."

I sat down limply. "But how—how—"

"How," he mimicked in a falsetto voice. "How? Because I've got a brain. That's why. When I had the case figured I sent for Muller. I told him what I knew, told him I could save his kid and would speak to the D.A. about *nolle prossing* his case if he'd help me. He did."

"But—how could Muller help you?"

"By doing what I told him to. He had a contact with Joe. A post-office box address. I had him write there enclosing a prescription. In the note he told Joe his kid suffered from heart trouble. If she didn't get the enclosed medicine at least three times a week, she'd probably die. Said if Joe wouldn't take the stuff to the kid, he, Muller'd talk."

"I still don't get it."

"Of course, you don't, you muddle-minded idiot. I put a tail on that box, on Joe. Not you or Battersly, but a guy with some brains from the Detective Bureau. Joe got the note. Joe knew, as I figured, a dead kid was no good to him at all. He high-tailed it with the medicine to the hideout where he was keeping the kids. My tail followed him: The joint was raided five hours ago."

Apologizing to Allhoff was like eating a succulent dish of fertilizer. I did it.

"But, sir," said Battersly, "I still don't understand this business about Hadderman and Petroni. About the shooting, sir. About—" He indicated the door behind which Hadderman lay growing cold in a pool of his own blood. Allhoff filled his cup with coffee. "All right, my weak-minded aides," he said. "I'll explain it. In the first place I didn't like Frankie Hadderman. If he was dead I'd feel better. Besides, there was going to be trouble convicting Big Joe. He's got a lot of drag. The case was involved and it would drag in those little punks who did the killings for him.

"So it seemed to me that if Joe met Frankie, who already knew Joe was gunning for him, there might be a little gun play. If Frankie killed Joe, well, Joe was dead and we sent Frankie up on the ten-thirty train for the killing. If Joe killed Frankie, Frankie's dead and Joe gets the train ticket. See, I couldn't lose."

I nodded reluctantly. Once again Allhoff had come out on top. Then as I thought of something, a smile flickered about my lips. Allhoff, noting it, snarled at me: "Why the simian grin?"

"The commissioner," I reminded him. "You'll remember he's something of a stickler for civil rights and the routine method of doing things. You've stuck your neck out, Allhoff, and it makes me very, very happy. For the first time in your career the commissioner is going to fall on you like a ton of bricks. At last you've overplayed your hand."

Allhoff took his face from his coffee cup and said with wide-eyed innocence: "I don't quite understand, Sergeant."

The 'Sergeant' should have warned me. It didn't. "Why," I said confidently, "that business of a corpse in your bedroom. You know, it's illegal to arm a couple of thugs and let them shoot it out. Especially when it happens in a policeman's boudoir."

Allhoff suddenly looked like a very wise guy. "Me?" he said with phoney innocence. "I didn't do anything. Hell, I told Battersly to disarm Hadderman, to handcuff him to the steampipe. If he failed to lock the handcuffs properly, so that Hadderman retrieved his gun and blasted Joe when he came in, it's not my fault."

I eyed him angrily. "I know damned well what you did," I told him. "I saw that body. One handcuff, the one that'd been locked to the pipe, had been unlocked. You did it. You gave him back his gun and told him Big Joe was coming in after him."

"That's sheer speculation," snapped Allhoff. "The report will inform the commissioner of Battersly's negligence."

Battersly stared at him with morbid hating eyes. He didn't speak, but in his face there was all the concentrated bitterness of the oppressed peoples of the world. Allhoff saw it, too. For one of the few times in his life he averted his gaze.

"All right," he said briskly to cover up. "Get that corpse out of my bedroom. I can't go to sleep with a corpse!"

My eyes followed Battersly as he walked into the bedroom. One of those two, I reflected, would one day, go to sleep with a corpse—on his conscience.

COFFEE FOR A KILLER

A KILLER WITH MONEY TO
BURN, SETS A MATCH TO A
MURDER FLARE-UP THAT LAYS
A SMOKE-SCREEN BEFORE THE
WHOLE POLICE DEPARTMENT—
TILL INSPECTOR ALLHOFF,
COFFEE CONNOISSEUR, STIRS UP
GROUNDS FOR AN INDICTMENT
IN A STEAMING CUP OF HIS
FAVORITE BREW.

CHAPTER ONE
BRAINS VS. STOOLIES

I **SAT** gloomily at my desk staring at the travel page of the evening paper, feeling very much like the German High Command standing at Calais gazing at the Dover cliffs across the channel. Pictorially, Miami Beach, palm lined and glistening in the sunlight was very, very attractive. The siren words strung together by the Chamber of Commerce press agent added fuel to the discontent in my breast. With a sigh I dragged my mind back from the waters of the ocean and dumped it in the lap of reality.

I looked around the room in utter disgust. It was four o'clock of the afternoon and the lights were already lit. The chipped and soiled wood of the walls encircled the frenzied disorder of Allhoff's apartment. Dirty dishes floated in the sink like a fleet of dispirited garbage scows. Allhoff's soiled linen which had been worn at least once, lay scattered across the floor. Cigarette ash and paper which had missed the waste basket formed sporting hazards for the cockroaches in their march toward the garbage can. The general atmosphere was one of gloom, dirt, disorder and melancholy.

Directly in front of me, Battersly's blue-uniformed bent back arched over his desk as he applied every brain cell to following the adventures of his favorite comic strip detective. On my left sat Allhoff.

His swivel chair was pulled as far up to his desk as possible. His chest was pressed against its top. On his left the stained coffee pot gurgled on its electric base. Before him lay a sheet of yellow paper on which he made meaningless marks with a pencil as he stared broodingly off into space.

The feeling of depression that was upon me lifted somewhat as I watched him. After several years, I was quite fed up with Allhoff's being right, thoroughly tired of his instinctive diagnosis of whatever problem the commissioner laid in his lap. This time, however, he had established a record. For forty-eight hours he had been as completely baffled as the veriest rookie on the force. There was no sympathy in my heart.

"Perhaps," I said aloud, "you're slipping."

He made a sound like a misanthropic panther. He picked up the coffee pot

They proceeded to beat the bejeezus out of Battersly.

and filled his cup. He ladled in sugar with a prodigal hand. He drained the cup before he answered.

"Am I a police inspector?" he demanded. "Or a yogi? Can I solve a murder that doesn't make any sense after they've burned up all the clues? The whole thing's ridiculous. I don't see any point in anyone's killing Murdock."

"He was a banker, wasn't he? From what I hear bankers have lots of enemies. Industrial and communistic."

"Enemy or not," snapped Allhoff, "why didn't the killer take the dough? Killing a banker at his home on a night when he happens to be carrying ten grand in cash is logical enough. But why scatter the dough all over the floor and leave it there? It doesn't make any sense at all."

I lit my pipe and from sheer boredom pursued the conversation.

"Are you sure the butler was telling the truth about the money?"

"Of course. He found the body, stabbed. He saw the dough all over the floor. When he called Murdock's wife, she saw it, too. Then while they wait for the coppers to get there the mysterious fire breaks out. Burns all the dough, half the furniture, and has begun to cremate the body when the firemen arrive."

BATTERSLY TURNED his attention from Dick Tracy and offered a contribution.

"Do you think the fire had anything to do with the killing? Or was it just accidental?"

"How the devil do I know?" said Allhoff testily. "The fire inspectors say there was gasoline in the room. But I don't know. Damn it, I don't know anything. I wish to God I'd never heard of the case."

He refilled his cup with coffee the color of Pluto's blood, and glowered menacingly at the far wall. I puffed at my pipe and grinned at his back.

It was not, I knew, the abstruse angles of the case that had him sore. He was nursing a personal insult. His ego, his pride, had been wounded. Heretofore, whenever the commissioner had handed a case to Allhoff, it had been all Allhoff's. No one else got a tithe of credit nor an ounce of authority.

This time, however, recognizing that there was absolutely nothing to work on, the commissioner had assigned two men to the case. He was playing two angles. Allhoff had brains and was, without doubt, a reasoning creature. Gebhart had stoolpigeons. The commissioner had assigned them both to the Murdock killing with orders to work independently. If intelligence failed to bring up the solution, perhaps the stoolies would come through, and vice versa. The commissioner, quite sensibly, was playing the percentage. But to Allhoff it was a mortal blow.

There was no living person whom Allhoff liked. There were several whom he hated. There were at least two whom he hated with every bit of the venom stored up in his twisted little soul. One of these was Gebhart. For twenty years, while both of them were rising to inspector's rank, they had fought. Allhoff detested Gebhart as a moron whose promotions depended solely on the fact of his obtaining a better class of stoolies. Gebhart hated Allhoff as a muscle man always fears the brains he cannot understand. They had double-crossed each other continually for two decades. On at least three occasions they had locked themselves in the detectives' room and proceeded to hammer each other into insensibility.

And now the commissioner had thrown a crowning insult at Allhoff by implying that Gebhart had as much chance of breaking the Murdock murder as himself. To add injury to that insult Allhoff, in some forty-eight hours, had accomplished precisely nothing. I knew he was eating his miserable heart out with worry that Gebhart would get something first.

About fifteen minutes before quitting time, I heard the footsteps on the stairs. Allhoff's nose was buried in his coffee cup as a sharp rap sounded on the panels of the door, and without waiting for an answer, Gebhart walked in.

With him was a girl—a brassy blonde of indeterminate age. She was pretty as polished rock is pretty. There was nothing soft about her face and she carried her shapely body like a flag. Allhoff took the cup away from his nose and set it down clatteringly in the saucer. He glared at Gebhart who grinned back mockingly at him.

"This, baby," he said to the girl, "this slum is where the brains of the police department hangs out. Sort of needs a feminine touch, don't you think?"

"Damn you," said Allhoff thickly. "What are you doing here?"

Despite the challenge in his tone, Gebhart maintained his bland amiability.

"This is Miss Whalen," he announced. "My girl friend. Had a date with her so I brought her along."

"Brought her along for what?" snarled Allhoff. "If this is official business, state it and get the hell out."

Gebhart kept his smile. He waved the girl to a chair and took one himself. He crossed his legs and lit a cigarette. Allhoff still glared at him. I knew the depth of his emotion as I watched his hand tremble when he poured more coffee.

"Say," said Gebhart, as if he'd just thought of it, "ever hear of a guy called Murdock?"

Allhoff froze with the cup lifted halfway to his lips. His eyes narrowed and his voice was taut as a spring when he spoke.

"Stop clowning, damn you! What about Murdock?"

Gebhart looked up. "Why," he said with phoney innocence, "he's dead."

THE WHALEN girl laughed uproariously and Gebhart joined in. Allhoff put down his cup and slopped coffee in the saucer.

"Very funny," he said with heavy sarcasm. "Very, very funny. And now that you've given us our laugh, will you kindly take your doxy and get out of here."

I wasn't quite sure what he meant by that last and Gebhart wasn't either. However since Allhoff was staring at the blonde we both gathered that it was an insult directed at Gebhart's lady friend. Gebhart stood up and now his mocking smile was gone.

"I'll get out," he said, "when I tell you what I came up here to tell you. I'm here to tell you about Murdock."

"You've told me he's dead," said Allhoff. "That I already know."

"That's all you *do* know. *I* know who killed him."

Allhoff's face became white. He said, "It's a lie," in the tone of a man who was very much afraid it wasn't.

Gebhart laughed. When he spoke his voice was high, excited and vicious.

"It's true," he said. "So true it's going to break your miserable little heart. For years you've been throwing your weight about this man's police department. For years you've been boasting that you're the only guy with an ounce of competence. Well, this time, I've licked you. You haven't even got a clue yet and I've broken the case. Maybe you'll shut up for a while now, Inspector."

"You will get out of here," said Allhoff speaking like a machine gun, "and with you, you will take your ———"

This time there was no doubt he meant the blonde and there was no need of etymological research to find the definition of his word. The Whalen girl flushed and took a step toward him. Gebhart put a hand on her arm, said, "I'll handle this, baby," and towered suddenly over Allhoff's desk.

"You lousy little bum," he roared. "For years the whole damned department has hated your guts. But I've hated 'em more than all the others put together. For years I've tried to put you in your place and now, by God, I've succeeded. I've broken the Murdock case and you haven't moved an inch on it. What about the great Allhoff brain now? Sometimes I think your legs are longer than your mind."

For a moment there was a silence in the room tense as a coiled spring, vibrant as the instant before an air raid alarm. Allhoff put a hand on his desk and slowly pushed his chair back. At the edge of his chair where his knees should have been, two leather pads abruptly terminated his thighs. Battersly made a strange hissing sound as he sucked in air and broke the silence. Allhoff's voice came deeply from his chest like that of an avenging angel.

"For that," he said, "you will apologize on your knees."

The blonde laughed off key. "Apologize? To a runt like you? He could lick you with one hand."

Allhoff's right arm moved rapidly. He opened a desk drawer and closed it again. His Police Special was in his hand and its muzzle drew an accurate bead on Gebhart's heart.

"Can he lick *this?*" said Allhoff.

Gebhart looked at the gun and his jaw was set firmly. The girl's eyes were wide and worried. Battersly stared at the tableau like a peasant at a skyscraper. I put down my pipe, stood up and said sharply, "Allhoff!"

"Keep out of this, Simmonds," he said, without taking his eyes from Gebhart. "You," he went on, "you and that trollop will apologize. On your knees!"

Gebhart stood uncertainly staring at the gun. The blonde put her hand on his arm.

"He wouldn't dare," she whispered. "Tell him to go to hell. He wouldn't dare."

But Gebhart knew Allhoff better than that. For that matter, so did I.

"Now listen, Inspector," said Gebhart placatingly, "maybe I said too much. Maybe I—"

"Your knees," said Allhoff. "You and your doll there."

GEBHART LOOKED at the gun, raised his eyes and looked at Allhoff. There was maniacal purpose in Allhoff's face. His little eyes were hot and bitter. Gebhart swallowed something in his throat. He put his hand on the girl's arm, and as he sank to his knees he dragged her down with him. There was murder in his gaze as he said slowly: "I apologize, Inspector."

Allhoff nodded, transferred his glance to the Whalen girl. "And you?"

I saw Gebhart's fingers tighten on her arm. She nodded her head quickly. "Me, too," she said. "I'm sorry."

"All right," said Allhoff. "Get out!"

They rose slowly to their feet. Flushed humiliation was in Gebhart's cheeks. The girl was plainly angry but fear kept her silent. They walked slowly to the door. There, Gebhart turned around.

"I'm going to get you for this," he said in a low husky voice. "I'm going to get you if it takes the rest of my life."

"Get out!" Allhoff said again, and reached for the coffee pot.

I was prepared for his explosion as soon as they left the room. It was apparent that he was keeping a volcano clamped down inside him. He had been controlling himself, maintaining an icy calm before Gebhart and, knowing him as I did, I knew he couldn't keep it up much longer. He didn't.

The instant the footfalls died away on the stairs, Allhoff swung around in his swivel chair and faced Battersly. He pounded his fists on the arms of his chair and raised his voice in a surging roar.

"Curse you!" he shouted. "Because of you, because of your arrant cowardice, I'm put in a position where morons like Gebhart can insult me. I devote my brain and body to the police department and you take half the latter away from me. You—"

He pulled obscenity out of his vocabulary like a street cleaner pulling filth from a clogged sewer. His face was red as bougainvillea, his fists flailed the chair arm, his leather stumps kicked convulsively in the air.

Battersly sat with averted face before his attacker. Like a disciple of Gandhi, he bent before the onslaught meekly, without retaliation. Then, when Allhoff's profanity beat against my ears until I could stand it no longer, I took a hand myself.

"Allhoff," I said, "for God's sake, lay off. You'll drive us all crazy including yourself."

He paused for a moment to take breath. Then he turned on me. I shrugged my shoulders and went back to my desk. At least I had diverted his thunderous sentences from Battersly to myself. I went back to the travel page of the evening paper. Some seven minutes later, Allhoff, out of breath and epithet, shut up. He sipped more coffee sullenly, sibilantly.

THIS, I reflected on the way home in the subway, had been going on for more years then I cared to remember. It had had its genesis half a decade ago, during a raid on an upper West End Avenue rooming-house. The stool-pigeon grapevine had reported that a trio of gangsters wanted in a dozen states were hiding out at a certain address in the nineties. Allhoff had been assigned to lead the raiding squad.

Battersly, a raw rookie in those days, had been ordered to effect a rear entrance, disable the operator of the Tommy gun which, we'd been informed, commanded the stairway facing the door. Battersly got in, all right. Then, at the zero hour he developed an understandable case of stage fright, with the net result that he fled up the stairway to the roof at the precise moment Allhoff came battering through the front door.

Allhoff charged into some twenty-odd lead slugs coming with high velocity from the barrel of the Tommy gun. Most of them lodged in his legs below the knee. A week later, gangrene set in and an hour after that came the amputation.

Of course, a legless police inspector violated every item in the civil service book. But the commissioner was of no mind to lose his best man on any technicality. He arranged that Allhoff should live in this tenement slum because of its proximity to headquarters. He arranged further that the city, through devious bookkeeping devices paid Allhoff his old salary. And with perhaps too grim a sense of justice, he had granted Allhoff's demand that Battersly be assigned as an aide. I had been thrown in the deal to keep peace between them.

Mine was a futile task. When Allhoff's legs had gone, something of his mind had gone along with them. Not that he was stupid, but there were occasions when I considered him far closer to insanity than many inmates of public institutions. Hatred and bitterness rankled in his heart and almost all of it was directed at young Battersly. He never missed a chance to extract revenge.

Personally, I would rather have walked the beat on the farthest outpost of Staten Island than loaf at a desk here. But the commissioner insisted upon this assignment and I'd spent too many years building up my pension to throw it away now.

CHAPTER TWO
MONEY TO BURN

I ARRIVED at the tenement the following morning as Allhoff emerged from his bedroom, unwashed and drowsy-eyed. He didn't speak. He never did until he'd absorbed at least a quart of the strong brackish brew he fondly believed was coffee. He dragged himself up into his chair, handed the coffee pot silently to me and opened the bottom desk drawer.

I filled the pot with water and returned it. Allhoff opened the can he had taken from the drawer and cursed loudly. At that moment, Battersly came in, shaved and primped, his brass buttons gleaming resplendently. He saluted and headed for his desk. Allhoff's thundering voice stopped him.

"I don't ask much of you," he roared. "I do the brain work here, Simmonds handles the papers and reports. All I require from you, when you've finished keeping up with the comic strips, is that coffee and sugar be kept in the joint. You can't even do that adequately."

He held out the empty coffee can accusingly as if it were a murder weapon.

Battersly bit his lip and frowned. "It was half full yesterday, sir. I swear it was. I looked. You *couldn't* have used it all. It—"

"It's empty now," snarled Allhoff. "Get me another can. And for God's sake, hurry."

He took a worn leather purse from his pocket and extracted a quarter. Battersly put the coin in his pocket and ran down the stairs. Allhoff stared gloomily at the wall and a series of low growls came out of his dry throat. A cocaineless hophead suffered less than Allhoff minus his quota of caffeine.

His fingers drummed angrily on the desktop as time went by and Battersly did not return. A good fifteen minutes elapsed and still Allhoff had no coffee. His fingers were beating a rapid tattoo now and he was muttering to himself. Silently, I cursed Battersly. He possessed a gift for getting Allhoff in black moods. I steeled myself for the explosion which would inevitably occur when Battersly returned.

A moment later the door opened. I heard Allhoff's intake of breath as he prepared to unload a verbal barrage on Battersly's tardy head. But as he looked up he held his wrath.

Battersly stood panting in the doorway. His cap was gone. As were two buttons from his uniform. His collar was ripped and his tie askew. One eye was developing slowly but with certainty into a shiner and blood dripped from his nose on to his chest. His hair was ruffled and there were a pair of nasty scratches on his cheek.

He took a brown paper parcel from under his arm and laid it on Allhoff's desk.

"The coffee, sir," he said.

"My God," said Allhoff, "and did you go through the German lines to get it?"

"I was ganged," said Battersly. "A mob of tough guys beat me up."

"Why?" I asked.

Battersly shrugged. "I don't know. I can't figure it. Just for the hell of it, I guess."

Allhoff was staring at the wrapped-up coffee can on his desk. There was a frown upon his brow. He looked up at Battersly and said: "Exactly what happened?"

Battersly dabbed at his red nose with a handkerchief. "Well," he said, "this mob of guys—there was five of them—was hanging out a couple of doors away from the grocery store. They never paid me any attention when I passed them the first time. Then I came out of the grocer's after buying the coffee—and that's the funny part of it."

"Uproarious," said Allhoff sarcastically. "What's funny about it?"

"Well, they got me when I came out of the grocery store. See? They let me go when I passed right by them. Then they get me afterwards."

"What happened then?"

"They began to slug me. Two of them held my hands so I couldn't go for my gun. The others slugged me. They knocked off my cap, knocked the coffee from under my arm and proceeded to beat hell out of me. I was half out when they quit. They was a block away when I got up. One of them had my cap. I saw him wave it at me before they scrammed around the corner of Broome Street. Souvenir, I guess."

ALLHOFF GRUNTED again. I was mildly surprised that he showed no elation. The idea of Battersly's getting smacked around certainly should have appealed to him. Battersly went into the bathroom to wash his face. Allhoff remained in his brown study until Battersly reappeared, then he suddenly banged his fist hard on the desk. He opened the drawer and put away the coffee. He looked around at me and said: "Simmonds, get me a glass of water."

I stared at him. "You mean you're not going to have coffee?"

"I haven't time. I'm working now."

I went to the sink and filled a glass. "Working on what?"

"These guys that beat up Battersly." He took the water, drank it and stared thoughtfully at the door.

I watched him and felt like a guy who has seen something drop *up*. Allhoff, foregoing his coffee, was a phenomenon happening not more than once in a lifetime.

"Battersly," said Allhoff. "Go across the street. Look through all the pictures in the gallery. Carefully."

"Yes, sir," said Battersly. "What am I looking for, sir?" He waited, puzzled.

"The guys that beat you up, you idiot. Get over there, see if you can pick any of them out."

Battersly went out while I stared at Allhoff in amazement for the second time in five minutes.

"I'm rather surprised," I told him, "at your zeal in wanting to put Battersly's assailants behind the bars."

"Battersly," he said, and the contempt in his voice was eloquent. "I don't give a damn about Battersly's assailants. Why should I?"

"Then what are you worrying about it for? The whole thing's obvious enough."

He swung around in his swivel chair and glared at me. "Is it?" he snapped. "Then go ahead, explain it."

"There are plenty of hooligans in this town who think it's smart to beat up coppers. It happens once a week. You know that."

Allhoff sighed the sigh of a man whose patience is sorely strained. "So that's all you get out of it."

"What else?"

He vouchsafed no answer. He stared at the wall like a professor of mathematics who in a few moments will have figured out how to square a circle.

After two hours Battersly returned. He laid a small square photograph on Allhoff's desk.

"That was one of the guys, Inspector. It was the only one I could recognize."

Allhoff picked up the photograph and examined it. "Frankie Splayton," he said. "All-around punk. Picked up four times. Robbery, D. and D., narcotics. Convicted twice on the last charge. Simmonds, what've you got on him?"

I got up, went to the filing cabinet at the side of the room. After a moment's rummaging, I told him: "Not much beside what you already know. He's a satellite of Danny Raleigh's."

"Ah," said Allhoff. "Raleigh, eh?"

Battersly and I exchanged glances. I shrugged. What was going on in Allhoff's head was utterly beyond me. And this time, I suspected it was also beyond Allhoff.

Battersly and I went back to our desks, leaving Allhoff still staring blankly into space. The three of us remained that way until my telephone rang. I picked it up and listened.

"Allhoff," I said when I had hung up, "I have some news you'll be delighted to hear."

He came out of his trance and cocked an inquiring eyebrow.

"It seems your pal, Gebhart, hasn't broken the Murdock case at all."

Allhoff uttered an oath which I decided was aimed at Gebhart rather than at me.

"That was a message from the commissioner. He wants you to bear down on the case. It seems Gebhart got some information from a stoolie which seemed to crack it open but it turned out to be phoney. Which news, I assume, fills your ears with honey."

Perhaps it did, but from his attitude it wasn't noticeable. His frown had grown more corrugated, and his register of profound thought more marked.

"Raleigh," he said suddenly. "Danny Raleigh. Counterfeiting was one of his prime activities, wasn't it?"

I nodded. "That and forgery. With perhaps a killing thrown in here and there. Why?"

"Good God, I'm beginning to see it."

"See what?"

THE TELEPHONE rang again before he could answer. I listened to the message and relayed it.

"Things are happening. There was another murder, precisely like Murdock's—except they've got the guy who did it."

"The hell they have," said Allhoff. "What's the details?"

"Guy by the name of Weldon. Stockbroker. Took some eighteen thousand dollars home with him. Shot in his study. His wife heard the shot. Rushed into the room. Saw her husband dead, dough scattered all over the floor. Went to call the coppers. While they were on the way, a fire broke out in the study. They rescued the corpse but half the house burned down before the firemen got it under control."

"Interesting," said Allhoff. "But what's this about them getting the guy who did it?"

"There was a guy who'd lost all his dough in the market. Rightly or wrongly he blamed Weldon for his losses. Swore before witnesses, he'd kill him. Was picked up near the Weldon house right after the crime. They've got him over at headquarters now. Homicide says it's cold."

"That's indicative that it isn't," said Allhoff, who had his own opinion of Homicide. "Call 'em back. Tell 'em to send that guy over. I want to see him."

I transmitted the message. At least I'd sooner having him working on the Murdock case which made some sense, rather than on the weighty problem of who beat up Battersly, which didn't.

Fifteen minutes later a burly Irish cop dragged a pale, scared little man into the office. The copper saluted Allhoff and announced: "This is Smith, sir. The prisoner in the Weldon case."

Allhoff waved Smith to a chair. Smith sat down as if he expected to be electrocuted there and then. He was a thin little guy who looked undernourished. He had a pair of wild eyes and at the moment fear had been poured into them. His fingers moved nervously at his sides.

"I didn't do it," he said to Allhoff. "I don't care what they say, I didn't."

Allhoff regarded him appraisingly and nodded his head. "I wouldn't be at all surprised if you didn't. What's your version of it all?"

Smith shifted nervously in his chair and spoke in a high-pitched voice.

"Weldon robbed me. Sold me worthless stock in enterprises controlled by him. Sure, I said I'd kill him. He took every cent I had. But I didn't do it."

"What were you doing in the neighborhood of his house?" asked Allhoff.

"I went to ask him for money. I only wanted a stake. Enough to get started again. After all he took from me, I figured maybe he had heart enough to give me that much. I was going to see him. I got in the lobby of the house and they pinched me."

"How much did Weldon leave you?"

"Three hundred bucks," said Smith bitterly. "Three hundred bucks in the bank and less than ten in my pocket. I got a wife and two kids, too. I got—"

Allhoff waved him to silence. "All right," he said to the copper, "take him away."

"Wait a minute," yelled Smith. "Aren't you going to help me? I tell you I didn't do it. I tell you—"

"Stop telling me," said Allhoff. "I know damned well you didn't do it."

"Then why—"

"You've got to go back to the can, anyway," said Allhoff. "I'm not quite ready to spring you yet."

The Irish copper dragged him away, while Smith audibly voiced his opinion of the police department.

Allhoff drank coffee morosely for the rest of the day. Basking in his silence, Battersly and I made no attempt to engage him in conversation.

THE FOLLOWING day was Thursday and the package came. It was an oblong parcel, perhaps five by eight inches. It was wrapped securely in brown wrapping paper and bore a vast number of colored stamps. And since Allhoff had never received any mail in all my memory, I accepted it with a surprised air, from the postman.

"Have you a birthday coming up?" I said as I laid it on his desk. "Looks like a present from a wealthy pal judging by all the stamps he's plastered over it."

Allhoff looked up from his coffee. He picked up the package and turned it over slowly in his hands. He grunted, then said: "Your powers of observation are improving, Simmonds. There's a buck's worth of stamps on this. Two bits would have carried it."

He studied the exterior of the package like a philatelist, making no attempt to open it.

"Well," I said, curiosity gnawing at me, "aren't you going to see what it is? Or are you afraid it's a bomb?"

He looked at me sharply. "A bomb," he said with a sudden inhalation. "A bomb, eh?"

I was surprised at his sudden serious air.

"I have no relatives," he went on. "As you are well aware I have no friends. I can think of no one who might send me anything at all through the mails."

"So," I said, "why not dump it in a bucket of water and then open it?"

His swift glance at me held contempt.

"It's lucky you're not on the bomb squad. Water's no damned good half the time. Oil is what you use." He turned his head in Battersly's direction. "Battersly. Here, take this across the street to Sergeant Averill on the Bomb Squad. Tell him to douse it in a pail of oil, then open it. Wait there until you get his report."

I blinked at him. Allhoff was no one's sucker and he wasn't a guy with any trend toward panic. Yet here he was taking my kidding suggestion as grimly as a scary old maid. Battersly got up, took the parcel with an odd inquiring glance at me and left the room. Allhoff returned broodingly to his coffee. I shook my head and clucked at him.

"And do you look under the bed for burglars at night before retiring?" I asked solicitously.

"Idiot," he snarled. "If a man tries once to kill you and fails, it's logical he'll try again."

I opened my eyes wide at that. "Who tried to kill you? When? How?"

For reply he sucked down coffee noisily. Then after the cup had clattered back into the saucer, he said slowly: "That Danny Raleigh. His last rap, as I remember it, was counterfeiting. But he beat it in a federal court. It was bad stuff he'd been passing. Easily spotted."

"Well," I said, "what about it? What's that got to do with some guy trying to kill you?"

But now he ignored me completely. He concentrated on his coffee and pretended I wasn't there. I sighed, after a while, and went back to my desk.

BATTERSLY RETURNED, taking the outside stairs two at a time. He burst, flushed and breathless into the office.

"My God," he said, "what do you think, Inspector?"

Allhoff and I looked at him. I remarked that Allhoff seemed calm and in no wise curious about Battersly's excitement.

"It was a bomb," cried Battersly. "Set to go off when that package was opened. It really was, Inspector."

"Sure," said Allhoff with the air of a man who has just been told that two and two reach a total of four.

"Good Lord," I said, "who'd be sending you a bomb? We're not even working on a case, except that screwy Murdock thing and we certainly haven't made any progress there."

Allhoff yawned. "Listen," he said, "you think you can get me some heroin from Narcotics?"

"Some *what?*"

"Heroin. It's a mixture compounded of so many parts morphine, combined with—"

"I know what it is. I just wondered if I heard you properly. What do you want heroin for?"

"Just get me some and shut up," said Allhoff. "Five or six ounces should be plenty."

"Five or six ounces," I said as I moved toward the door. "My God, the whole damned town can get high on that."

As I crossed the street to headquarters I reflected upon a very peculiar circumstance. Allhoff had appeared vastly more interested in the fact of simple assault upon Battersly than he was in an attempt upon his own life. Pondering this I was one bewildered police sergeant when I brought him back his six ounces of heroin.

Casually he tossed the drug into a desk drawer. Then turning to Battersly and myself, he said: "Tomorrow morning I want a number of people here. I want them here early. Get 'em before they've had a chance to get their breakfast, if you can. Here's the list. First, Gebhart and that blonde of his, second, Gebhart's mother and a Mrs. Charles Latrobe of Neptune Avenue, Coney Island. That's Gebhart's married sister."

"My God," I said, "what is this? A communion breakfast for the Gebhart clan?"

"Third," he went on, ignoring me, "I want Frankie Splayton and Danny Raleigh. I don't care how you two guys split them up—you can get more coppers or a wagon if you want to—but Battersly'd better pick up Raleigh."

"Why?" I said.

"Because he's a tough guy, Sergeant," said Allhoff mocking. "And unless I'm very, very wrong, he's not going to want to come at all."

I scratched my head. "I don't see this," I told him. "What are you going to solve? The mystery of who beat up Battersly?"

He smiled without mirth. "Among other things. I shall also solve the mystery of who killed Murdock, who killed Weldon, who tried to kill me."

He reached for the coffee pot as Battersly and I stared at him in bewilderment.

"Is that all?" I asked with heavy irony.

"No," he said over the top of his cup. "Before you go home, roll a typewriter over here where I can get at it with a modicum of effort. Thank you."

I rolled the typewriter-stand across the room and my thoughts were no more lucid after his last order. Allhoff hadn't touched a typewriter for at least a year. On the way home in the subway I decided that he had either gone utterly mad or that he expected to pull some very odd rabbits from the hat on the morrow.

CHAPTER THREE
THE AFFABLE ALLHOFF

IT WAS a little after eight thirty in the morning when Battersly and I herded our motley collection into Allhoff's tenement apartment. None of them, I think, had had their breakfast and indignation hovered over their heads like a cloud. Indeed, it had taken a telephone call to the commissioner himself before Gebhart had agreed to come along with me. Gebhart's mother, a plump blonde of indeterminate years, was annoyed and his sister was loudly proclaiming the fact that she, as a citizen, knew her rights under the Constitution.

Gebhart's blonde glared sullenly at Allhoff as she came in the room. It was apparent that she had neither forgiven nor forgotten the humiliation he had forced upon her during her last visit.

Battersly's customers, it seemed, were no more delighted to greet Inspector Allhoff at this hour in the morning than were mine. Splayton looked exactly what he was. A small-time punk dressed in a green suit of extreme cut. His face was pasty, his eyes shifty. He cringed as he came into the room, glanced about furtively, obviously terrified that he had been dragged here in order that Battersly could extract brutal revenge for the beating he had undergone the other day.

Danny Raleigh was a crook of vastly different caliber. His clothes were conservative and tailor made. His bearing was jaunty, though tempered with shrewd alertness. He eyed Allhoff appraisingly, then cast a swift, veiled glance at Gebhart. Battersly stood with his back to the door like a jailer as the group herded itself into the little room.

The thing that staggered me was the arrangements Allhoff had made for his involuntary guests. Chairs were grouped about his desk in a semi-circle. More amazing, they had been freshly dusted. Laid out on the desk blotter stood six coffee cups, shining and white. Obviously they had been recently washed and with soap. Obviously, too, since Battersly and I had just arrived, they had been washed by Allhoff—a fact which sent several precedents crashing into pieces upon the floor.

Six teaspoons, bright and polished, lay by the sides of the cups. Even the coffee pot, I noted, had been burnished to brightness for the first time in its venerable career. Dazed, I went over to my desk. Inspector Allhoff apparently was entertaining at breakfast, which was rather like a professional hermit suddenly becoming an Elk.

Allhoff had been reading a sheet of typewritten paper when we had come in. Now, he placed it face down on the desk and smiled with what I'm sure he thought was beneficence. Actually he looked like a panther in need of a dentist. When he spoke there was oil, honey and glycerine in his tone.

"I am very sorry," he said, "to disturb you all at this hour. However we all have certain duties as citizens—duties which, I'm sure, you'll be only too happy to discharge."

Mrs. Gebhart alone seemed slightly mollified by these words. Splayton, the punk, still looked as if an invisible rubber hose was suspended above his head. Danny Raleigh watched Allhoff through half closed lids as a zoo keeper might watch a dangerous animal.

Gebhart's sister and the Whalen girl retained their air of outraged dignity, while Gebhart, red-faced and angry said: "Save the editorial, Allhoff. There may be some departmental reason for you dragging me down here this morning. But, forcing my family to come also, is sheer malice. You did it to annoy me because you hate my guts."

I WAS watching Allhoff closely and when he didn't get angry, I came to the conclusion that he was playing a very deep game indeed.

"Now, Gebhart," he said mildly, "this is very important. It's a murder case. You as a policeman know that solving such cases is the most important thing there is to us. A little inconvenience doesn't matter. Now," he waved his hands toward the chairs, "will everyone sit down, please?"

Everyone sat down with an air of not committing themselves.

"Now," said Allhoff, "you'll remember, Gebhart, there was a case a few days ago which you announced you'd solved."

I remarked that Danny Raleigh's eyes had steel in them then. Gebhart slapped his knee angrily.

"Damn you," he said. "Must you gloat this early in the morning? I made a mistake, that's all. My information was incorrect. You know quite well, I admitted my mistake. I didn't solve the Murdock case at all."

"You're much too modest, Inspector," said Allhoff, an odd lilt in his voice. "You *did* solve it."

Gebhart's womenfolk looked at Allhoff, then back at Gebhart. Splayton, the punk, still cringed in his chair, apparently paying no attention to the conversation. I kept my eyes on Raleigh. He was always a dangerous man and at that moment be looked more dangerous than usual.

Nevertheless my ears were all for Allhoff. In our several years association, I had heard him say some crazy things. This, however, was a new high in illogic. The idea of Gebhart actually solving the Murdock murder, a feat which would have given him a splendid opportunity to crow over Allhoff, and then denying it, was utterly incredible.

Gebhart's mother voiced my thought. "Are you crazy?" she asked. "Why would my boy deny such a praiseworthy thing as that?"

"Ah," said Allhoff ministerially, "who can fathom the motives of a human heart?"

Danny Raleigh stood up. "Look here," he said briskly, "I ain't been formally arrested. Unlike Gebhart, I ain't here on the commissioner's orders. I was brought here strong-arm and it ain't right. See? I ain't going to stay."

Allhoff lifted his eyes to the door where Battersly's bulky frame still stood.

"You were brought here strong-arm," he said, "and you'll stay here strong-arm. Sit down." For an instant his air of phoney affability had left him but he turned it on again a moment later. "Of course," he went on, "I realize we're all a little out of sorts since we haven't had our breakfasts. A nice cup of coffee will fix us all up."

Now he was talking like Uncle Don and the effect was like Boris Karloff telling a bedtime story. He opened the bottom drawer of his desk. He withdrew a brown paper-wrapped parcel, tied with white string. He opened it and placed the coffee can it contained upon his desk.

"Lucky," he said, "I have enough coffee for you all. I saved this can the other day. Always like to have some in reserve in case of guests."

That, of course, was an outrageous lie. He never had any coffee in reserve. He never had any guests, either, for that matter.

He ladled coffee into the percolator with a lavish hand, never considering that his guests' taste might incline to a weaker brew than his own. He turned the electric plate on full, then turned, beaming, back to his audience. I followed his gaze in time to intercept a swift glance between Raleigh and Inspector Gebhart. Allhoff's roving eye fell upon young Splayton.

"Well, well," he said with heavy affability, "that's a nice suit you're wearing, son. Where'd you get it?"

I braced myself and wondered if my ears were playing tricks on me. Allhoff's sartorial interests were those of a nudist. Moreover, he was not in the habit of engaging guys like Splayton in polite conversation. Splayton shifted uneasily in his chair and regarded Allhoff with suspicion.

"Yes, sir," said Allhoff, like an insurance salesman. "It certainly looks good on you. I don't know whether I admire the cut or the fabric more. Come over here, let me feel the material."

SPLAYTON STOOD up and approached Allhoff like a child who, when promised candy, expects to be struck. Allhoff swung his chair around facing him. He stretched forth his fingers and examined the cloth of Splayton's suit. He nodded his head in approval. Gebhart's sister watched him for a moment, then blew up.

"This is a ridiculous outrage," she snapped. "Personally, Inspector, I think you're insane. You bring us here before breakfast, then force us to listen while you admire a badly-made, cheap suit. Now, tell us what you want us for immediately, or I shall leave. Coppers or no coppers."

Allhoff looked at her with a jaundiced eye. Yet his voice retained its blandness as he spoke.

"Very well," he said, feeling the side of the coffee pot to see how it was heating. "I apologize for wasting your time. I shall proceed to the point at once. It begins almost a year ago in a federal court."

He paused and drew a deep breath. I observed Raleigh and Gebhart staring at the opened coffee can on Allhoff's desk. I regarded it questioningly myself. Never since I had known him had I seen him save a can of coffee. This one certainly hadn't been bought this morning.

"Yes," went on Allhoff, "Raleigh, here, was in a little trouble with the federal boys. They claimed he'd bought a lot of counterfeit dough from someone. They claimed further that he and his henchmen were passing it at a great rate. Moreover, it wasn't very good money. It was so badly printed that even a Brooklyn delicatessen clerk would have little trouble in realizing its phoniness."

"If you're anything at all," said Raleigh, "you're a city cop. I don't see how a federal rap interests you. Besides, just for the record, I beat that rap. The jury acquitted me."

"Indeed they did," said Allhoff almost cheerfully. "They also left you with a vast number of counterfeit dollars on your hands—dollars for which you'd paid good hard cash, perhaps twenty per cent of their full face amount. That left you with the problem of cutting your losses. The stuff was so bad you didn't dare try to pass any more of it. It was too dangerous. Then you thought of an angle."

The percolator gurgled as the first spurt of coffee hit against its top. Gebhart started in his chair.

"It wasn't a direct angle," continued Allhoff. "But it was something. Instead of that counterfeit dough being a total loss you managed to devise a scheme to use it. After your flyer in the queer you went back to your usual operations of larceny, and murder, adding a crime which the records imply was novel for you."

Raleigh looked from Allhoff to the coffee pot and back again.

"What crime?"

"Arson. That, too, like your use of the phoney money was an indirect crime, though. It—"

"Inspector Allhoff," said Mrs. Gebhart, "I am an old woman. Yet no one has ever accused me of senility. But I don't understand what you're talking about."

"Right," said Gebhart standing up. "I've heard enough of this, Allhof. You're a crazy old man. We're staying here no longer. Come along, all of you."

Gebhart's womenfolk stood up, relief showing on their faces. Allhoff's gaze traveled to Battersly, at the door.

"Battersly," said Allhoff, "you will draw your gun."

Battersly did so with all the enthusiasm of the Italian Army charging.

"You will permit no one to leave the room. That's an order. Gebhart, sit down."

Gebhart glared at Allhoff. His women watched him uncertainly. Then slowly he sat down. The distaff side of the family followed suit.

"I was speaking to you, Raleigh, of the Murdock and Weldon killings," Allhoff resumed conversationally. "I was about to explain the tie-up between them, arson and counterfeit money."

The percolator was bubbling merrily now. Allhoff glanced at it once, then transferred his caustic gaze to Raleigh again.

"As I said," he went on, "you, Raleigh, returned to simple murder for a living. Somehow, through your spy system, your stool-pigeons, you found out when certain citizens were about to take large sums of cash home with them for one reason or another. Whereupon you cased the house, entered, murdered them and stole the money."

There was a moment's silence. Then Raleigh said: "It's too pat, Inspector. You may as well accuse me of being a fifth columnist. You can do it as glibly and with just as much reason."

"Now," said Allhoff, ignoring the comment, "you murder Murdock and Weldon, you steal their money. You also remove all suspicion from yourself by a judicious use of arson and your counterfeit bills."

FOR THE first time since he had begun to talk a slow light dawned in my brain. "You mean," I asked, "that Raleigh planted his phoney money, permitted someone to see it, then returned to the house and set it on fire? In that way he would destroy the counterfeit money so that no one would suspect it wasn't genuine. And he would also make the murder look as if it had a personal motivation."

"Precisely," said Allhoff. "Naturally when the police learned that the actual cash was not stolen they would never go looking for a professional crook such as Raleigh. On the contrary, they'd search for someone with personal motivation. As for instance that poor guy they've got in the can now for the Weldon murder. What's his name? Smith."

I thought it over for a moment and decided it sounded logical.

"Of course," said Allhoff, "Raleigh intended to commit these murders anyway. The phoney money, the arson was incidental. However, since he had the queer on hand, it was a good time to use it. In theory it was supposed to keep suspicion away from him. Actually, it pinned the whole thing right on his dapper shirt front."

"How?" said Raleigh in an expressionless tone.

"Because," said Allhoff, "it was the burnt money that set my brain cells to functioning. The second fire, under precisely the same circumstances as the first seemed something more than coincidental. If the fires were deliberate it seemed odd to me that any man would burn good money. The next thought was whether or not it *was* good money. There it lay in my mind until Splayton here attacked Battersly. Splayton was known as your man, Raleigh. You, in turn, were known to have a load of counterfeits on hand. With that tie-up, I figured it out."

Now Allhoff was going too fast for me again. True, what he had said sounded plausible. Yet, apparently he had no proof at all. Further, there was a bomb to be explained and why Battersly had been attacked at all. Danny Raleigh drew a deep breath.

"All right, Inspector," he said. "Since you know all this, since you have me dead to rights, since your evidence is—"

Gebhart swung around in his chair. His face was gray.

"Raleigh," he said, "shut up. He knows nothing. He's guessing. He can't prove anything."

Raleigh met his eyes for a long uncomfortable moment. Gebhart flushed. Raleigh said: "I thought he could prove everything. I thought he knew from—"

"He knows nothing," said Gebhart. "Nothing. Keep your mouth shut and you're clean."

"I thought—" said Raleigh again, and there was flaming rage in his eyes.

"We all make mistakes," said Allhoff and there was a suspicious oiliness in his voice.

He picked the percolator off its base and proceeded to fill all the cups in front of him.

"What we all need is a good hot cup of coffee," he said amiably. "You'll excuse me. I've already had mine."

Young Splayton stared at Allhoff, wide-eyed. Gebhart bit his lip and Danny Raleigh looked around the room as if hoping reinforcements would come through the walls. No one made a move to reach for his coffee.

"Come, come," said Allhoff. "Coffee, Miss Whalen?"

The Whalen girl who hadn't spoken since she had come into the room, shook her head dully. Gebhart's sister said icily: "I pick my company." Gebhart's mother shrugged her ample shoulders.

"Thank you, Inspector," she said. "Since I've had no breakfast, I'll take it."

CHAPTER FOUR

GOOD TO THE LAST DROP

ALLHOFF HANDED her the thick cup with ceremony. Danny Raleigh lit a cigarette and I remarked the shaking of his fingers. Splayton had now taken his gaze from Allhoff and was regarding Mrs. Gebhart with a glazed and horrified stare.

Mrs. Gebhart lifted the cup to her lips and I heard Splayton inhale sharply. Then Gebhart was on his feet. His right hand lashed out and slapped hard against the thick cup. Coffee spattered his mother's dress and the wall. The cup rolled to the floor.

Mrs. Gebhart stared at her son in inarticulate astonishment. Gebhart breathed hard like a man who has just run a hundred yards. Splayton slumped down in his chair. Allhoff bowed satanically.

"Thank you, Gebhart," he said mockingly. "That tells me all that I wanted to know."

Gebhart stood glaring at him. It dawned on me that I seemed to know less about what was going on than anyone else in the room. I said so, loudly. I added: *"What* was all you wanted to know, Allhoff?"

"Who was trying to kill me. Who sent me a bomb and a pound of poisoned coffee?"

"Well, who did?"

Allhoff grinned. Now all the simulated affability had gone from his face. There was sand, not oil, in his voice as he answered me.

"Pause, Sergeant," he said. "Pause and reflect. Battersly goes out for a tin of coffee. On the way *into* the store he passes a mob of hoodlums, captained by young Splayton here. They do not molest him. On the way *out* he gets jumped on and slugged."

"All of which indicates you're about to be poisoned," I said ironically.

"Exactly," said Allhoff. "When Battersly returns here, bruised and bearing the wrapped coffee can, I observe, as you should have, that it is wrapped with white string. As far back as I can remember, that corner store has been using black string to wrap parcels with. A small thing, perhaps. But coupled with the odd circumstance of Battersly's beating, worth investigating."

"So you investigated," I said. "With what result?"

"The laboratory informed me that the coffee had been removed from the can, soaked in a cyanide solution and replaced. The attack on Battersly was to create a diversion, knock the package out of his hand and plant the other one, the poisoned one, in the street."

"Who would want to poison you?" I asked. "And why?"

"I asked myself that three days ago," said Allhoff. "Splayton might want to poison me, but he doesn't possess the nerve. Splayton ties up with Raleigh. Raleigh, who kills for money, wouldn't be murdering me free of charge, merely for the practice, would you, Danny?"

Raleigh didn't answer. He was staring at Gebhart and the expression on his face wasn't pretty.

"Gebhart," I said suddenly. "Gebhart wanted to kill you. You mean he hired Danny? You mean he—"

"No," said Allhoff. "He didn't hire Danny. I doubt that Danny would have tried it for money. He frightened Danny into it."

Raleigh wasn't the sort of guy who frightened easily and I said so.

"He's afraid of the chair," said Allhoff. "Did you ever see one of them who wasn't?"

I sighed. "Can you tell it in monosyllables?"

"Sure," said Allhoff. "You remember Gebhart came in here with his woman to sneer at me because he'd solved the Murdock case? You'll also remember that a day later it developed he'd made a mistake. To quote him 'his information was faulty.'"

"So?"

"He lied the second time. Not the first. Somehow, probably through his farflung stool-pigeon system, he learned the truth of the Murdock killing. For all I know, he had evidence to prove it, too. But after the humiliating half-hour he spent up here, he decided my death was vastly more important to him than a murder solution."

"So," I said, "he told Raleigh what he had, promised to forget it if Raleigh got you."

ALLHOFF SIGHED heavily. "Simmonds," he said, "you'd make as bad a crook as you are a copper. Gebhart wouldn't tell Raleigh that. If Raleigh thought Gebhart was the sole man who knew of his guilt, Raleigh'd kill

Gebhart, not me. No, Gebhart told Raleigh that I had broken the case, that I was waiting a few hours to clinch it. So Raleigh planned to kill me. He may have planned to kill Gebhart later. I don't know. When Raleigh's coffee didn't work he descended to the crudity of mailing a bomb."

Raleigh was standing up now. His face was turned in Gebhart's direction.

"You louse," he said. "Why don't you do your own killing? Why don't you—"

"Wait a minute," said Gebhart, gray-faced. "Wait, Danny. Don't you see it's all conjecture? He hasn't got a square inch of evidence. He can't prove a thing. If we stick together we'll beat it. There's not one single item he can present to a Grand Jury."

There was a hollow silence in the room, broken only by the sound of Mrs. Gebhart's weeping. His sister sat staring stonily ahead, while the blond Whalen girl linked her arm through Gebhart's. Raleigh, eyelids narrowed, tapped his fingers thoughtfully on the back of his chair.

"I'll get you for this, Gebhart," he said. "I'll get you sooner or later. In the meantime, though, we'll stick together. You're right, he hasn't any evidence at all."

Allhoff grinned like a storm trooper in the Dachau camp.

"Don't bet on it," he said. "You women may go. Battersly, take Raleigh and Gebhart across the street. Book them for murder, attempted murder and anything else the desk sergeant may suggest."

"Wait a minute," said Gebhart, "you can't do this. You've no proof. We'll be sprung in an hour."

"I'D HAVE the proof in less than that," said Allhoff. "Battersly, take 'em away."

Raleigh shrugged. "All right," he said. "Why stand there and argue? Since he has nothing, my lawyer'll have us out before lunch. We'll go quietly."

The women filed from the room. Battersly, escorting Gebhart and Raleigh, followed. Young Splayton stood up, relief on his face, and headed for the door.

"You!" said Allhoff. "Sit down."

Splayton turned around anxiously.

"You ain't finished with me yet?"

"Hell," said Allhoff. "I haven't started with you. Do you think I'm going to let you smack my assistant around and get away with it? Come here."

Splayton approached Allhoff's desk like a sparrow charging a rattlesnake. Allhoff turned over the typewritten sheet of paper before him.

"Now," he said, "this is a written draft of all the things I have just said. It explains everything. The Murdock and Weldon killings, the poisoned coffee, the bomb, and Gebhart's hand in these matters. Since you are as well informed of these things as I am, I must ask you to sign it."

Splayton blinked.

"You mean, a confession? You mean you want me to turn rat on the boss?"

"I am uninterested in your verminous tendencies," said Allhoff. "I want you to sign this paper. It'll make you a state's witness and you won't take the rap you quite well deserve."

Splayton shook his head doggedly. "No, sir," he said emphatically. "I ain't no rat and I ain't no dope. Why, the boss just said you ain't got no proof. If I don't sign that you can't do nothing to me."

"No?" said Allhoff and he conveyed an awful lot of threat in the single word.

Splayton shuddered. "Go ahead," he said. "Beat me up. I still won't sign it. I ain't as yellow as you think. I been beat up before and I ain't talked. I can stand a beating for five, six hours, I can."

"Yes," said Allhoff slowly. "And can you take a beating for fifty years?"

"Fifty years? You can't hold me more than forty-eight hours. I know the law."

"Do you?" said Allhoff. "Do you know, then, what happens to a guy who's already carrying two convictions on a dope rap? Do you know what happens to him the third time? He never gets out, except in a hearse."

SPLAYTON SHOOK his head violently. "I'm clean on that. I'm taking no chances. I ain't touched any stuff since my second conviction.

Allhoff shrugged and turned to me. He said: "Arrest him, Simmonds."

I took a step forward. "For what?"

"Possession of narcotics."

"I tell you I ain't got any dope," yelled Splayton. "I ain't handled dope since—"

"Search him, Simmonds."

Something was beginning to filter into my brain. I put my hand in Splayton's right-hand coat pocket first—I found what I expected to find. I held it out to Allhoff.

"An interesting little package," he said. "What do you think's in it, Splayton?"

Splayton stared at him. His face was ashen. He knew damned well what was in the paper package.

"It's a frame," he cried. "You planted that on me when you was feeling the material of my suit. They'll send me away for life."

Allhoff picked up a fountain pen. "Not if you sign this," he said. "We'll forget what we found in your pocket."

Splayton's indecision lasted less than twenty seconds. He grabbed the pen as if it were a life preserver. He scrawled his name across the bottom of the paper.

"Can I go now?" he pleaded.

Allhoff shook his head. "You're much too valuable," he purred. "You go to the can as a material witness. And don't change your mind in the Grand Jury room. I'll just keep this junk, in case."

Battersly came back into the room as I asked Allhoff a final question.

"Why the women?" I said. "Why was it necessary to bring Gebhart's mother, sister and mistress down here. Just to see him squirm a little more?"

Allhoff smiled happily. "In part. The most important thing was that I had to have someone Gebhart really cared for, consent to have a cup of coffee. It's quite possible that they might have refused. The more people I had here, the more chance that someone would try to drink the poison. When Gebhart knocked the cup from his mother's hand, I knew that once again I was right."

His smugness, as usual, was annoying, but there was nothing to do about it.

"Take this mug over to the D.A.," he said to Battersly. "On the way back, get me a can of coffee."

Battersly said, "Yes, sir," and stood expectantly at the side of the desk.

"Well," snarled Allhoff, "what the devil are you waiting for? A written memo?"

"No, sir. You usually give me the money first. Of course, I don't mind laying it out, though. I—"

Allhoff's fist hit the desk like Thor's hammer.

"*You* don't mind laying it out! By God, you'll pay for it yourself. Look what you brought me last time. Poison! You expect me to pay for my own poison. Get out of here and use your own money. This is the second time you've tried to murder me! You lousy yellow, low—"

Battersly scurried from the room, dragging Splayton with him. A torrent of adjectives flowed down the stairway behind him. I went back to my desk and stared grimly out the window.

Some day, I thought, some one *will* kill him. I wondered quite seriously if it would be I.

THE CORPSE THAT WASN'T THERE

OFFICERS SIMMONDS AND BATTERSLY, STARTING OUT TWO JUMPS AND TWO CLUES AHEAD OF THE LEGLESS, COFFEE-SWILLING INSPECTOR ALLHOFF, JOYFULLY ANTICIPATE A QUICK SOLUTION OF THE MURDER IN ROOM 1201— FOLLOWED BY PROMOTION AND ESCAPE FROM THEIR BITTER BOSS. THEN ALLHOFF THE OMNISCIENT POSES A RIDDLE: "WHY WERE THE WATER FAUCETS REVERSED IN THE MURDER CHAMBER?" AND, PLUMBING THE DEPTHS OF THIS WATER-PIPE PUZZLE, THE TWO LUCKLESS DICKS FIND THEIR RED-HOT CLUES TURNING COLDER THAN THE MURDER VICTIM'S CORPSE.

CHAPTER ONE
A CORPSE IN MY LAP

I LEFT the house a little after eight o'clock that morning. I walked toward the subway with the taste of buttered toast and my wife's farewell kiss upon my lips. Despite the bracing autumn air there was no spring in my stride. Mentally I was grappling with what was a perennial problem, almost an obsession, with me. For possibly the thousandth time in my police career, I was frowningly engaged in figuring the angles on a transfer.

For five years I had worked with Inspector Allhoff. And in those five years I had aged ten. Fifty times I had applied for a transfer. Fifty times the commissioner had said loudly, "No!" Now, I pondered the problem again with the desperate defeatism of a convict working on an escape from Alcatraz.

As I approached the marquee of the Lafayette Hotel, I had reached the melancholy conclusion that I was licked. My only avenues of escape from Allhoff were his sudden and heartwarming demise, my own arrival at retirement age, or direct aid from heaven. Then as I passed the hotel doors heaven took a hand in the person of Ralph Bardon.

Bardon rushed suddenly out into the street. His hair was disheveled and his eyes were wide. He looked like a man who was about to begin beating his breast in public.

"There's never a copper around," he said to the ornately uniformed doorman, "when you want one. I—"

Then he swung his head around and saw me. "Simmonds," he said. "Thank God!"

His right hand clenched into a fist and
smashed twice into Dawson's face.

I regarded him oddly. I'd known him for several years.
He was part owner and manager of the hotel. He was an
Elk and a solid citizen given neither to hangovers nor
hysterics. But at the moment he looked very much like a

man who has just seen a corpse. It developed a moment later that he had.

"Sergeant," he said to me. "Murder! And in my hotel. Not in thirty years—"

I knew that speech. I'd been hearing it from hotel men and rooming house keepers for years. I held up my hand to stop him and said: "Why don't you call Homicide? They—"

"I've called them. What am I supposed to do in the meantime? The crossword puzzle in the *Mirror?* I tell you, Sergeant, in all my thirty years, I never—"

"All right," I said wearily. "All right. Where's your corpse? I'll take a look at it."

He seized my arm and galloped me into the hotel. I accompanied him up to the twelfth floor. Bardon opened a door dramatically, flung out his hand, and said: "There! And, Sergeant, in all—"

"I know," I said. "In all your thirty years in the hotel business. Now you go down to the bar and have a drink. I'll take over here until Homicide arrives."

HE LEFT me with no reluctance whatever. I walked across the room to the bed and took a professional look at the corpse. From the point of view of a maniacal killer it was all very interesting. The face looked as if the Gestapo had handled the job on direct orders from Berchtesgaden. The skull had been smashed in as if a moderately sized building had fallen on it. The nose was neatly flattened up against the cheeks. The hair was matted with blood and the sheet on which the body lay resembled a cardinal's robe that had been dipped in cochineal.

It was a nasty mess. I sat down, my back to the corpse, and lit a cigarette. I reflected that in all my years as a copper this was the first time a dead man had just fallen in my lap. I had often wondered about these fictional detectives and journalists who were constantly being hit on the head by corpses falling from the fourth-story windows; who, through some apparently accidental inevitability, walked into murder and intrigue as an Irishman walks into a Saturday night brawl.

Well, at last it had happened to me. Not that I had any intention of performing some miracle of detecting—not that I intended to put my hand on the case at all. I would sit here quietly until Homicide arrived, then go downtown where Allhoff would continue his life work of driving Battersly and myself quietly crazy. I smoked my cigarette slowly and pondered the wide chasm existing between the detectives of fiction and myself.

Then I saw the fountain pen top. It was colored a rich green. It bore a gleaming gold clip on its side and it lay beneath the writing desk. I stood up. I maneuvered my way across the room with my back still to the corpse. I picked up the pen top and examined it. I glanced down at the desk. Scrawled upon a piece of the hotel writing paper was a telephone number in the Wickersham exchange. I folded the paper and put it in my pocket.

My heart was beating rapidly now. An idea, daring and radical, was gestating in my mind. A murder had been committed in this room. The commissioner, in common with most of his predecessors, didn't like murder. He was very partial to the men who solved them.

I thought for a moment of Muller. Muller, a detective-sergeant, had cleaned up a Brooklyn killing single-handed only a week ago. Muller had then drawn a month's vacation with pay, a citation, and a promotion. Now, here I stood, first man on the scene of a killing, with two clues in my hand. Suppose I held the fountain pen top, the scribbled telephone number out on Homicide? Suppose I turned up the murderer myself, alone and unaided? That certainly should be worth a transfer in any commissioner's book.

My right hand closed tightly over the pen top as the door was flung suddenly open and Lieutenant Marsden walked into the room. He looked at me in surprise not unmixed with disgust.

"Don't tell me Allhoff's on this damned case already?"

I reassured him. I told him as my pulse quickened that the case was all Homicide's. I bade him good-bye and hastened out of the room. I went downstairs and conducted the first wholly private investigation of my departmental career.

The desk informed me that the dead man was one George Green, registered from a small town in North Carolina. The switchboard told me that he had made one phone call the night before, that the number did not answer. A bellboy mentioned the fact that Green had tossed him a dollar for carrying the bags upstairs. All this was routine enough until I interviewed Room Service.

The graying clerk who handled the telephone there scratched his head.

"Green?" he said. "It's 1201, isn't it? Yeah. A bit of a nut. Eccentric, I guess. Called up late last night. Ordered two soft boiled eggs. Said they must be six minutes. Then he phoned down and squawked like hell because the eggs were hard. Who the devil ever heard of six-minute eggs, soft boiled?"

I sighed deeply, lit my pipe and went away. Perhaps, Sherlock Holmes could have gone right to work on the material I had. Frankly, none of it made any sense to me.

However, I wasn't discouraged. I had a phone number to work on and I was looking for a man who'd lost the top to his fountain pen. If I found him, fine. I'd win my transfer. If I didn't, it was Homicide's rap. I was in the enviable position of a man who has something to gain and not a red cent to lose. I eschewed the subway and took a taxicab downtown.

IT WAS twenty minutes to ten when the stairs leading to Allhoff's tenement apartment creaked beneath my foot. A moment later I entered Allhoff's combination office and living-room. As always the first impression I received, crossing the threshold, was one of superlative disorder. The floor was unswept. The wastepaper baskets were overflowing. The sink was a gray mausoleum brimming with dirty dishes.

Allhoff's laundry lay piled against the west wall, climbing dispiritedly day by day. The garbage can, beneath the sink, was again yielding up free lunch to myriad cockroaches. The bedroom door was ajar, revealing an unmade bed, twisted sheets and a blanket trailing on the floor. There was an air of mustiness in the room which filled my nostrils. I sighed heavily and sat down at my desk.

Allhoff regarded me with baleful little eyes over the rim of a chipped coffee cup. On his desk the electric percolator gurgled spasmodically. Allhoff slammed the cup down in its greasy saucer. I felt his gaze on me but did not look up.

Across the room from me, young Battersly leaned against the wall and read the comic papers with the desperate boredom of a man who has absolutely nothing else to do. I shuffled papers on my desk and tensed myself for the sound of Allhoff's harsh voice against my eardrums. It came like the sound of a machine gun with laryngitis.

"I will not be put upon," he said. "I shall not have my authority flouted."

I looked at him. To someone who didn't have to spend eight hours of each day in his presence, the idea was funny. He was never put upon. He was never flouted. He was feared more than the mayor himself. He was an arrogant combination of Napoleon, Heinrich Himmler, and Donald Duck. I relit my pipe and said: "Who's flouted you?"

Allhoff picked up the coffee cup, drained it and set it down again.

"You," he snapped. "You're forty minutes late. You'd never dare pull that sort of stuff in any other department. You take advantage of me because I'm easy."

Easy? Allhoff was as easy as a problem in calculus to a Kallikak with a nervous breakdown. I took the pipe from my mouth and said as much.

"Damn you," said Allhoff. "You're insubordinate as well. You're thoroughly incompetent. So, for that matter, is Battersly. I don't know why I'm stuck with such a lousy pair of assistants. How would you like it if I sent you over to rot in Staten Island? Two hours' travel a day. Decaying out there in the sticks. How would you like that?"

I met his eye squarely. "I'd love it," I said. "When do I go?"

Battersly looked up from his paper, a gleam of hope in his eyes. There was none in mine. I knew rhetoric when I heard it. Allhoff was certainly going to give me no transfer—and as for Battersly, he would work in this room until the day when either he or Allhoff died.

Allhoff opened his mouth to speak again, then closed it as we heard footfalls on the creaking stairs without. A moment later, there was a staccato rap on the door. In response to my shouted invitation, two men entered.

THE FIRST of them was stocky, well-dressed, and over-groomed. He strode rather than walked and he exuded an air of authority. He stood before Allhoff's desk, regarding the gnome-like figure sitting huddled over in his chair, his chest pressed against the edge of the desk. He said, crisply: "My name's Winters. I have a note here from the commissioner. This gentleman is Robert Dawson."

Dawson, who was well over six feet tall, bowed and smiled sadly. Allhoff uttered no word of greeting. He ripped open the envelope Winters had handed him, scowled and read it. He threw the note in the general direction of the wastepaper basket, looked up, and said antagonistically: "So the commissioner wants me to do a little job for his friends, eh? All right, where did you lose the dog?"

Winters blinked at him. "Dog?" he said. "What dog?"

Allhoff registered phoney surprise. "No dog?" he said. "Amazing. Don't tell me the case is more important than that. When the commissioner unloads his friends on me, I suspect political motives. The last time was a ward leader who'd lost his wallet. Having some influence he insisted on having the best man in the department on the job."

He drank a deep draft of coffee, and added with pleasurable reminiscence: "I had him thrown out of the office."

Winters' well-manicured finger tapped Allhoff's desk irritably. "See here, Inspector," he said. "I'm a well-known man in this town. I'm here on a rather important case. I expect at least courtesy."

Allhoff waved a grimy hand in my direction. "He wants courtesy, Simmonds. Give him some. If later, he wants some intelligence also, turn him back to me."

He buried his nose in his coffee cup and sipped noisily. Winter's face turned the color of the purple hibiscus at dawn. He opened his mouth wide and took a deep breath. I prepared to enjoy the invective he was about to hurl in Allhoff's face. Then Dawson, whose melancholy smile persisted, came into the conversation.

"Inspector," he said like a Balkan diplomat addressing Hitler, "I can well understand the impatience of a man of your talents with some of the picayune matters given you. This, however, is a rather important affair. Mr. Winters here, called his friend the commissioner only to be certain that the best brains in the entire department would be available to us."

Allhoff put down his coffee cup and grinned like a ninety-year-old ingenue who is the recipient of a pass from a football player. He bowed like an actor. He indicated two rather crummy chairs.

"Gentlemen," he said. "Sit down."

I regarded him with disgust. There were times when it seemed to me that all you had to do was tell him that he was intelligent and he'd write you a check.

Dawson and Winters sat down. The latter still appeared annoyed. Dawson, his face still wreathed in ineffable sadness, did the talking.

"I'm afraid, Inspector, we are confronted with the case of a missing man and quite possibly a murder."

"Missing Persons and Homicide," said Allhoff pleasantly. "The two most incompetent bureaus in the department. I shall be happy to show them up again. Now what's it all about?"

"The missing man," said Dawson, "is named Edwards. He is an old prospector. He was due in from Cripple Creek early yesterday morning. I was to meet him. When he failed to arrive, I got in touch with Cripple Creek. He left all right. He boarded the train. Yet he never arrived."

Allhoff took it very calmly. "Probably picked up a floozy in Chicago," he said. "What about the murder?"

"A cousin of mine," said Dawson. "Killed last night in a Bronx hotel. He came up from North Carolina yesterday. I just identified the body."

I took the pipe from my mouth and blinked. My pulse picked up a beat. I said: "Bronx hotel? North Carolina? What was his name?"

"Green," said Dawson. "George Green."

Allhoff twisted his neck around and glared at me. He said through contorted lips, "Go ahead."

"Go ahead what?"

"Go ahead and tell us who killed him. Sergeant Simmonds, the great detective! Asks one single question and knows all the answers. If you're taking the case over, go right ahead. If not, shut up."

I REALIZED I should have kept my mouth shut. I was on dangerous enough ground already, withholding evidence. Fortunately, there was a blow torch burning in Allhoff's soul at my temerity in daring to ask a question when he was handling a case. Otherwise, he would have been certain to ask my interest in the matter, to ask what the devil I cared about the corpse's name. I put my pipe back in my mouth and shut up.

Allhoff transferred his gaze from me to Dawson. "What," he asked, "is the connection, if any, between your dead cousin and this guy Edwards?"

Winters spoke impatiently as if he felt too much time was being wasted.

"Four of us were interested in a gold mine Edwards had found. Dawson here, Green, his cousin, Edwards and myself. There is no claim filed on the mine yet. Edwards is, to put it politely, not quite all there. He's a paranoiac. Delusions of persecution. Believes everyone is trying to steal his mine. He was to arrive yesterday, give us the location of the mine and collect the money for our interest. He didn't show up. In the meantime, Dawson's cousin Green, who just came in from the south to get in on the deal is killed last night in his hotel. We want you to find Edwards and Green's murderer. That's all."

"That's all!" said Allhoff. "Are you sure you don't want me to find out what became of Lord Kitchener and clean up the Elfwell case for you as well?"

Winters made a gesture of annoyance and futility. "I know it's puzzling," he said, "and difficult. That's why we asked the commissioner for his top man. If there is anything either of us can do to help you, don't hesitate to call on us. During office hours you can get me at the Drovers' Bank. My home address is—"

He reached toward his vest pocket. Then he said abruptly: "I forgot. My fountain pen is broken. May I borrow a pencil?"

Allhoff handed him a pencil and my heart stood still. I had a fountain pen top in my pocket. I was looking for the murderer of a man named Green. Before me was a banker who had had business dealings with Green and he was not carrying his fountain pen!

Allhoff took the paper with Winters' address. I half stood up and craned my neck reading it over his shoulder. It was on Madison Avenue in the fifties. I recalled the exchange of the telephone number I had taken from the Lafayette Hotel was Wickersham. That fitted, too.

Allhoff said: "All right, I'll think about this. I'll get the complete report from Homicide on Green's death. Undoubtedly, I'll want information from both of you. I'll get in touch with you. Dawson, leave me your address."

Dawson handed him a card. I fought to keep my mouth shut. I didn't want to arouse Allhoff's wrath again. Nor did I want to make him suspicious of what I was doing. But I had to ask one question. No effort of will could keep my vocal chords still.

"Mr. Winters," I said, "where did you spend last night?"

Winters raised his eyebrows and Allhoff gave me his prime, Grade A nasty look.

"Home," said Winters. "With my wife. Why?"

"Oh, nothing," I said, then to shut off Allhoff, I turned to Battersly. "Battersly, will you hand me those reports from the Alien Squad?"

Battersly obeyed blankly. Allhoff's eyes grew harder. He looked as if he were about to say something, but Winters spoke first.

"Battersly?" he said. "Is your name Battersly?"

Battersly admitted his identity.

"John Battersly?" persisted Winters.

Battersly nodded. Winters smiled cordially for the first time since he had been in the office.

"Congratulations on your game Sunday. I enjoyed it. I'm a great fan, you know. You kicked three goals, didn't you?"

THERE WAS a sudden silence in the room broken only by the swift sibilant intake of Battersly's breath. I looked over at Allhoff. His little eyes were glowing like two coals imported on a fast plane from hell. He licked his lips slowly with a pointed tongue. He said, and his vocal chords were oiled with venom: "He kicked three *what?*"

"Goals," said Winters. "In soccer. He's the best forward in the east. Aren't you, Battersly?"

Battersly didn't answer. His face was a sickly gray and his eyes were empty. I stood up, alarmed. Allhoff opened his mouth revealing all his stained teeth. Somehow he reminded me of a crocodile about to pounce on a rabbit.

"A forward," he said and his voice rose maniacally crescendo. "He kicked three goals, eh? And what, my fine athletic friend, did you kick them with?"

Battersly moistened his dry lips. Winters exchanged a bewildered look with Dawson whose melancholy had turned to puzzlement.

"What did he kick them with?" repeated Winters. "His legs. His feet, of course. Soccer, understand? You know soccer, Inspector."

Allhoff put his right hand on the edge of his deck. He pushed with all his strength. His chair flew across the floor on its rollers. The movement revealed for the first time to Winters and Dawson the macabre fact that Allhoff's body ended where his torso did. At the juncture where his thighs should have begun, there was nothing.

Two black leather stumps protruded over the edge of his chair. At the moment they wriggled horribly, dancing a rigadoon in the empty air. His fists, clenched and taut, pounded madly on the arms of the chair. His mouth was open and his larynx rattled like hail on a drumskin.

"He kicked three goals!" he roared. "With his legs and his feet. With those legs and feet? Whose? Damn you! Tell the pretty gentleman whose feet you actually used! You cowardly, yellow dog! You—"

He dived into the depths of his vocabulary and came up again with buckets of assorted obscenity. He poured them over Battersly hysterically. Twice, I attempted to stem the evil tide that gushed from his twisted lips. My voice was drowned out in his.

Then, physically exhausted, he stopped. He turned his head toward the open-mouthed Winters, the shocked and startled Dawson.

"Get out," he said. "If I want you I'll get in touch with you."

With no reluctance whatever they got out. Allhoff turned back to his desk. With a trembling hand he took the coffee pot off its base and filled his cup. He buried his nose in it and drank deep. Battersly stood cowering against the wall. His face was the color of dirty snow. His hands were tremulous, and though I could not see them I knew his knees were, too.

I breathed a deep sigh and lit my pipe. Five years of this same scene played over and over again with profane variations took almost as much out of me as Battersly. Then, I thought for a moment of the Green murder, of the fountain pen top and the telephone number in my pocket. I resolved that if I broke this case personally, I'd cut Battersly in on the credit. In the matter of a transfer, God knew, his need was greater than mine.

CHAPTER TWO

HOT AND COLD CLUES

ALLHOFF'S OUTBURST which had roared into my ears for the past five years had its genesis during a raid on a West End rooming house some time ago. In those days Battersly was a raw rookie facing danger for the first time. Allhoff was a seasoned, though misanthropic campaigner.

We had it from a stoolpigeon that the two thugs we were after had rigged a Tommy gun on the stairway dominating the door. Battersly's assignment had been to effect a rear entrance, attack the gun's operator from the rear at zero hour when the raiding squad came crashing through the front door.

The first part of the assignment he had carried out. Then, inside the house, he had undergone a quite understandable case of buck fever. He became suddenly panicky. Instead of attacking, he hesitated. During that vacillating moment, Allhoff, at the head of the raiding squad, came charging through the front door.

The Tommy gun went into immediate action, sending a score of bullets through Allhoff's legs before the squad disposed of the operator. A week later gangrene set in. Twelve hours after that came amputation.

Unfortunately Allhoff's legs were not the only organs that operation cost him. Part of his brain seemed to go with them. He emerged from the hospital bitter and brooding. Within him seethed a cauldron of hate, the fires of which were never low.

The commissioner was of no mind to lose one of his best men, legs or no legs. So he had arranged that Allhoff rent this tenement slum opposite headquarters and remain a member of the department *ex officio.* Allhoff had acceded to this request but had laid down one adamant condition. Battersly was to be his assistant.

This, then, had been the setup for the past five years. Allhoff devoted his life to extracting his revenge, losing no opportunity to make young Battersly pay for that one weak moment which had cost Allhoff his legs. I had been tossed into the combination, ostensibly to take care of the paper work, actually to lend a hand when Allhoff became too violent.

All in all, the three of us led a miserable life. I was thoroughly sick of it. That was the prime reason that I deliberately had jeopardized a clean career by withholding evidence in a murder case. There was nothing I would not do to ensure a transfer from this dank and miserable slum apartment where Allhoff dwelt with hate and venom in his twisted heart.

IT WAS a little after four o'clock in the afternoon when the complete report on the Green murder came in from Homicide. I glanced over the single-spaced typing on the onionskin sheets of paper and noted with marked satisfaction that Homicide was baffled.

With the two purloined clues in my own pocket, with the fact of Winters' broken fountain pen, plus the check I had done at lunch and discovered that the Wickersham telephone number was listed as Winters' residence, I figured I'd have little trouble breaking the case before Homicide had even evolved a tenable theory. Even better, before Allhoff had got his stained teeth into the case at all.

Allhoff watched me as I scanned the report. He removed his coffee cup from his mouth. "All right," he said. "Give."

I took a deep breath. I quoted and summarized. Almost everything contained in the paper I already knew. At the bottom of the final page I came across a fresh fact which set my heart to beating wildly.

"They found fingerprints," I told Allhoff, "on the bathroom faucets. They didn't belong to the dead man. They belonged to none of the hotel employees. They belonged undoubtedly to the murderer."

"So what?" said Allhoff. "If the killer has no record that means nothing. We can't go around printing every guy in town."

"There's something else," I said. "Though it's equally unimportant."

"Give me a fact," said Allhoff. "It's more valuable than your opinion."

"The bathroom faucets were reversed. The hot tap was fixed to the cold water and vice versa. Bardon, the manager, says he can't understand it."

Allhoff wrinkled up his brow and poured himself another cup of coffee. The fact that he was registering deep thought with absolutely nothing to work on, rather amused me. I was pretty sure, by now, that I had almost the entire answer to Green's death. For the first time in my life I was entering the stretch some eight lengths in front of Inspector Allhoff.

I looked across the room toward Battersly. He sat, the newspaper open to the comic page on his knees, staring broodingly out the window. There was something shocking about the expression of utter despair and futility upon so youthful a face. His eyes were blank and though he sat upright I had a distinct impression that his back was bowed.

I smiled at him and felt a warm glow inside me. Battersly didn't know it yet but he was going to get half credit in the solution of a murder case which had baffled Homicide, an ordinary enough occurrence, and defeated the great Inspector Allhoff, which wasn't.

Allhoff poured two more minims of caffeine into his system. He said abruptly: "What about those faucets? Does the report mention what kind of faucets they are?"

I picked up the onionskin again. Homicide wasn't very efficient, true. But they were damned thorough. They even mentioned the color of the dead man's shirt.

"Sure," I said. "It's all here. But I could have told you that. They use those bar-shaped modernistic faucets at the Lafayette. Those single lever affairs. Why?"

Allhoff grunted and returned to his coffee. He was silent for a long moment.

"It's damned funny," he said at last. "There are a number of angles I can see in this damned case. On the other hand, there are at least an equal number that I can't."

He drew a deep sigh up from his intestines and shook his head. I grinned happily. There were a number of angles I could see, too. Only one that I couldn't. And I knew where to look for that.

"After all," I said pleasantly, "no one's infallible."

HE SPUN around in his chair and glared at me. He said, "I am." He reached for the telephone, picked it up and said: "Get me Cripple Creek, Colorado. Chief of police, if they have one." He hung on to the wire and stared at Battersly and myself. "You two, get out," he snapped. "Go home. The atmosphere is more conducive to clear thinking without the presence of a pair of nitwits like you guys. Lam."

Nothing loath we lammed. Downstairs. I steered Battersly into Noonan's for a drink. He sat staring moodily into his beer. I drained my rye, set down the glass, and tossed the panacea for all his troubles in his lap.

"Listen," I said, "how would you like to be a hero?"

"At what?" he said bitterly. "Soccer?"

I shook my head. "A police hero. A headline copper. With the newspapers showering praises on you. With the commissioner handing you a bow. With yourself in so solid that you could probably wangle a transfer into any precinct, any department you wanted."

He looked up, a faint glimmer of interest in his eyes.

"Are you kidding?"

"I'm not kidding. I walked into a murder today. That Green murder that they've saddled Allhoff with. I believe I've got it tied up and in the bag. I'm certain I know whose fingerprints those are. Homicide and Allhoff will never figure it. All that's lacking is a motivation and unless I'm badly mistaken we can dig that up at this guy Winters' house. I'll cut you in."

Battersly's beer was forgotten now. The dull weariness that constantly glazed his eyes was gone. For the first time in years, he was eager and alert.

"Sergeant," he said, "God knows I'm grateful. This is the greatest break anyone ever gave me. What are the details?"

Benignly, like a scoutmaster who has bestowed another Eagle badge on a promising lad, I told him what I had.

"You see," I concluded, "everything points to Winters. There's the fountain pen angle. There's the fact of that phone number. I'm certain those are his fingerprints. We need motive. We're going to his house now to look for it."

Battersly ordered another beer. He looked suddenly thoughtful.

"But," he objected, "Winters apparently has an alibi. You asked him what he did last night. He said that he stayed home with his wife."

"Wives don't furnish very good alibis," I told him. "We can probably break that down. It's bound to fall anyway if the fingerprint angle holds up."

Battersly lifted his beer. I raised my rye. Our eyes met. We spoke no word. Yet I knew that each of us in his heart was drinking to the downfall of Inspector Allhoff.

I FELT the nervousness of a playwright on the eve of an opening as I rang the bell of Winters' Madison Avenue apartment. A rigid butler opened the door. He informed us that Mr. Winters was not in. Mrs. Winters was. Since that was the way I preferred to play it, I considered this an omen.

Janet Winters received us in the drawing-room. She was a tall, dark girl with provocative black eyes. There was, rather to my concern, a great deal of poise about her. I made my identity known. She took that calmly enough. I wracked my brains trying to remember the Allhoff technique for breaking down self-possessed young women. I achieved no good result. Battersly, I observed, wasn't going to be much help either.

He stood, hat in hand, eyes fixed on Janet Winters. He rather resembled a shy freshman calling on the campus belle. I sighed, cleared my throat and plunged in.

"Mrs. Winters," I said. "There is no reason for alarm."

She raised two delicate eyebrows. "Do I give the impression of being alarmed, Sergeant?"

She most certainly didn't.

"I called to see your husband," I went on. "With your permission, I'll wait for him. In the meantime I'd like to ask you a question or two."

She lit a cigarette with long slim fingers. "All right, go ahead."

"Your husband, I understand, spent last night at home?" I asked without much hope.

Janet Winters took the cigarette from her mouth. "As a matter of fact, Sergeant, he didn't. Why do you ask?"

In that moment I felt like a guy who has picked the daily double three days in a row. For once in my life, I felt shot with luck. Far from having the difficult task of breaking down Winters' alibi, his wife had calmly done it for me and tossed the fragments in my lap.

"Oh," I said, suppressing my excitement. "Can you tell me what time he went out? What time he returned?"

"He left a little after nine. He came in quite late. I was in bed at the time. It must have been well after midnight."

I exchanged a glance with Battersly. At that moment we both saw the same vision. An eight-hour tour of duty in a precinct as far removed from Allhoff's tenement as departmental geography would allow.

I thanked Janet Winters profusely for her help. I asked her again if she minded our waiting for her husband. She rose to her feet. She said, graciously: "Not at all, Sergeant. Perhaps you'd be more comfortable waiting in his study. If you'll follow me—"

I followed her, elation soaring in my heart. Battersly, his eyes shining, closed fast on my heels.

The first thing I saw on the study desk, after the door had closed, was the cigarette holder. Exultantly, I picked it up with my handkerchief. Battersly watched me with a conspiratorial air.

"Undoubtedly," I told him, "Winters' prints are on this. We can compare them with those prints Homicide took off the faucets in the Lafayette bathroom."

Battersly nodded. He turned to a steel filing cabinet against the east wall. He said, a touch of grimness in his tone: "We need a motive, don't we, Sergeant? Perhaps, we can find it here."

I stowed the cigarette holder away carefully in my pocket. A sudden hunch struck me.

"Look in the G file," I said. "See if there's any correspondence there."

"G?"

"For Green. George Green."

Battersly went through the files like a pirate digging for buried treasure. He extracted a sheaf of letters. He held them with trembling fingers as he ran his eyes across the page. Then he uttered an oath that was more a prayer of thanksgiving than blasphemy.

"Sergeant," he said excitedly. "It's here. He's been fighting with this guy Green about who should have control of that gold mine. Here, read some of this."

I pored over the correspondence. I gathered from the earlier letters that Green and Winters had never met—that Green had an out-of-town investor's suspicion of Winters, a baron of Wall Street. As the dates on the letters grew more recent, the context grew more acrimonious.

Green accused Winters of attempting to get control of Edwards' mine, whereas, he, Green, had been promised majority stock several months ago for lesser money. Green pointed out that since he had grubstaked the prospector, Edwards, though with no written contract, he was entitled to control.

Winters had replied to him angrily. Green retaliated by hinting there was a scandal somewhere in Winters' life, and threatening to expose him when they met in New York.

Then in a letter written less than two weeks ago, Winters angrily denied the scandal charge and threatened to thrash Green if he tried any blackmail. There was more in the same key.

I stuffed the letters in my pocket. "We're in," I announced gleefully. "We have our motive. Winters meets Green when he gets to town. They quarrel. Winters kills him. If the prints on this cigarette holder check with the ones Homicide already has, we've a case as cold as any Allhoff ever solved himself. Come on."

"Aren't we going to wait for Winters?"

"Why? We have everything we need. We're going down to headquarters now. Fingerprint division. Tomorrow morning, unless I'm badly mistaken, we'll have Allhoff's back against the wall."

AT NINE THIRTY the following morning, the telephone on my desk jangled. It was Fingerprints.

"Simmonds," said Dutch Slagle, "the marks on the cigarette holder you left here check with those hotel faucets. Homicide wants to know what the hell Allhoff's got. They're scared to ask him."

I said in an unnecessarily loud voice: "Allhoff's got nothing. Battersly and I have it. We'll present the whole case wrapped up and tied with a neat pink ribbon to the D.A. before lunch."

I hung up. I looked around to see Battersly grinning at me, and Allhoff glaring over the chipped rim of his coffee cup.

"Did I understand you to say that you were solving a murder case?"

"Battersly and I. The Green ease."

He looked at me as if I had announced I had just squared the circle. Then he threw back his head and laughed. The laugh nettled me.

"Go ahead," I said. "Have a jolly time. Your ego won't take it so well when we break the case before you've even got around to a theory."

"A theory," he said. "I have a theory. It's a cast-iron theory. But there's a missing piece. There's one angle I simply can't figure."

I gave him my smuggest expression.

"We have all the angles figured," I told him. "We're ready to turn the Green killer in now."

"Green?" he said. "What about this guy Edwards?"

"What about him? That's for Missing Persons. Battersly and I've been working on a murder case."

He regarded me strangely. He ran his fingers through his hair. "You have the confidence of a man who knows nothing."

"On the contrary, I have the confidence of a man who knows everything."

He filled his coffee cup. Oddly enough he remained calm. The explosion I had anticipated wasn't forthcoming. He emptied the cup and said: "What do you propose doing about it?"

"With your permission, Battersly and I will go out. We will bring Winters, his wife and Dawson down here. Then I'll solve your murder for you."

He lit a cigarette and looked at me for a long time.

"Go ahead," he said. "I haven't been amazed in years. Perhaps it's a pleasant sensation. But if you two guys, with your limited minds can solve a case I can't figure, I'll stop being a copper and go in for crossword puzzles in the tabloids. All right, go ahead. Send out your invitations."

Battersly and I marched from the room as if each of us carried a royal flush in his hip pocket.

CHAPTER THREE
A RUDE AWAKENING

I FELT like an actor on a first night who is certain he is starring in a hit play. I was exultantly nervous. I believed that I held in my hand the key which would release me from the handcuffs chaining me to Allhoff's side. Across the room Battersly watched me with shining eyes. I was glad I had cut him in. I had never, in five years, seen him look so alive.

Allhoff sat crouched over his desk, his face expressionless. He poured coffee incessantly and drank it with an ugly gurgling noise. Winters, smoking an expensive cigar whose fumes gave fragrant battle to the normal mustiness of Allhoff's apartment, sat upright in a battered Windsor chair. He appeared, I observed, magnificently unworried.

Dawson, gaunt and melancholy, lounged back on our decrepit sofa. His fingers intertwined themselves nervously. He watched Allhoff drinking coffee much in the manner of Emily Post regarding a shoat toying with the day's garbage.

Between them, silken knees crossed, was Winters' wife. Even in the murky atmosphere which framed her, she remained beautiful. Her face was serious enough but there was an ineffable mockery in her black eyes which seemed to laugh at us all.

Allhoff suddenly slammed down his cup. He said, rather like Pontius Pilate washing his hands of the whole business: "There was some loose talk, Simmonds, about your solving a murder case. Go ahead."

"*Our* solving a murder case," I said. "Battersly is in on this."

Battersly flashed me a glance of gratitude and I felt, for a moment, like Sam Rover of the Eagle Patrol who has just done his good deed for the day.

"You mean," asked Winters, "that you've discovered who killed Green? That you've found Edwards?"

I met his eyes squarely. "I know who killed Green," I said evenly. "I don't know anything about Edwards."

Allhoff clucked with phoney sympathy. "An oversight, undoubtedly," he purred. "After cleaning up a murder case, Simmonds can handle a missing person in stride. He'll probably take ten minutes off this afternoon and dig up Edwards for you."

I held my tongue. At the moment I could afford to be magnanimous. I cleared my throat and stepped into the center of the room. I had seen Allhoff play this scene a hundred times. I intended to play it along his pattern.

"Now," I said, "let's begin at the beginning."

Allhoff's eyebrows lifted themselves in the general direction of the ceiling. "It's customary," he murmured *sotto voce.*

I summoned all my dignity as I ignored him. "George Green," I began, "comes to town from North Carolina. He is interested in a mining deal. He's invested money through his cousin in this guy Edwards' mine."

Allhoff filled his cup. "By the way," he said and the mockery was thick in his tone, "whatever *became* of Edwards?"

I gave him my most freezing look which had no effect at all.

"Green," I continued, "registers at the Lafayette Hotel. While there he is visited by someone who is also interested in the mine. Someone who has quarreled with him about who owns how many shares of it."

Still playing it according to Allhoff's technique, I glanced about the room, then brought my eyes to bear upon my suspect. Winters was watching me, a frown upon his brow. The man, I decided, had nerves. He evinced neither nervousness nor guilt.

I continued: "I have in my possession letters proving motive absolutely. The fingerprints Homicide discovered on the bathroom faucets, I have checked. Homicide couldn't find out to whom those fingerprints belonged. Battersly and I did."

I LOOKED over at Battersly, and in retrospect I must admit we bowed like two ham actors before the exit. Winters' brow was screwed up like the plans of the Italian General Staff. Dawson was regarding me intently. Janet Winters' eyes were still mocking. She possessed an odd quality of making a man feel like a fool even when he was quite sure of himself.

Allhoff registered mild boredom. He embraced Battersly and myself with his gaze and muttered: "Battersly and Simmonds, the bloodhounds of the law! The underworld trembles! Go on, Sergeant."

"All right," I said. "We have the motive. We have, in the hotel bathroom, the fingerprints of a man who denies he was ever in the room. Which is evidence enough to convict even a man of your standing, Mr. Winters."

I stood there like a lawyer who has just produced evidence which the Supreme Court is eating out of his hand. I turned my face in Allhoff's direction and gloated silently. Winters got up out of his chair and looked at me as if I were a congenital idiot.

"Do I understand that you are accusing me of killing Green?"

"Exactly," I said. "We have the motive. We have your fingerprints."

Allhoff swallowed a cup of coffee with the sound of a plugged sewer during a heavy rain.

"Hasn't Winters an alibi?" he asked. "Didn't he spend the evening of the murder at home with his wife?"

"Of course," snapped Winters. "Thank God there's someone around here with an iota of intelligence."

I cleared my throat and spoke very much like Ely Culbertson playing the thirteenth trump.

"Winters was not at home that night. Was he, Mrs. Winters?"

Janet Winters drew a deep breath. Her face was most serious, yet the odd mocking glint remained in her deep black eyes.

"No," she said softly. "He was not."

Winters stared at her as if someone had hit him on the head with an invisible club. His mouth was open and his eyes gaping.

"Janet! Are you mad? That was the night we played backgammon together. We went to bed a little after midnight."

Janet Winters met his eye. She shook her head almost imperceptibly.

"I do not consider that my conjugal duties demand I lie to the law," she said evenly. "When murder is involved my conscience insists upon the truth."

Winters expelled air from his lungs with the sound of a deflating tire. He turned to Allhoff, wide-eyed.

"Inspector," he said. "I don't understand this? Am I being framed?"

Allhoff shrugged his shoulders. "I haven't the slightest idea," he said amiably. Then to me: "Simmonds, is the gentleman being framed?"

"The Grand Jury won't think so," I said. "Battersly and I have a case as solid as any you ever solved."

"Look here," said Winters desperately. "This is insane. Now think, Janet. You remember that night. You must—"

"Yes," said Allhoff quietly. "Think, Mrs. Winters. Are you sure you're not making a mistake? Your husband's life may well be at stake."

"Are you prompting her?" I asked indignantly. "Because we've broken this case under your very nose, are you trying to get Mrs. Winters to lie?"

Janet Winters shook her head. "I won't lie," she said evenly. "This is a murder case. I have been brought up to believe that murder is a hideous crime. Not even to save my husband would I lie."

"All right," I said. "Battersly, take Winters downstairs and book him. I'll take my evidence over to the D.A."

Allhoff emptied his coffee cup. "Just a minute," he said. "There's one thing I'd like to know, Simmonds."

"What?"

"Those fingerprints which were in Green's bathroom. Homicide found them. They couldn't find out to whom they belonged. Winters has no criminal record. How did you happen to get a sample of Winters' prints and compare them?"

To answer that question truthfully was to get myself into one hell of a lot of trouble. I said: "I worked on some private clues which apparently escaped Homicide."

"Apparently," said Allhoff dryly. He lifted his head and stared for a moment at Dawson. Dawson had sat silent throughout the entire proceedings. He smiled sadly and shook his head as if commiserating with Winters.

Allhoff spoke commandingly. "Dawson, come here!"

Dawson raised first his eyebrows, then his gaunt body. He walked across the room and stood at Allhoff's side.

"Bend down," said Allhoff.

Dawson stooped over until his face was within six inches of Allhoff's. Allhoff's voice, suddenly savage and crescendo, filled the room.

"I don't like you," he screamed. "You and your damned smug smile. Are you pitying me because I'm a cripple? Do you consider me an inferior object because I have no legs? I can't stand your damned attitude any longer. I won't. I won't!"

WITHOUT WARNING he lifted both his hands. His left curled around the back of Dawson's neck. His right clenched into a fist and smashed twice into Dawson's face. Blood and two teeth fell down upon the floor.

For an instant I stood stunned. God knew Allhoff's conduct was unpredictable enough. But this was utterly unheard of. I took a step across the room as Janet Winters' voice rang out.

"You dirty sadistic little beast! I'll report you for this. I—"

"Allhoff," I said, seizing his arm. "For God's sake!"

Dawson backed away. He dabbed at his face with a handkerchief. He wiped off some of the blood but none of the astonishment and rage.

"Are you crazy?" he demanded thickly. "By God, if it weren't for the fact—"

"Sure," said Allhoff with amazing calm. "If I had my legs you'd beat me up. Isn't that it?"

"My God," said Winters querulously, "is everyone insane?"

I didn't answer. I was still regarding Allhoff. There was a bland smugness about him I didn't quite like. The only explanation for his outburst that I could evolve was the fact that he was so enraged at his own case being broken under his nose that he had gone suddenly amuck.

"Well," I said again. "Book Winters, Battersly. I'll—"

Allhoff ladled sugar into his coffee with a prodigal hand. "Just one more minute," he said with strange quietness. "I discovered this morning, Simmonds, that you were in Green's hotel room when Homicide arrived."

"Right." I gave him the details.

"So you went to work independently on this case, eh?"

"I had Battersly's help."

"You figured that if you two solved it you could gloat over me. Is that it?"

"It is not. I like you so little I don't even want to gloat. I want a transfer. So does Battersly. Perhaps, with this murder case wrapped up and in the bag the commissioner might see it our way."

"A transfer," said Allhoff slowly. "A transfer. And you were the first copper at the scene of the crime. And you solved it. Always, of course, with Battersly's aid." He was silent for a moment. Then an expression of demoniac glee distorted his features. He lifted his fist and brought it smashing down on the desktop. He opened his mouth and peals of gargantuan laughter resounded through the room. "Click!" he roared. "Click! That's the missing piece."

Bewildered I shook my head and looked around the room. Janet Winters regarded Allhoff as if he were something that had just crawled out of a swamp. Dawson holding his handkerchief to his face blinked dazedly.

Winters held his hand to his temple as if he were desperately trying to understand what was going on. Battersly asked me for his cue with his eyes.

"Allhoff," I said politely, "have you gone mad?"

His laughter ceased abruptly. "Wait a minute," he said and there was an unholy glint in his eyes. "I am fighting an internal battle."

"Go ahead and fight it," I said. "In the meantime, Battersly, take Winters—"

"No!" roared Allhoff. "No one is to leave this room until I say so. I've got to make a decision."

There was something so completely dominant in his tone that no one moved. He sat, hunched over his desk, the center of a great silence. His brow was corrugated and his stubby forefinger beat a thoughtful tattoo on the desktop. Finally he unleashed a sigh that came from the very bottom of his being.

"No," he said, "I won't do it. There's a lot of copper in me after all. A sort of a compulsion to make a criminal pay for his crime no matter how satisfactory it would be the other way."

"Allhoff," I said, "you're talking Choctaw."

"I'll put it into English. I'll tell you who killed Green. I'll tell you what became of Edwards from Cripple Creek. I have solved the case, Sergeant. Without, I may add, Battersly's help."

I shook my head. "I know what you're doing. You're putting up a desperate fight to save your face. You can't go behind my case. You can't go behind my evidence. It's sure-fire."

"I can go so far behind it," he said viciously, "that you'll find yourself facing charges, Sergeant. That odd cloud you may notice hovering over your head is the endangering of your pension rights."

I FELT a slight quiver at the pit of my stomach. Allhoff was rarely wrong. And I *had* withheld vital evidence. But how, I asked myself, could he possibly know that? How could he conceivably crack the case I'd built up against Winters?

He filled his coffee cup. He emptied it. He took a deep breath. He said: "To quote yourself, Sergeant, let's begin at the beginning."

"You mean the night Green was murdered?"

"I mean the moment Edwards stepped off the train from Colorado."

"But he didn't," said Dawson.

"The hell he didn't," said Allhoff. "He arrived on schedule."

"Then where is he?" asked Winters excitedly. "Perhaps he can throw some light on all this. Where is he?"

"In Woodlawn Cemetery," said Allhoff, "lying in a coffin with a ton of earth over him."

I gaped at him. How he'd found this out, I had no idea. "You mean," I asked, "that it was a double murder? Green and Edwards?"

"No, Dick Tracy. I don't mean any such thing. Since you were at the hotel before I got any information, I guess you had the same clues to work on that I did. More, as a matter of fact. But, with your customary stupidity, you blew them."

"What clues?" I was frankly nervous now. "How did I blow them?"

"You found a corpse registered as George Green from North Carolina, didn't you?"

I nodded.

"You probably found out that he ordered soft boiled six-minute eggs for breakfast. Moreover, it's quite likely that a bellboy told you Green tossed him a dollar tip."

This was all true enough and I said so. Allhoff refilled his coffee cup. He sighed as if exasperated with the utter stupidity of the world.

"Well," he said, "Green wasn't Green. He was Edwards."

Winters gasped. Battersly glanced at me but I did not meet his eye. The hollow sensation at the pit of my stomach spread to the lower intestines.

"How could Green be Edwards?" said Dawson through his bleeding mouth. "That's ridiculous."

"No more ridiculous than a six-minute soft boiled egg," snapped Allhoff.

"Look," I said, "would you kindly take a moment to tell what in the name of God eggs have to do with it?"

"Sure," said Allhoff. "Edwards came from Cripple Creek. That's about ten thousand feet high. The boiling point of water is much lower than it is at sea level. It would take six minutes to cook a soft boiled egg in Cripple Creek."

I blinked and digested this information. Allhoff grinned at me happily.

"Then there's the dollar," he said. "No one apparently thought to ask that bellboy how a flimsy dollar bill could be tossed at him. Yet Homicide assures me 'tossed' was the word he used. Obviously it was a silver dollar. There are more silver dollars in use around Denver than anywhere else. I immediately arrived at the conclusion that Edwards was Green."

I thought it over and took heart. I nodded reassuringly in Battersly's direction.

"That doesn't touch our case," I said. "Edwards or Green. He was murdered, wasn't he? So my cast-iron evidence makes Winters the killer of Edwards instead. In effect, it's still the same case."

"In effect," said Allhoff, "you're a blundering slow-witted lout whose screwing around has almost sent an innocent man to the chair, made a fortune for a murderer and dragged yourself and Battersly into the stinkingest departmental trial that ever gave off an odor."

I didn't know precisely what he was driving at. But somehow I wished I was a long way from here. There was a certain gloating assurance about him. I remembered his reputation for being right, my own for being wrong. I bit my lip. I said: "Will you explain all this?"

"Willingly and loudly. Since Sherlock Simmonds and Doctor Watson Battersly have stepped down, Inspector Allhoff will take over. Hold on to your hats everybody, here we go!"

CHAPTER FOUR
PROF. ALLHOFF'S
MURDER CLASS

THERE WAS a breezy confidence about him that I didn't like at all. He tilted his coffee cup, spilling the last three drops upon his chin. He leaned back in his chair and began to talk with all the apodeictic authority of an isolationist senator.

"This guy, Edwards, apparently finds a gold mine. He is, as Dawson has told us, as Cripple Creek has wired us, a bit of a nut. He'd been gypped out of mines before this and now he's panicky about city slickers. He doesn't even file his claim. He comes to New York to sell part of it for a lot of cash. Dawson, who knows him, is supposed to meet him at the station."

"And," I murmured, taking heart, "today is Tuesday. We know all these facts."

"Thus far you do," said Allhoff. "Now I'll give you some more facts. Facts which completely escaped you. Edwards *does* arrive on that train. Dawson *does* meet him. Dawson takes him to the Lafayette Hotel. But before doing so he pours a lot of slime in the old guy's ear. He plays on the old man's delusion of persecution. He tells him that big operators from Wall Street are out to steal his mine. That extreme caution is called for."

Dawson took the crimson handkerchief from his lips. He said: "This is ridiculous."

Allhoff ignored him. He continued.

"To this end Dawson persuades Edwards to mask his identity. This, says Dawson, will fool the crooks who are after the mine's location. Dawson, his old pal, has it all fixed. Edwards is to assume the person of one George Green, Dawson's cousin from Carolina. Edwards, who apparently trusts Dawson, agrees. Dawson loads Edwards with papers and stuff which will identify him as Green and takes away everything which might identify him as Edwards. Then he registers him as Green at the Lafayette Hotel and tells Winters that Edwards never arrived."

I considered this. It sounded all right, but for the life of me, I didn't see that it interfered with my case against Winters.

"What about the fingerprints?" I said. "What about Winters' prints on the bathroom faucets?"

"Ah," said Allhoff, "you mean those very odd faucets? The one marked hot on the cold water tap and vice versa?"

"What's so significant about that? It often happens."

"Not in first-class hotels," said Allhoff. He leaned across the desk and fixed Winters with his index finger. "Now, Winters, it is true, isn't it, that recently your wife decided to change your bathroom fixtures? She brought home samples for you to examine?"

Winters blinked. "My God," he said, glancing at his wife. "Yes, yes, Inspector. That's true. I—"

Allhoff's upheld hand silenced him. "The fact of those faucets being reversed started me thinking that perhaps the fingerprints had been planted on them *before* they were taken into the hotel. That's exactly what happened. Our killer in his haste accidentally reverses them when he screws them into the water pipe."

"You mean," I asked, "someone was trying to frame Winters?"

"With your help," said Allhoff, "yes. We have these bitter letters about the mine between Green and Winters. That makes a motive. The theory is that Winters called on Green to straighten things out, they had a fight and in a rage Winters killed him. The fingerprints in the bathroom prove it. Hell, you figured that all out yourself, Simmonds. That was exactly what the killer wanted you to do."

"I still don't get it," I said. "What's the murderer's motive?"

Allhoff cocked an eyebrow in Dawson's direction. "Do you care to tell him, Dawson, or shall I?"

Dawson took the handkerchief away from his mouth. He said again, "Ridiculous." I noted, with a sinking heart, that he didn't say it with a great deal of conviction.

"Edwards is dead," said Allhoff. "Only Dawson now knows the location of the mine. Moreover, Dawson has the dough that Winters put up. He's already claimed he'd forwarded it to Edwards in Cripple Creek. He also has something else."

Winters glared at Dawson. Then he turned his head and regarded his wife with an odd mixture of fear and wrath.

"What else has he?" he asked and he was obviously fearful of the answer.

"Mrs. Winters," said Allhoff.

THERE WAS a hush in the room broken only by the swift intake of Janet Winters' breath.

"It had to be," said Allhoff. "If a man is using his wife to front for him on a phoney alibi, he certainly has it fixed with her first. Winters told us at once that he spent the night of the murder at home with his wife. His wife denied it. Then when I checked on those faucets it was clear her hand was in it, too. Why?"

"Why?" I echoed weakly.

"Because she's been having an affair with Dawson. Because if Winters burns for murder she and her lover get the money. This figured obviously. A few moments ago I proved it."

"How could you prove such a charge as that?" snapped Janet Winters.

Allhoff grinned satanically. "With Dawson's teeth. You sat quiet and still while your husband was being railroaded to the electric chair. You made not the slightest protest. Yet when I smacked Dawson, you unleashed a howl. Obvious, wasn't it?"

Janet Winters bit her lip. I focused my eyes on the far wall and called every brain cell into action. If Allhoff was right and I was wrong, I was going to find myself in more trouble than a rugged individualist at Camp Dix.

"Wait a minute," I said. "What about this Green? Where is he? And why should Dawson have gone through that business of switching Edwards' identity? Couldn't he have framed Winters for killing Edwards with the same result? Why all this business of substituting the identity of the two men?"

"A fair question," said Allhoff. "Green exists only in Dawson's mind and on the police blotter. That switch was done for reasons of motive. Dawson couldn't possibly cook up a motive for Winters' murdering Edwards. Edwards demanded a certain price for an interest in his mine. Winters was prepared to pay it. Edwards, who I gather was rather illiterate, would not engage in any angry cor-respondence. No, Dawson needed this Green whom he invented. Green, a supposed business man, ostensibly gets into this bitter financial controversy with Winters. Dawson, of course, is actually writing these Green letters, having them forwarded by some stooge of his in Carolina.

"I've been in touch by phone with the coppers in that Carolina town Green was supposed to come from. They found out from the post office that letters addressed to Green were being picked up from a certain box. They got the guy who was picking them. They found the original of Winters' letters in his possession. He talked at the drop of a rubber hose."

Winters sighed heavily.

"What I fail to understand," he said, "is if those finger-prints of mine were planted in the hotel, how did Dawson figure they'd be traced to me? After all, the police can't go around checking prints with every person in New York City."

I exchanged a glance with Battersly. There was something cold and unpleasant at the pit of my stomach. Allhoff drained his cup again and looked at me like the devil about to light a particularly hot fire in Hades.

"The Sergeant wanted a transfer, didn't you, Sergeant?" he said mockingly. "The point Winters just made had me troubled for a while. If the killer left Winters' prints, it was obvious he must also leave some clues which would lead Homicide to Winters. I'm quite sure he did. What did you do with them, Sergeant?"

I SAT down, feeling as if there were water instead of blood in my knees. I saw Allhoff's unholy grin through a haze. He had me cold and completely. If I got out of this with less than a fine of two months' pay, I'd consider myself lucky.

I took a deep breath. I murmured a silent prayer to the patron saint of dumb police sergeants. I took the pipe from my mouth with a trembling hand and told him everything. As I spoke I was aware of Battersly's eyes upon me. He looked rather like a little boy who has discovered that his father has lied to him.

Allhoff heard my recital, his face twisted up, and gleaming mockery in his eyes.

"So," he said as I finished, "you withheld evidence, eh, Sergeant? And Battersly was in this, too."

"No," I said. "He really wasn't. He—"

"You said he was," said Allhoff mercilessly. "You said it three times before witnesses. Of course, the matter will be reported. It'll probably cost you both a degree of seniority and a month's pay."

I did not meet Battersly's eye. Yesterday I had lifted him up beautifully. Today, I had dropped him with a thud.

"You see," Allhoff went on, "Dawson figures it simply. As a relative, he identifies Green. The body is buried and no questions asked."

Across the room, Dawson cleared his throat. "Inspector," he said, "you're a master of conjecture. You'll need more than conjecture in a jury room."

"I have a witness," said Allhoff. "Haven't I, Mrs. Winters?"

For the first time since I had known her, Janet Winters revealed a measure of uncertainty. She glanced quickly toward Dawson, then back at Allhoff.

"You see," said Allhoff, "when I figured this plumbing business, I had a couple of boys from the detective bureau—not my own assistants here, of course; they were too busy working out the case for themselves—canvass the hardware shops in your neighborhood. It was simple since the faucets you bought had to be the same type as those used in the Hotel Lafayette. I discovered the store where you purchased those faucets, Mrs. Winters. I discovered further that the hardware dealer has an identifying mark on all his merchandise. That's enough, with the rest of the evidence to make a very tight case against you, Mrs. Winters. If you can explain it all without involving Dawson, you're most ingenious. If you can't, you'd better involve him now. Being a woman and a witness for the state, you'll probably save your life."

Dawson leaned forward on the couch. Janet Winters avoided her husband's eye and looked squarely at Allhoff.

"I've always been a realist," she said evenly. "So I see your point, Inspector. I do involve Dawson. And right now."

Dawson said, "Janet!" But she didn't look at him. She regarded Allhoff with her deep black eyes and it seemed to me there was some hatred in them—some hatred and a great deal of respect. "Maybe," she said, "I should have married a man like you."

"In my day—" said Allhoff, so softly, so reminiscently, that for an instant I was shocked. Then he broke off abruptly. He snapped: "Battersly, get me a copper. Take Mrs. Winters and Dawson out of here. Book them across the street."

Battersly moved dully toward the door. All the hope he had glowed with yesterday was gone. He moved like a beaten man. I felt like a louse. Allhoff drank coffee noisily like Goering toasting the fall of Paris.

THE THREE of us sat alone in the office. Allhoff chuckled without turning around.

"Why don't you boys get in touch with Eddie Hoover?" he said mockingly. "I understand he needs men badly."

I didn't answer him directly. I mentioned something that had been on my mind for the past few minutes.

"About that hardware store—" I said. "Isn't it odd that each dealer should carry identifying marks on every piece of material?"

"Odd?" said Allhoff. "It's impossible. But what woman would ever know that?"

I shook my head. Whenever he tried a bluff it seemed to work. When I tried one, I invariably fell on my face.

"There's one more thing," I said. "Do you recall before you began your explanation you announced you were conducting an internal struggle? After that you said that there was a lot of copper in you after all. What was it all about?"

Allhoff spun around in his chair. He balanced his coffee cup delicately on the stub of his right thigh.

"Oh, that," he said. "I was wondering if I ought to teach you guys a lesson. I was considering letting you get away with your case. Letting Winters burn. Then I would produce my own evidence. You certainly would've looked like a couple of first-rate idiots then."

"You actually considered that?"

He grinned. "Why not? I think it would have been damned funny."

"Allhoff," I said very seriously. "Why don't you see a psychiatrist? Consider, for God's sake, your mental health. You don't think it's normal, do you?"

His eyes lit up. His twisted smile spread over his face. "How's my mental health?" he said, and there was a hysterical note in his voice. "Oh, I can't kick, Simmonds." His voice rose like a siren blown by a maniac. His fist beat furiously on the desktop. "I can't kick, damn you! *I can't kick!*"

A BED FOR THE BODY

IT WAS GREAT NEWS FOR KILLERS! INSPECTOR ALLHOFF— TRAPPED ON THE WRONG SIDE OF THE MURDER FENCE! IN FACT, ONLY A GRADE-A MIRACLE COULD SAVE THE LEGLESS, COFFEE- TIPPLING SCOURGE OF THE UNDERWORLD FROM THAT SAME HOTSEAT HE HAD SO HOSPITABLY RESERVED FOR SCORES OF OTHERS.

CHAPTER ONE
THE EXECUTIONER'S
FRIEND

IT **WAS** a quiet afternoon. Outside the snow fell like confetti, blanketing the ugly architecture of police headquarters across the street. Dark clouds covered the sky and filtered a crepuscular light down upon the city. In Allhoff's tenement apartment the cluster of three fly-specked bulbs overhead had already been lit.

On my left, Allhoff's back was hunched over his desk. I saw his claw-like hand reach out suddenly toward the stained coffee pot which gurgled dispiritedly on its electric base. He poured eight ounces of a thick black liquid into a cup the color of a dirty sheet. He drank it with a sibilant unpleasant sound.

Battersly, tall and rather handsome in his uniform, sat in a swivel chair directly before me. He pored over the evening paper, studying the comics with the intensity of Einstein devoting his time to the fourth dimension. I toyed with a pencil and idly read a headline which informed me that Roy Anthony would be killed on schedule and impersonally by the sovereign State of New York, a week from today.

I glanced over at Allhoff and reflected idly that he was the high priest who had sent Anthony to be sacrificed on the altar of law and order in the Sing Sing death house. I reflected further that the state executioner should split his

"Hell,"—Anthony's voice came through the door—"you've got me cold."

fees with Allhoff. Certainly he supplied more work than any other individual in the entire department. I had often wondered how he felt about it. As a matter of fact I had often wondered how Allhoff felt about anything at all.

The door opened suddenly. I looked up. My hand swung toward the desk drawer which contained my Police Special. My movement stopped as suddenly as it had begun. I had no desire to die without drawing any of my pension money.

Battersly tore his eyes away from the fantastic adventures of Dick Tracy and faced reality. Allhoff put down his coffee cup. His little yellow eyes stared toward the doorway, toward the well-dressed man who stood there, toward the muzzle of the automatic which was in his hand.

Allhoff spoke first. "Anthony," he said, "you're crazy. Your brother's going to burn next week. If you blast me with a howitzer you can't prevent it."

GEORGE ANTHONY came into the room and closed the door softly behind him. He was a big man with graying hair and shrewd black eyes. His clothes were well-cut and expensive. His manner, even under these unusual circumstances, was assured. Two decades as a successful corporation lawyer had engendered in him a poise not easily dissipated. He sighed, sat down in a chair, and maneuvered his automatic so that it could easily swing in the direction of any one of the three of us.

"I'm not here on a mission of revenge," he said quietly. "I simply want to talk to you."

"Must you talk over a gun barrel?" demanded Allhoff.

"To you, yes. Normally, you'd throw me out of the place before I could say what I have to say. The gun is to compel your attention."

Allhoff glared at him. There was, I conceded, a degree of truth in Anthony's words. Allhoff's short temper, his absolute refusal to discuss anything connected with his work, were well-known. But the idea of having a gun held on him in his own filthy flat was going to infuriate him. Battersly caught my eye and I joined him in a sigh. Neither of us cared to have Allhoff infuriated at any time.

"The Governor," said Anthony, "is considering a commutation of my brother's sentence to life imprisonment."

Allhoff reached out and poured himself a cup of coffee. The hand that held the percolator trembled. It was rage, I knew, that caused that tremor, not fear.

"Very interesting," he said. "However, I am not responsible if a politician makes an ass of himself."

Anthony sighed. He looked around the chaotic room. Allhoff's laundry formed a dirty pyramid against the east wall. The dishes in the sink were reminiscent of a struck cafeteria kitchen. The bedroom door was open revealing an unmade bed and a mound of twisted sheets that attested to both Allhoff's complete contempt for the germ theory and a most restless sleep of the preceding night.

"Look," said Anthony, "I have the names of five of the jurors who convicted my brother upon a petition asking leniency. I have the signature of the D.A. who prosecuted the case. The Governor has hinted that if your signature, as the copper who dug up the evidence, is on the petition he'll consider it favorably."

Allhoff drained his coffee. "Your brother," he said, "murdered a man in a fight about a woman. The laws of this state say that a man must die for that. I've done my job. I'm through with the case. Now will you put up that gun and get out?"

"No," said Anthony. "I owe it to myself and to you to give you every chance."

I stirred uneasily in my chair. I didn't like the turn the conversation was taking. If Anthony meant by that last remark that he was going to demand Allhoff's signature at the point of his gun, I was very much afraid there was going to be some shooting. Allhoff was as obstinate as a stone wall.

"Look," said Anthony, "consider this: My brother Roy is sitting in the death cell. He is a sensitive educated man. He is about to die a miserable ignominious death for a single impulsive move. You can spare him. A mere scribbling of your name upon a piece of paper will save his life."

Allhoff looked as yielding as the R.A.F. He said with shocking humor: "The executioner is a friend of mine. He'd never forgive me if I did him out of the hundred and fifty bucks he'll get for burning Roy."

Anthony winced. "The evidence was circumstantial," he said. "It isn't fair that a man's life should be taken."

Allhoff snorted. "Circumstantial?" he said. "What evidence isn't? Do you believe there's a place called Africa?"

"Of course. Why?"

"Have you ever seen it?"

"I know people who have."

"Hearsay," snapped Allhoff. "Not permissible in any courtroom. Your knowledge of Africa is based on circumstantial evidence. Almost all human knowledge is. Now will you get the hell out of here?"

"For the last time," said George Anthony, "will you sign my petition? I'm asking you for your signature. That's all. If I don't get it, you'll regret it for the rest of your life."

ALLHOFF LOOKED squarely into the gun muzzle. "If you're threatening my life," he said, "it's your move."

Anthony stood up. "I'm not threatening your life. I asked you something. You've refused. That's all."

"The hell it is," said Allhoff. "Possession of a gun is illegal in this state. I'll turn you in for it."

"I have a permit."

"You have no permit to bring it up here and hold it on me. You'll get up to three years on the Island for it."

"I don't think so," said Anthony softly. "You see, Inspector, the gun isn't loaded. I merely used it to force you to listen to me. If the department knew that I'd stuck up the great Inspector Allhoff with an unloaded weapon, it'd get a laugh it has waited for many years."

Allhoff's eyes blazed. He had been calm enough when he believed his life in danger. Now that there was a threat of laughter turned against him he became furious. His fist belted down on the desk and coffee slopped over the side of the chipped cup.

He opened his mouth, dug deeply into the darker recesses of his vocabulary, and threw a choice assortment of oaths at George Anthony. Anthony stood calmly under the verbal barrage. He slipped his gun into his pocket, opened the door and disappeared into the hallway outside.

Allhoff swore viciously until he was out of breath, then reached for the percolator with an angry hand.

"That guy," he muttered between loud sippings, "he ought to be up there with his brother. By God, I'd like to get something on him. I'd even frame him. Coming in here with an empty gun. By God—"

His voice mumbled on, uttering slurred and violent threats against George Anthony. I glanced over at Battersly and grinned. Apparently the storm of his wrath, for once, was not aimed at us. It was characteristic of Allhoff that his anger was caused principally by the fact of Anthony's gun being unloaded. Death and danger he could face coolly enough, laughter and loss of dignity he could not.

Our second visitor of the afternoon carried no gun. Yet he had not been in the room three minutes when I recognized that he was destined to threaten my peace of mind infinitely more than George Anthony had.

He came in a few moments before Battersly and I prepared to depart for the day. He was young, brash and breezy as a gale. His clothes looked as if they had been designed by a tailor in Elkhart, Indiana, who had been told by a traveling friend what the actors were wearing on Broadway.

He entered the room without knocking and turned a one hundred percent personality smile on Allhoff. He said, "Good afternoon," with all the phoney affability of a telephone operator apologizing for giving you the wrong number. He beamed broadly at us all as if he were the firm's star salesman, which, it developed later, he was.

"My name," he announced, tossing a card on Allhoff's desk, "is Burroughs. Elmer Burroughs. You'll be very glad I came, Inspector Allhoff."

Allhoff took his nose from his coffee cup. He looked up at Burroughs like a man who was prepared to wager a minimum of a million dollars that the last statement was a downright lie. He picked up the card from the desk. Without glancing at it, he tore it carefully into eight pieces and threw it into the waste-paper basket. He lowered his eyes again and deposited his nose back in the cup.

The effect of this insulting pantomime on Burroughs was three millimeters less than nothing. His smile broadened. He took a folded pamphlet from his pocket and spread it open on Allhoff's desk. He said with the vulgar arrogance of the professional salesman: "Just take a look at this. You'll thank me for the rest of your life. I'm the man you've needed ever since you had your accident."

At that last word Battersly looked up, horrified. I felt a lump of ice fall inside my lower intestines. Allhoff looked at Burroughs over the rim of his cup. Burroughs, as unaware of the tension in the room as a corpse, rattled on.

"Yes, *sir.* I represent the Orthopedic Shoe Company. We have shod thousands of club feet, deformed feet, all kinds of abnormal feet for fifty years. With eminent satisfaction, too. And we let no grass grow under our *own* feet either."

He paused here for the laugh, as undoubtedly called for in the salesbook. Failing to get it, he continued.

"Look at this pamphlet. You'll see our shoes are made of the best iron and leather. Built up for short feet, reinforced with steel. Wear them, Inspector, made up to your own specifications, of course, and you'll walk as you ever did. Now, if you'll tell me the precise nature of your trouble we can get down to business."

HE STOOD there, bland as a mirror and very pleased with himself. He looked like a sunbeam as the thunder clouds gathered, all unaware that its existence will be terminated in another instant. Battersly stood up now, his back to the wall in both a figurative and literal sense. I sat still, my brain desperately trying to function, but every cell remained paralyzed at the enormity of the things Burroughs had said. We all looked at Allhoff, Battersly and I like a couple of air raid wardens waiting for a time bomb to burst.

It did.

Allhoff slammed down his cup with a sound as ominous as the first shot fired by the *Wehrmacht*. He put two trembling hands on the edge of his desk. He pushed his swivel chair out sharply. It moved halfway across the floor on its rollers. At the edge of the chair where his legs should have begun, were a pair of furiously wriggling leather stumps. They beat thrashingly against the empty air. His little yellow eyes glared across the room and I had the impression I was seeing hell through a lens. His lips were parted, revealing yellow teeth that were hungry for Burroughs' throat. He took a deep breath and when he spoke his voice rose in vibrant crescendo that broke just about two points this side of hysteria.

"You grinning extrovert!" he shrieked. "Is this your idea of a practical joke? You gorilla's offal. You lousy low scum. You—"

He paused for a moment and drew another Breath. In that instant he conjured up several obscenities I had never heard before. He unloaded them through twisted lips. Battersly's face was white and his eyes were troubled. I felt a sickness at the pit of my stomach. I stood up and said sharply. "Allhoff!"

He paid no attention to me. He hurled the entire netherworld of his vocabulary at Burroughs. Then, finally, out of breath, he stopped. Burroughs stood before the desk calmly. For the first time in my life I witnessed someone taken aback not one whit by Allhoff's savage attack. True, his smile had vanished. His debonair attitude had not.

"Sorry," he said without contrition. "I guess someone down at the office made a mistake. However, no harm done, Inspector. We put out the best artificial legs in the business. Here, let me show you—"

Allhoff's howl of stark rage sounded as if it had come from the jungle. He fumbled with trembling hands at his desk drawer. I knew what he was groping for. I sprang across the room and seized his wrist at precisely the same moment his fingers closed over the butt of the revolver.

"Get out," he screamed. "Get out or I'll kill you. If you ever come in here again, I'll kill you on sight. Get out! Get out! Get out!"

The final two syllables sounded like the high-pitched screeching of a tortured violin. At last Burroughs lost some of his poise. He saw Allhoff's hand on the gun in the desk drawer. He knew the margin of safety reposed solely in my ability to cling to Allhoff's wrist. He turned and fled down the stairs. I removed my fingers from Allhoff's wrist and stood back. I was tense and my teeth bit my lower lip. The worst, I knew, was yet to come.

Allhoff swung slowly around in the swivel chair and looked at Battersly. Battersly, his back still against the wall, faced Allhoff as he might have faced a firing squad. Allhoff uttered two sentences which disposed of the morals of Battersly's mother. Then he said: "You louse, you sent him here."

That was as ridiculous as it was unjust. The last man in the world to have countenanced Burroughs' presence in this place was Battersly. I said as much.

"Damn you," yelled Allhoff, throwing all logic to the winds, "you were probably in on it, too. Neither of you lose any opportunity to attack me. You're a couple of stinking parasites living on a legless man. Battersly's yellowness cut 'em off, and you, Simmonds, are on his side. You're a pair of—"

Any self-respecting printing press would have balked at printing the next five hundred words. He hit Battersly savagely with every profane phrase in his book. In a number of digressions he did not neglect me. Then he shut up as suddenly as he had begun. He swung around to his desk again, poured himself another cup of coffee and drank it, loudly and greedily.

Battersly, pale and with his fingers trembling, sat down again and picked up his paper. I sighed heavily, returned to my desk and filled my pipe. These outbursts were an ancient story to me. Yet I would never become inured to them if I spent the rest of my life in Allhoff's company, which I prayed fervently, might heaven forbid.

THE ODD environment in which the trio of us spent eight good hours a day in each other's company had its genesis in a raid of several years ago. Back in the days when Battersly had been a raw rookie with less than six months' service and Allhoff an Inspector with two good legs.

A stoolie had informed us that a couple of thugs we had long wanted were hiding out in an upper West End Avenue apartment. He informed us further that a Tommy gun mounted on the stairway commanded the door against a raid.

Battersly's assignment had been to effect a rear entrance, to attack the gun operator from the rear at zero hour just as Allhoff led the main squad through the front door. Battersly had effected the entrance, all right. Then he had become suddenly panicky, and fled up the stairs instead of carrying out the rest of his orders.

Allhoff had charged through the front door in time to receive a blast of machine gun bullets through his legs. Gangrene had been followed closely by amputation.

But the commissioner had been of no mind to lose his best man. Circuitous bookkeeping kept Allhoff on the city payroll at his old salary. He had taken this tenement slum, primarily because it was so close to headquarters, secondarily because it made not the slightest difference to him, how or where he lived.

With a sense of savage poetic justice he had demanded and received of the commissioner the services of Battersly as his assistant. In that capacity the younger man never had a chance to forget that devastating moment of cowardice which had cost Allhoff his legs.

Realizing that Allhoff's mind had become twisted where Battersly was concerned, I had been sent over here to pour oil on the waters whenever they became too troubled. I was getting very tired of it. However, I had to stick it out. I saw no point in sacrificing a pension at this stage of my career.

CHAPTER TWO
FIVE DAYS OF GRACE

ARRIVED at the tenement the following morning a little after nine o'clock. Battersly was already at his desk. Allhoff sullenly imbibed his first pint of coffee. The flat was in its usual chaotic disarray.

However, as I took my seat I noted a single odd circumstance.

Allhoff's bedroom door was closed. If memory served me correctly, it had never been closed before. Each weekday morning I had stared directly across my desk to see a pile of disheveled and dirty linen piled on a mattress that sagged like the back of an ancient pack mule facing me in the bedroom.

At the moment, I paid the matter scant attention. I turned to the morning reports on my desk and went over them. Battersly engaged himself with Winchell, and Allhoff poured liquid into his stomach like a camel who is going off on a long weekend.

Shortly after ten o'clock, footfalls sounded outside. Preceded by no knock, the door opened and Inspector Chalmers strode in. Allhoff lifted his head and I lifted my eyebrows. There was no love lost between these two men. To my knowledge Chalmers had never been in this room before in all his life. As a matter of fact, nearly all official business came to us through the commissioner direct. The rest of the department, aware of Allhoff's temper, were content to leave him alone anyway.

Chalmers looked around with morbid interest, like a man in a zoo.

"Ah," he said, laying the sarcasm on with a trowel, "charming little place you have here, Inspector. Who's your decorator?"

Allhoff replaced the percolator on its base with a bang.

"What the hell do you mean coming in here without knocking? What the devil are you doing here anyway?"

"I assure you," said Chalmers looking like a man who is smelling a very bad smell, "it is not a matter of choice. I am here on orders."

"Whose orders?"

"The first deputy commissioner."

"All right," said Allhoff. "If you got any orders, carry them out and get the hell out of here."

"Very well, Inspector," said Chalmers with exaggerated politeness as he walked across the room.

I watched him curiously. What possible orders he might have which led him into Allhoff's miserable apartment was beyond me. My gaze followed him with interest as he came to a halt outside Allhoff's bedroom door. He put his hand on the knob and pushed. Nothing happened. He turned around again and held his outstretched palm in Allhoff's direction.

"The key, Inspector."

Allhoff stared at him. He seemed puzzled which, in my book, was odd.

"The key?" he said. "You mean you have orders to go into my bedroom?"

"Correct, Inspector."

Allhoff shrugged and blinked. "Are those monkeys across the street trying to frame me?" he asked. "They haven't enforced the adultery laws in this state since Steuer got sore at a witness eight years ago."

It was my turn to blink. That last statement implied that there was a woman in Allhoff's bedroom. Personally, I would sooner have gone looking for one in a Franciscan monastery than on Allhoff's sagging mattress.

"The key," said Chalmers again. "I remind you, Inspector, I am under orders."

"The commissioner will hear of this," said Allhoff. "The key, Inspector, is on the inside of the door. If you knock, it will be opened."

CHALMERS RAPPED sharply against panels. Battersly and I watched him, fascinated. If, after all these years, Allhoff had a girl, I was damned interested in seeing what she looked like. Chalmers knocked again. Nothing happened.

"This," said Allhoff testily, sliding down off his chair, "is a damned outrage. Do I go snooping around the first deputy commissioner's bedroom, prying into his private life? I'm going to raise hell about this."

It was all happening too fast for me. If Allhoff had any private life he had kept it better hidden than the plans for the United States Navy bomb sight. He crossed the room and pounded heavily on the door.

"It's all right," he said loudly. "It's me. Open the door."

The door remained closed and there was no sound whatever from behind the panels. Chalmers looked at Allhoff oddly.

"I have my orders, Inspector," he said punctiliously. "Shall I break the door down with your permission or without?"

Allhoff scratched his head. He appeared to be thinking deeply. He took a long breath.

"With my permission," he said at last. "I smell a faint odor of halibut somewhere. "

Chalmers moved two paces away from the door. He charged against it, striking the panels with his shoulder. The ancient lock gave way. The door swung open. I stood up and craned my neck. There was someone in Allhoff's bed. I winked at Battersly and walked toward the room.

If, after all these years, Allhoff was going in for sex, I was most anxious to see with whom.

Chalmers put his hand on a dirty sheet and threw it off the bed. All of us stared down at the thing his gesture had uncovered. For there, head cradled on Allhoff's pillow, was Elmer Burroughs. His throat had been cut neatly and with dispatch. Blood stained the gray sheets. And Burroughs' head lolled crazily and loosely on his neck.

Chalmers said with vast satisfaction: "Ah, I thought so."

Dazed, I turned my head and looked at Allhoff. His face looked like old parchment. There was, for perhaps the first time in his life, a shadow of fear in his eyes. He said, "My God," twice and very slowly.

"Undoubtedly," said Chalmers with a gloating note in his voice, "undoubtedly, you can explain the presence of a corpse in your bed, Inspector?"

"I can," said Allhoff sharply. "But I won't."

"Ah," said Chalmers mockingly, "for some noble reason, no doubt."

"For a damned expedient reason," said Allhoff. "No one would believe me."

"It's quite likely that you'll burn for this," said Chalmers as if he relished the idea.

ALLHOFF BREATHED heavily. He turned suddenly and walked into the other room. He stretched forth his hand and slopped coffee into his cup. He drank it like an Alpine traveler gulping brandy from a Saint Bernard's collar. Then he swung around in his chair and faced us. Chalmers' face was wreathed with satisfaction. The boys across the street would be very happy at the crashing sound of Allhoff's downfall. Battersly's register was utter bewilderment. He stared blankly around the room, trying to grasp a situation which was too much for him. I slowly considered all the angles and moved step by step nearer to nothing at all.

"At last," said Allhoff bitterly, "I appear to be making several people happy. You have found a body in my bedroom. It is the body of a man with whom I quarreled yesterday— a man whom I threatened to kill. My loyal assistants will gleefully testify to that fact. They will, moreover, be delighted to tell you, that when they reported for work this morning my bedroom door was locked—a circumstance which has never happened before."

"Wait a minute," I said, "before you assume we'd crucify you for the sheer pleasure of it. We're both prepared to testify that George Anthony was in here yesterday, too. That he threatened you subtly for refusing to sign the petition for his brother's commutation. There's a possibility, faint as it may be, that you're being framed."

"Thank you," said Allhoff with ornate irony. "But that won't do. It would obviously be impossible for Anthony or anyone else, to plant a corpse in my bedroom without my knowledge. Especially since I have not been out of the house. Moreover, the fire escape ladder which leads to the street can be lowered only from upstairs. So the body could not have been brought in that way. The trap door to the roof is locked and always has been. I think you'll find it untampered with if you look. And finally, if you check you'll discover that Anthony has an alibi riveted together. I wouldn't be surprised if he spent last night with several solid citizens, all of unimpeachable reputation."

"Thank you," said Chalmers, "for riddling whatever defense your lawyer might pick up."

I looked at Allhoff keenly. "Are you admitting you killed Burroughs?"

"No," said Allhoff. "Nor denying it."

Chalmers moved across the room. He put his hand on Allhoff's shoulder—a gesture I had thus far seen only in the movies. He said: "I arrest you, Inspector, on suspicion of first-degree murder. Will you accompany me across the street to headquarters?"

For the past fifteen minutes the fire had gone out of Allhoff. He had been strangely subdued. He had the air of a beaten man. But now the old spirit flamed in him. He turned on Chalmers and the snarl on his face would have impressed a wolf.

"No," he shouted. "I shall not accompany you to headquarters. For years I've been getting you cretins across the street out of jams. For years I've been doing your work for you. For years I've saved your faces, saved the reputation of the department. Now, by God, I've got a case with a far bigger stake than ever before—my own life. And I'm going to work on it. I'm not going to rot helplessly in a cell while the D.A. builds up a sure case against me. I'm not going to jail and I'm not going to burn. I can't solve a case while sitting in the Tombs. If I'm locked up now, I'll burn. The whole damned department won't lock me up, either."

He ripped open the desk drawer. He whipped out his thirty-eight. Chalmers gaped at him. I stood up.

"Allhoff," I said, "are you crazy? You can't hold off the entire department with a gun. If you drive Chalmers out of here, they'll send over a squad. They'll—"

"Shut up," snapped Allhoff. "Get me the commissioner on the wire."

I SHRUGGED, picked up the phone, and put the call through. He spoke to the commissioner from the extension on his own desk. He did not, during the conversation, cease to threaten us with his gun. After some five minutes he hung up.

"All right," he announced, "the commissioner has seen it my way. My arrest is to be held off for five days. Because, as he says, of my past record, this is to be done. If you want to check that, Chalmers, you may use my phone."

Chalmers, who already knew the answer, having overheard Allhoff's end of the conversation, shrugged.

"Five days is all right with me," he said. "If you can get yourself out of this in five days, you're almost as good as you think you are."

His smile of triumph still unimpaired, he left the room. Allhoff put his gun on his desk, sighed heavily and reached for the percolator.

"As a matter of routine," he said to me, "check George Anthony's alibi. You'll find, I think, it's very close to perfect."

I picked up the telephone and went to work. Some fifteen minutes later, I reported: "After Anthony left here he was in his office all afternoon. After that he went to a banquet of the Second Baptist Church deacons. He stayed at a friend's house all night. The only unaccounted for time is some twenty minutes of the late afternoon when he left his office alone, then returned. That would give him no time for planting a body here."

"No," said Allhoff, "I knew damned well it wouldn't."

He stared at the wall over the chipped edge of his coffee cup. It seemed to me that the bend of his back had increased its arc. The drooping lines around his mouth were etched deeper. There was a shadow in his eyes, a shadow of defeat that had never been there before.

Battersly lit a cigarette with unsteady fingers and stared at Allhoff's back. Perhaps at last the thing had happened which would free him from Allhoff's thrall forever. I puffed at my pipe, shook my head and wondered.

True, Anthony was a natural suspect. But events seemed to have precluded his having anything to do with the corpse in Allhoff's bedroom. Allhoff himself had broken down what slim evidence there was to connect the crime with the lawyer whose brother was in the death house.

Whether or not Allhoff had slit Burroughs' throat I did not know. Certainly he was capable of murder either coldbloodedly or in hot passion. Certainly he had threatened Burroughs. Certainly he had made no explanation of the corpse on his mattress. It was, I reflected, quite possible he had killed Burroughs early in the morning, had intended keeping the body in his bedroom until night, when it could be disposed of. And the clincher, it seemed to me, was that Allhoff was worried and anxious. He had lost the arrogant air of superiority which was as much a part of him as his twisted little mind.

After a long while he drew a heavy sigh. "I think," he announced, "that I've put the parts together. The difficulty is whether I can make anyone see the whole as plainly as I see it myself."

That was rather too cryptic for me and I said so.

"Here's what you two are to do," said Allhoff. "Check on this guy Burroughs. Find out who his relatives are, with particular attention to two points. Look for a girl. A tall, dark, damned good-looking girl. Black eyes and hair. An upturned nose. Possibly she's an actress. Anyway you may be sure she'll have one hell of a lot of poise."

I blinked. "Is this the crystal ball method of detection?" I asked. "How can you know this?"

He didn't answer me. "The second relative is probably some old guy with dough. He's probably dying. Maybe by now he's dead. Get going, both of you. And hurry. I haven't a great deal of time."

Battersly and I got up. As I reached the doorway, I noted that Allhoff's gun was still on the desktop. I said curiously: "Why did you pull that gun? If the commissioner had turned you down you didn't expect to hold off the entire police department, did you?"

Allhoff slammed down his coffee cup. "Can I solve a case in a cell? Can I solve a case without authority? If the commissioner had turned me down I was as good as burned."

"Still," I said, "why the gun on Chalmers?"

"I don't intend to die in a chair," said Allhoff. "It'd give too damned much satisfaction to too many people. That gun wasn't meant primarily for Chalmers."

It dawned on me slowly how deadly in earnest he was. "You mean?" I said.

"Never mind what I mean. Get going. There's damned little time."

CHAPTER THREE
QUIZ PROGRAM

THERE WERE a dozen names and addresses scrawled on a telephone number card at Burroughs' apartment. We checked them first. I put through two fruitless calls to people who proved to be neither relatives, dying old men or gorgeous girls. I had decided that Allhoff's crystal ball theory wasn't doing so well, when Battersly, who'd called the third name on the list, hung up the phone and turned to me, astonishment written on his face.

"Sergeant," he said, "I just called a guy named Latham. He's a great-uncle of Burroughs. He couldn't come to the phone himself because he's too sick. I spoke to his secretary. He wouldn't talk much but when I told him I was a copper he said that Latham was quite well-to-do."

We stared at each other for a long time. There was awe on Battersly's face not unmixed with fear. "Sometimes," he said slowly, "I think that guy's a witch."

"Maybe," I said. "But I'm sure he wouldn't like the gender. However, if he was that good on the old guy, write down the names of all the women on that list and we'll go calling."

The instant the door opened I knew it was she. Her name was Hazel Repass. She was tall and straight and aphrodisiac. She was dark, with black eyes and an upturned nose. Battersly gaped at her like a yokel at a dirty postcard.

I displayed my badge. "Officers," I said. "May we come in?"

She bowed graciously. "Of course. I hope nothing's wrong."

Nothing was wrong, but I was astounded as to how damned right Allhoff had been. The first question I asked her was on my own hook.

"Do you know a man named Allhoff? Inspector Allhoff?"

She shook her head slowly. "Allhoff? No. I don't know any policemen at all. Is he a policeman?"

"Maybe not," I told her. "Sometimes I think he's a seer. Anyway, do you know a guy called Burroughs?"

"Elmer Burroughs? Yes. He's a third cousin of mine. We don't see much of each other, though. Why do you ask?"

"Well," I said. "He's dead."

Her gorgeous eyes opened wide. "Elmer dead? How? When did it happen?"

"This morning. The department will give you the details later. I've done all I'm supposed to do."

She plied me with questions, however, until I was forced to answer. She was dabbing her eyes with an Irish lace handkerchief as we left.

We went back to the office and reported to Allhoff who listened to us as if he were in a daze. He dismissed us with a wave of his hand. He seemed to take no triumphant pleasure in the fact that his guess about the two relatives had been correct.

"Go home, both of you," he said wearily. "I've got to think."

It was an order we obeyed with alacrity.

THE FOLLOWING morning we found Allhoff already out of bed and embarking upon his second quart of coffee. He paid us no attention for a good hour. Then he said abruptly: "I've had that Latham on the phone. He's expected to live less than a week."

Which information threw absolutely no light upon anything so far as I was concerned. I asked: "Have you made any real progress? Are you clean on Burroughs or not?"

He turned his head around and glared at me. "I'm clean," he said, "though I doubt if anyone in this office believes me. I know how, why and when Burroughs was killed. It's the evidence I'm worried about. Here."

He handed me a sheet of white paper with typing on it. I glanced at it, puzzled, said: "What's this?"

"George Anthony is coming here this afternoon. I've sent for him. However, I'm not going to see him. I'm locking myself in the bedroom. You will tell him I went out. That I changed my mind about seeing him anyway.

You will ask him the questions I have typed out for you. You will study them, commit them to heart. He mustn't see you reading from the paper."

I looked down at the paper again. "Allhoff," I said, "are you crazy? This concerns that messy Talbot divorce case."

"Learn them by heart," said Allhoff. "Immediately."

I shrugged my shoulders. The Talbot divorce case had been plastered all over the front pages of the tabloids some few months ago. Talbot was a millionaire whose vices were only equalled by the vices of his wife. Anthony had been Susan Talbot's lawyer, but since he never handled divorce cases he had handed the proceedings over to a colleague. In its day the Talbot case had been a very juicy morsel of gossip.

Slowly I read Allhoff's typing.

1. You are, of course, familiar with the Talbot divorce case?
2. Who handled it? You, personally?
3. Was Susan Talbot as good-looking as she was supposed to be? Was she guilty of all those indiscretions?
4. I understand there's a very undercover story to the effect that Talbot spent a fortune to keep the name of a famous movie star out of the proceedings?
5. There's also talk that you split the fee with the counsel on that case. As a matter of fact, I understand it can be proved by a letter Talbot wrote to the Bar Association squawking?
6. I'm not permitted to make private calls on this phone. Allhoff's funny about it. Would you mind making a call for me in the booth across the street when you leave?

I put the paper down on my desk. I said: "Allhoff, this is the weirdest yet. Why the devil must I speak all this jargon to Anthony?"

"Because," said Allhoff and his tone was grim, "because I order you to. Make it as casual as possible. Tell him you've always been interested in that Talbot case. He'll probably be so relieved that I'm not here he'll be cordial. Ask him anything else you like. Ad lib along to make it sound reasonable. But be certain to intersperse those questions. Every single one of them. Commit them to memory. Don't make any mistake."

He turned back to his coffee. I shrugged my shoulders and pored over the ridiculous questions. I was not, I discovered, a very quick student.

IT WAS late afternoon when George Anthony entered the room. Battersly was downstairs in Noonan's getting a sandwich and Allhoff was behind the closed door of the bedroom. Anthony, perfectly groomed as usual, came in with a frown.

He said, irritatedly: "I hate this damned place. I don't see how anyone lives in it."

He sat down and seemed considerably cheered when I informed him Allhoff wasn't going to see him. I drew a deep breath and began talking about the Talbot case.

Anthony, as Allhoff had predicted, seemed to thaw once he had been told Allhoff was out. He discussed the famous case quite freely with me for some time. I managed, at no little cost of mental agility, to get in all of Allhoff's written questions.

We parted, after a half-hour, cordially. Then, the instant the door closed behind Anthony, Allhoff rushed feverishly out of the bedroom.

"Get out," he said. "Get out! Don't let Battersly come back either. I've got to be alone now. Both of you come in about noon tomorrow. You'll have to stay overtime. Now go, I've a hell of a lot to do."

Puzzled, I donned my hat and coat. Never had I seen Allhoff so terribly excited. Though in the light of what I was about to learn on the morrow, I cannot say I blamed him.

IT HAD been dark for almost three hours. By now my dinner had been removed from the table and put in the icebox against my arrival. Early in the afternoon Allhoff had decreed the overtime for both Battersly and myself. I sat at my desk, smoking and yawning. Battersly scanned the front page of the evening paper.

Allhoff sat brooding and silent at his desk. His face was grayer than usual and age and weariness sat intangibly though not invisibly upon him. I regarded him with an odd pity in my heart—an emotion I had never believed he could arouse in me.

He had one more day of grace to vindicate himself of murder. Frankly, I did not believe he could do it. As far as I could see he had made no progress at all. There was a tenseness and air of anxiety about him that had never been there before.

As I watched him I noted something else. He was not drinking coffee. The percolator sat simmering upon its electric base and there were two clean cups on the desk. It had been a good three hours since he had last poured a dose of caffeine into his system, a circumstance which had not existed since he was thirteen years old.

Battersly looked up from the paper. He said, with all the tact of a gynecologist questioning a patient: "Well, I see Roy Anthony dies tonight."

I glanced at him sharply, then at Allhoff apprehensively. Allhoff turned slowly around in his swivel chair. I was relieved to see no trace of wrath upon his lined face.

"Perhaps he won't be alone," he said quietly. "Perhaps some other people will die tonight as well."

There was a cryptic fatalism in his manner that somehow chilled me. I looked at him closely. Knowing him as I did, I sensed he had something in the back of his head—something deadly, malevolent.

He sighed heavily and slid off his chair to the floor. His stumps thudded across the floor toward the bathroom. He entered and slammed the door behind him. Battersly cast the newspaper aside in disgust. He stood up.

"Well," he said, "if we're going to sit around here waiting for God knows what, all night, I may as well have a cup of Java."

He crossed the room to Allhoff's desk and picked up the percolator. He filled one of the clean cups. As he lifted it to his lips, the bathroom door opened and Allhoff stood upon the threshold. He saw the cup in Battersly's hand and froze to immobility in the doorway.

There was an odd burning speculative light in his eyes which puzzled me. He drew a deep breath. He stared at the moving cup in Battersly's fingers as if fascinated by the sight. Then as Battersly's lips touched the edge of the cup, Allhoff took a step forward and spoke explosively.

"Put it down! Put that cup down! Who the devil invited you to help yourself to my coffee?"

Battersly lowered the cup in amazement. Allhoff was constantly attempting to foist a cup of ink-like coffee upon anyone who would drink it. This sudden reversal was entirely out of order.

"Dump it in the sink, wash the cup and return it to me, you—"

He hurled an epithet at the amazed Battersly and clumped across the floor to climb back into his chair. Battersly washed the cup and replaced it on the desk. He looked at me inquiringly. I shrugged my shoulders. Allhoff, doubtless, was under a greater strain than usual. That was enough to harass an ordinary man, much more so Allhoff.

As I saw it, he was going to be indicted for first-degree murder within the week. What little defense he may have been able to put up he had destroyed himself. He was going to the dock with a stronger case against him than many he had himself built against those whom he'd sent to the chair.

I HEARD someone coming up the stairway outside. I exchanged another glance with Battersly and waited expectantly. The reason we were working overtime should become apparent now. The door opened. McCarthy, a sergeant attached to headquarters, came into the room. With him was Hazel Repass.

Battersly's eyes focused upon her. Her hat and dress were red and her dark beauty radiated in the dismal setting. Allhoff nodded to her. He said: "Get out, McCarthy. Sit down, Repass."

Repass sat down, poised as a queen in a pigsty. She crossed her legs and Battersly's stare became a gape. She lit a cigarette and said: "Why did you have me dragged here, Inspector?"

"I wanted to be sure you'd come," said Allhoff. "I haven't much time."

"Never mind," she said with a gentleness which imparted a viciousness to her words, "you *will* have, Inspector. Plenty."

I waited with some apprehension for the Allhoff temper to flare. It didn't.

"I want to ask you," said Allhoff heavily, "if you are willing to send a man to the electric chair?"

She lifted plucked eyebrows. "Why not? You've sent several there yourself, haven't you?"

"They were murderers," said Allhoff stonily.

"Well?" said Repass and there was a wealth of meaning in her intonation.

Allhoff sighed and ran his fingers through his hair. Hazel Repass watched him with mocking lips and mordant eyes. I felt rather like a man in a maze. Obviously there was something clashing between them. What it was, I couldn't figure. I wasn't sure that Allhoff could either. Usually when he was sure of himself, he was cocky and arrogant. Tonight he had all the assurance of a tired eagle watching the *Luftwaffe* roar by.

Allhoff's hand reached out in familiar gesture toward the coffee pot. His fingers suspended themselves in midair just this side of the handle. He shook his head and withdrew his hand again.

I blinked. If the strain was so great that Allhoff was forgoing the solace of caffeine it was a historical moment.

"Look," he said to Repass. "You're not getting away with it."

Repass, I observed, did not ask what "it" was. She said, "Really?" with the air of one who neither admits nor denies anything at all.

"No," said Allhoff. "I have the evidence to send a con-federate of yours before the Grand Jury. In order to make it easier for himself he's going to talk."

Repass exhaled smoke insolently in Allhoff's direction. "That old gag," she said. "I'd heard you were more tal-ented, Inspector."

"All right," said Allhoff. "I'll let you hear it for yourself."

He took a heavy silver watch from his pocket. He glanced at it. He turned around in his chair. He said to Battersly and myself: "Take her in the bedroom. Hold her there by force. Gag her so that she can make no noise. Lock the door and all of you stay there until I tell you to come out."

Battersly stood up and looked at Repass uncomfortably. To drag off a woman accused of no crime, especially one as good-looking as Repass, was a delicate job. I was some-what hesitant myself. Then Repass resolved the situation for us.

"Of course," she said, "you know all this is illegal, Inspec-tor. I suppose you're working on the premise that it won't matter whether or not you're broken after the next few days. All right, I'll go quietly. Merely to save that handsome lad embarrassment."

Battersly flushed like a bloodstained rose. The three of us trooped into Allhoff's filthy bedroom. We closed the door behind us.

CHAPTER FOUR

NEW SHOES
FOR ALLHOFF!

HAZEL REPASS looked around the bedroom over a wrinkled nose. She sat down gingerly on a tired old chair, looked at the rumpled bed and said quite coolly: "Who's been sleeping in those sheets? Jeeter Lester?"

We didn't answer. Abashed, I took a clean silk handkerchief from my pocket.

"I'm sorry, Miss Repass," I said. "But we're working under orders. I haven't any idea what this is all about. However—"

"I understand perfectly," she said evenly. "Do whatever the inspector requires of you. Sort of a doomed man's last wish, you know."

I adjusted the handkerchief about her mouth. Battersly stood, looking extremely uncomfortable, with his back to the door. I sat on the edge of the bed, speculating madly on what Allhoff was up to. Repass sat upright in the chair as calm as if she were in a beauty parlor.

I heard the outer door open suddenly, heard footsteps in the other room. A chair leg scraped over the floor and George Anthony's voice said irritatedly: "I hate this damned place. I don't see how anyone lives in it."

Allhoff said, "Under the circumstances your solicitude is remarkable," and I noted that the anxiety seemed to have left him. He spoke in his usual insulting sardonic drawl.

"Anthony," he went on, "this is an important night for both of us. You received my note? You have digested my evidence?"

"Yes."

"Very well. Did you kill Burroughs?"

"I did not. I can tell you who did."

I saw the Repass girl stiffen in her chair. Battersly stared at me in utter amazement, an expression reflected in my own eyes. If Allhoff was about to obtain a confession in the Burroughs murder it was the most miraculous rabbit he had ever pulled out of a hat.

"Well," said Allhoff, "since we both know her name you needn't mention it. She's rather beautiful in a way, too."

"She's a beautiful girl," said Anthony. "But she's guilty as hell. Though you'd not suspect it to look at her."

Repass gasped through the gag. She lifted her hand to her mouth as if to remove the handkerchief. Remembering Allhoff's instructions, I held her wrists firmly.

"She did it," said Allhoff musingly, "for personal reasons of finance, primarily. However she was delighted to plant the body on me to divert suspicion from herself. You were glad to work out the details for her to revenge yourself on me for refusing to sign that petition about your brother."

"That is absolutely true," said Anthony dejectedly, "though I'm damned if I know how you found it out."

"That's beside the point," said Allhoff. "I've already showed you I've enough evidence to send you away for life for your part in the job. I have scarcely any evidence against the girl. If you'll pin it on her it'll be easier for you."

"Hell," said Anthony, "you've got me cold. But where in the name of God did you get your information?"

Repass was sitting now as if there was a ramrod in her spine. I still held her hands. Her eyes blazed at the door panels as if she could see through them and hurl the venom in her pupils at Anthony outside. Battersly remained amazed. I had an odd sensation that something very screwy was going on. I had listened to the conversation between Allhoff and Anthony very carefully. There was something strange about it. Something was wrong. I could not, however, quite put my finger on it.

"I have my methods," said Allhoff from the other room. "I don't divulge them. Now, will you go across the street to headquarters and sign a full confession? You have, as I see it, no other choice."

"Immediately. Across the street. For whom do I ask?"

"McCarthy's waiting outside for you. He'll take you over. He'll see you get to the right person."

There was a long silence broken by a heavy sigh. Anthony said: "All right. Good-bye."

Footsteps sounded across the floor and evanesced down the stairway. Then there was a second silence. After which Allhoff said loudly: "All right, come in, you guys. Bring Repass with you."

I TOOK the silk handkerchief from the girl's mouth. Battersly opened the bedroom door. The three of us walked into Allhoff's presence.

The coffee cups, I noted, were still clean. My sensation that something screwy was going on became more pronounced. The idea of Allhoff eschewing coffee for several hours was almost incredible.

Hazel Repass stood before Allhoff's desk and stared at him with hard eyes. Her attitude seemed one of defiance, bewilderment, seasoned slightly with fear.

She said, shaking her head: "No, it's utterly impossible."

"What is?" said Allhoff. "That one criminal should tell the truth about another to make his own punishment lighter?"

"No," said Repass. "Not that."

"What then?"

"That you should've dug up enough evidence to force Anthony to confess."

Allhoff lifted his eyebrows and looked smug. "I did it," he said. "That should be enough. I have a suggestion to make to you. Go over to headquarters. Get your own confession in. Fast. Perhaps it will be done before Anthony's. It might avail you nothing. On the other hand you have nothing to lose. You're cooked anyway. There's no point in your saving his skin now."

Repass nodded. Her little chin was set firmly. There was, perhaps, a deeper shadow of fear in her eyes now, a trifle less arrogance in her manner, but she still remained a rock of steadiness.

She uttered an obscene epithet which sounded odd falling from her soft and shapely lips. "That rat," she said. "I'll talk. Take me over there at once."

Allhoff signaled Battersly with his eyes. "Take her over."

Battersly nodded. Repass' spike heels tapped a staccato across the floor. The door closed behind them.

I looked at Allhoff closely. I had seen him triumph a hundred times. I had seen him gloat and toss his ego around the room like a bouncing ball. Yet here he had apparently beaten the toughest case of his career, a case in which his own life may well have been at stake and there was nothing of the conqueror about him. A mantle of dejection sat upon his stooped shoulders. There was a tenseness about him—a strange and alien nervousness.

I said, more to break the silence than anything else: "You're not drinking coffee tonight?"

"Maybe," he said softly, "maybe later. One last cup."

He spoke as if the words held a profound significance which was beyond me. His hands moved nervously as he straightened up the desk. He took a sheaf of papers, put them together, opened a drawer of the desk to put them away. I looked over his shoulder as he did so. My eyes bulged suddenly. For in the desk drawer was a pair of shoes! A pair of new tan shoes in Allhoff's desk!

He turned his head slightly, looked at me and slammed the drawer shut. With an effort I kept my mouth the same way. Then as my brain whirled, grappling with the problem, the door opened and George Anthony walked in. I gaped at him. Things were happening so fast that before I had fairly recovered from one shock another piled on top of me. After all, Anthony had just been over to headquarters to register a confession branding him as a conspirator in a murder case. Under those circumstances headquarters rarely permitted one to walk out again under his own power.

Anthony's face was haggard and there were dark rings under his eyes. He glared bitterly at Allhoff, sank into a chair and said: "Well, what is it this time?"

Allhoff looked over at the coffee pot as if he were about to pour out a cup of the brew. Then he seemed to think better of it. He transferred his gaze to Anthony and there was a strange gleam in his eye.

"This," he said, "is the day your brother is to die."

"Have you invited me here to gloat?" demanded Anthony. He smiled without mirth. "Are you in a position to gloat? You've your own life to worry about now, Inspector."

"Listen," said Allhoff. "Are you still carrying that petition in your pocket?"

Anthony nodded. "What of it? It's too late now."

I SAT down and pulled at my pipe. By this time I had given up completely. What was the reason for Anthony's second visit? The reason for the shoes in Allhoff's desk? The reason for his abstinence from coffee? I passed my hand over my head feeling very like an idiot confronted with a problem in calculus.

"It's almost ten o'clock," said Allhoff. "It is almost axiomatic in this state that executions take place at midnight. If I sign you can phone the Governor. He can grant a stay by telephone, if he cares to."

Anthony's eyes lit up. "You mean," he said incredulously, "you'll sign?"

"Conditionally."

"Name it."

"I want you to sign a statement swearing that you know a girl named Hazel Repass. I want you to swear that you saw her on Tuesday last, between the time you were in this office and midnight. I want you to swear that she is known to you both as a personal friend and as a client."

Anthony screwed up his brow and considered for a long, long time. He said at last: "That's absolutely all you want me to swear to?"

"That's absolutely all."

"Then you'll sign my petition?"

"I'll sign it. You can call the Governor from this room."

Anthony drew a deep breath. "It looks all right to me," he said. "I'll sign."

Allhoff took a piece of typewritten paper from his desk. He handed it to Anthony. Anthony scrutinized it carefully. He scrawled his name across the bottom of the sheet. Allhoff took the paper back and handed it to me. "Witness," he said.

I read it cursorily and signed my own name. I handed it back to him and wondered if everyone was crazy but myself.

"Now," said Anthony, "my petition."

He took it from his pocket. Allhoff wrote his name upon it. Battersly entered the room.

"Say," he said excitedly. "Anthony crossed you. He didn't go over to headquarters at all. McCarthy said you never told him to wait. No one's seen him over there. Shall I have an alarm sent out? I—?"

Anthony spun around his chair and Battersly, startled, broke off. "Oh," he said, "I didn't know. I—"

Anthony eyed Allhoff suspiciously. "What's it all about?" he demanded. "What's this about an alarm? Why was I expected at headquarters? What does it mean?"

Allhoff ignored him. He glanced up at Battersly. "Did that canary sing?" he asked.

"Loudly," said Battersly, "and completely. But what I can't figure—"

"Damn you," said Anthony and there was apprehension in his tone, "what does all this mean?"

Allhoff's hand struck the desktop. The mantle of anxiety he had worn for the past week dropped silently to the floor. The old flashing hatred and contempt for humanity shone brilliant in his eyes. His head was held high and his lips contorted into a vicious sneer.

"It means," he said, loud and bitingly, "it means you'll live longer than midnight, Anthony. But not a hell of a lot longer, at that."

Anthony transferred his gaze at me. "Is he crazy, Sergeant?"

That was a question I had never satisfactorily answered in my own mind. I said so.

Allhoff took the percolater off its base. He held it out to Battersly.

"Here," he said. "Dump out this coffee. Throw the pot away. Throw these two cups away. There's a new pot in my bedroom closet. Fill it with water and bring it to me. Quick!"

Battersly did as he was told. I watched, puzzled. Anthony's frown indicated he was as baffled as myself. Allhoff set the new pot on the electric base. He dumped coffee in with a lavish hand. He waited for it to boil, like a hophead cooking opium.

"Look here," said Anthony, "what the devil this is all about, I don't know. I don't care much. But you promised I could use your phone. I want to call Albany."

Allhoff grinned horribly. "Go ahead," he said.

CHAPTER FIVE
A CUP OF KINDNESS

ANTHONY PICKED up the receiver, asked the operator to get him the executive mansion and hung up waiting for her to call back. Allhoff watched the coffee percolate, snatched up the pot with a trembling hand. He filled and drained his cup three times like a desert rat who has found an oasis. Then he breathed deeply and put the cup down with a bang.

"Now," he said, "I'll tell you why you're not going to die tonight, Anthony. I'll also tell you how and why Burroughs was murdered. Are you interested?"

I was intensely interested. I leaned forward in my chair eagerly. Battersly, I noted, was regarding Allhoff with a sort of awed loathing. Anthony looked extremely wary.

"A week ago," said Allhoff, "you came in here with a gun in your hand and a vicious plan in your head, asking me to sign that petition I've just signed. You had a revenge planned in case I refused. I did refuse and you put that plan into operation."

"What plan?" I asked.

"Burroughs' murder. Burroughs wasn't exactly a plant. He'd come up here leveling. But he'd been told to do it by someone who didn't tell him I had no legs."

"You mean," I said, "that Anthony sent him here?"

"No," said Allhoff, "you're not that dumb, are you Anthony? Hazel Repass sent him here. Anthony never even knew Burroughs. But he knew Repass and he sent Repass here later on that same day."

"When?" I asked. "I never saw Repass that day."

"You'd gone home. Repass arrived here a little before midnight. She unloaded a cock and bull story on me about her husband planning a murder. She wanted me to stop him, knew of me because of my reputation as the smartest copper in town. I was sucker enough to believe her. She threw hysterics all over the office and I put her in my bedroom after she faked a pass-out. I slept on the floor out here. That was precisely what she came here to maneuver."

Anthony's face was frozen marble. I tried to put it all together and had the success of a guy organizing an Irish Peace Movement. Battersly, looking as if he were about to burst, said excitedly: "That's how they planted the body. That's how they—"

Allhoff glared at him and he shut up. For a moment I wondered how one possessed of Battersly's mentality had come in with the answer before I'd figured it. Then I recalled with satisfaction that he had already seen the Repass confession.

"While I slept," went on Allhoff, "some guy you had hired, Anthony, delivered Burroughs to my bedroom via the fire escape. He was alive then, though either drugged or slugged into unconsciousness. Repass lowered the fire escape so that your man could bring up the body. Repass put him in my bed and neatly slit his throat. She exited then the same way that Burroughs had entered."

"How?" I asked. "Since that fire escape must be lowered from the top?"

"That last flight is weighted," said Allhoff. "It must be lowered from the top. It's no task at all to push it back up again if you have a window pole or any long stick. That's what Repass did."

"And that morning," I said slowly, "you actually expected to find Repass asleep in your bed when Chalmers broke the door down."

"I did," said Allhoff. "One of them phoned an anonymous tip to Chalmers. I found instead the body of a guy I'd threatened to kill before unfriendly witnesses."

That, of course, was a whack at Battersly and myself. I deemed it inadvisable to press the point.

"Why didn't you say so at first? Why didn't you say the girl was here that night?"

"Listen," said Allhoff with a touch of grimness, "I've been listening to killers tell tales as wild as the one I was stuck with all my life. I've never believed them. Why should I expect anyone to believe me? You wouldn't've, would you?"

I thought that over and said, "No."

"Well," said Anthony harshly, "and where do we go from here?"

"Well, there I was," said Allhoff, "stuck with a ridiculous story. The Repass girl would've denied ever having seen me in her life. I hadn't a clue to work on. I knew, Anthony, that you were in it somewhere. I knew, further, that you'd have a cast-iron alibi. I had no clue. I had no chance."

"But you've evidently pulled it out," I said. "So you must have had something to go on."

ALLHOFF POURED a pint of coffee down his gullet. "Sure," he shouted and there was bitterness and triumph in his tone, "sure, I had something to go on. A brain. The best brain in the whole damned department. A better brain than any lawyer who was trying to frame me. First, I thought it all out. When I went after my evidence, I knew exactly what had happened."

"Well, what?" I said impatiently. "I don't even know now."

"Figure it," said Allhoff. "Anthony is a smart guy. Why would he trust a woman on a thing like this? If he's simply hired a killer, why not do it through an agent and hire a man? Obviously because the girl had some interest in the murder. Possibly, I reason, she even did the murder. That fact would effectively keep her mouth shut about Anthony's part in it."

"You mean he hired the girl to do the killing?"

"No," said Allhoff. "It seemed reasonable that the girl gained personally through Burroughs' death. Anthony, for motives of revenge, was merely setting the stage for a client to do her own killing."

"What was her motive then?"

"Ratiocinate," said Allhoff. "Revenge didn't seem it. Burroughs was no Don Juan. That leaves dough."

"Don't tell me that lousy shoe salesman had dough."

"No," said Allhoff. "That's what I figured. He probably hadn't. That made it look like *potential* dough. Potential dough conjures up the idea of a will. Anthony is a lawyer. Click. Get it?"

"No."

Allhoff sighed and reached again for the coffee pot. He was more than making up for his hours of teetotalism. Anthony watched him through narrowed eyes.

"If it's a will," went on Allhoff, wiping his lips with a stained sleeve, "it implies Burroughs is a relative of Repass. I investigate. He is. It implies another and wealthy relative. I investigate. There is. He is also Anthony's client. A phone call to Latham who lies on his deathbed at this moment informed me that his dough goes to Burroughs. If anything happens to Burroughs, it goes to Repass. There's your setup. Simple?"

"You mean," I said, "that the setup existed all the time. Anthony was ready to use it if you refused to aid in the commuting of his brother's sentence?"

"At last," said Allhoff, "you have it."

"Except," said Anthony calmly, "as to evidence. Your story, Inspector, is as incredible as that first story you found yourself stuck with."

I screwed up my brow and got a headache. Only a few moments ago, I had heard Anthony concede that Allhoff had enough evidence to force him to confess. Now he contended that there was no evidence at all. Battersly looked like a very wise guy and, I reflected, it was probably the only time in all his life that he had reason to.

"Anthony," said Allhoff, "that Repass girl has saved your life, or at least postponed the taking of it."

"Speak English," said Anthony.

"The Repass girl has just completed a full confession over at headquarters. She's omitted nothing. You're an accessory before, during and after the fact of murder. In your business you know that the chair lies at the end of that charge."

Anthony blinked. "I don't believe a word of it."

"You will in a moment," said Allhoff. "Watch."

HE OPENED the second drawer of his desk. He withdrew the pair of tan shoes I had seen there earlier. He slid out of his chair to the floor. He made his way slowly and silently toward the door, the shoes held in his hands. We watched him, fascinated.

He opened the door and slammed it again. He bent down like an ape, the shoes fitted over his hands. He moved briskly toward his desk on all fours. His stumps made no sound, the shoes on his hands made a noise of normal footsteps. He reached the desk and climbed back into his chair.

"And what in the name of God," said Anthony, "was that supposed to be?"

"That," said Allhoff, "was you entering this room to confess to me your part in the Burroughs killing and to promise me that you would implicate Repass to cover yourself."

"Are you laying the foundation for an insanity plea?" said Anthony. But my own heart picked up a beat. For the first time I saw a tiny shaft of light.

"Listen," said Allhoff. He opened a second drawer of the desk. He withdrew a portable phonograph. He placed the needle on a record and started it. George Anthony's voice, clear and unmistakable, came from the machine.

It said: "I hate this damned place. I don't see how anyone lives in it."

Allhoff stopped the machine. He said: "I'd like to talk to you about the Talbot divorce case. Did you get that divorce for Susan Talbot?"

He let the record turn again. Anthony's voice said: "I did not. I can tell you who did."

Allhoff lifted the needle and moved it back again over the grooves it had just reversed. Now he asked another question. "Did you kill Burroughs?"

He released the record. Again Anthony's voice said: "I did not. I can tell you who did."

Anthony sprang from his chair. "Wait a minute," he yelled. "Those are the answers I gave Simmonds when he was talking to me about the Talbot divorce case."

"True," said Allhoff, "but Hazel Repass didn't know that."

I blinked. The utter enormity of what he had done stirred a reluctant admiration within my breast. At last I knew why I had sensed something phoney was going on. The words of Anthony which we had heard in the bedroom, I had heard only a few days before.

"You see," said Allhoff, "I told Repass you were going to sell her down the river. I put her in my bedroom and told her to listen to our conversation. Of course, you weren't here. But your voice was. For instance, Simmonds asked you if Susan Talbot was good-looking, if she really was guilty of all the indiscretions listed in the papers. I told you that the killer of Burroughs was beautiful. Your reply to both questions was—"

He let the record go again. Anthony's voice said: "She's a beautiful girl. But she's guilty as hell. Though you'd not expect it to look at her."

"To continue," said Allhoff, his voice rising excitedly, "Simmonds asked you if you got a cut of a split fee in that case. I told you I had evidence against you. You said—"

Again he released the record. Anthony's answer played back: "Hell, you've got me cold. But where in the name of God did you get your information?"

"Simmonds asked you to make a call for him across the street. I asked you to go over and sign a confession. You said—"

The record played again. Anthony's voice said: "Immediately. Across the street. For whom do I ask?"

"So you see," said Allhoff, "Repass hearing your voice answering my questions was convinced you were going to rat on her. She rushed across the street to beat you to it. To get her confession in first."

Anthony's face was ashen. There was a desperate note in his voice as he spoke.

"Then—what—what was the idea of asking me to sign that statement saying I knew Hazel Repass, that I saw her that afternoon?"

"I am taking no chances of a slip-up in this case," said Allhoff vindictively. "I never wanted a conviction so much in my life. You have some standing in this town. You might've denied even knowing the girl. I wanted a definite tie-up with her. That, coupled with the fact that you were Latham's lawyer, should close the slimmest loophole."

THE TELEPHONE jangled on Allhoff's desk. Anthony reached for it. "That must be my call," he said. "At least, I've salvaged something. After all, you signed my petition for the Governor."

He picked up the receiver. He spoke for a few minutes into the mouthpiece. As he hung up it seemed as if the hand of Time swept over his face and aged him eight years.

"You dog," he said in a low bitter voice. "You low lousy trickster. My brother's dead. Executed at six tonight. I bet you knew it all the time."

"Knew it?" screamed Allhoff, pounding the table with his fist. "You're damned right I knew it. I had it done. The warden's in my debt. You should know executions in this state are ordered done on a certain date at any time during the day at the warden's discretion. They're almost always done at midnight to provide for any last-minute reprieve. But they can be done at any time during the twenty-four hours. I had this one done at six tonight!"

Anthony sank back in his chair like a dead man, which, not to put too fine a point upon it, he was. Allhoff drained a cup of coffee greedily. He said: "Battersly, take him across the street. Book him."

Battersly helped George Anthony from his chair, escorted him from the room. I took my pipe from my mouth and said: "You took one hell of a long chance."

"How so?"

"Those phoney questions and answers. Suppose Anthony had replied differently?"

"So I'd rephrase my questions. After all, the questions you put to him were bound to result in certain replies. I simply had to make the second set of dialogue fit the answers to the first."

I nodded. Then I asked the thing that puzzled me more than anything else.

"Why did you suddenly go off coffee? What was the idea of throwing that old pot away?"

Allhoff drew a deep breath. "I told you they'd never send me to the chair."

"You mean," I said, "that your coffee was poisoned?"

I looked up to see Battersly standing in the doorway staring, horrified, at Allhoff.

"The coffee?" he said. "Poisoned? My God, I almost drank—"

Battersly's eyes met mine. I knew we were thinking the same thing.

Allhoff swung around in his chair. "I know what's going on in your heads," he snarled. "You want to know why I let Battersly live. Death's too damned good for him. That coffee was too simple a way out. It was too kind. A cup of kindness—" He cackled insanely. He lifted his voice and sang.

"We'll take a cup of kindness yet for auld lang syne."

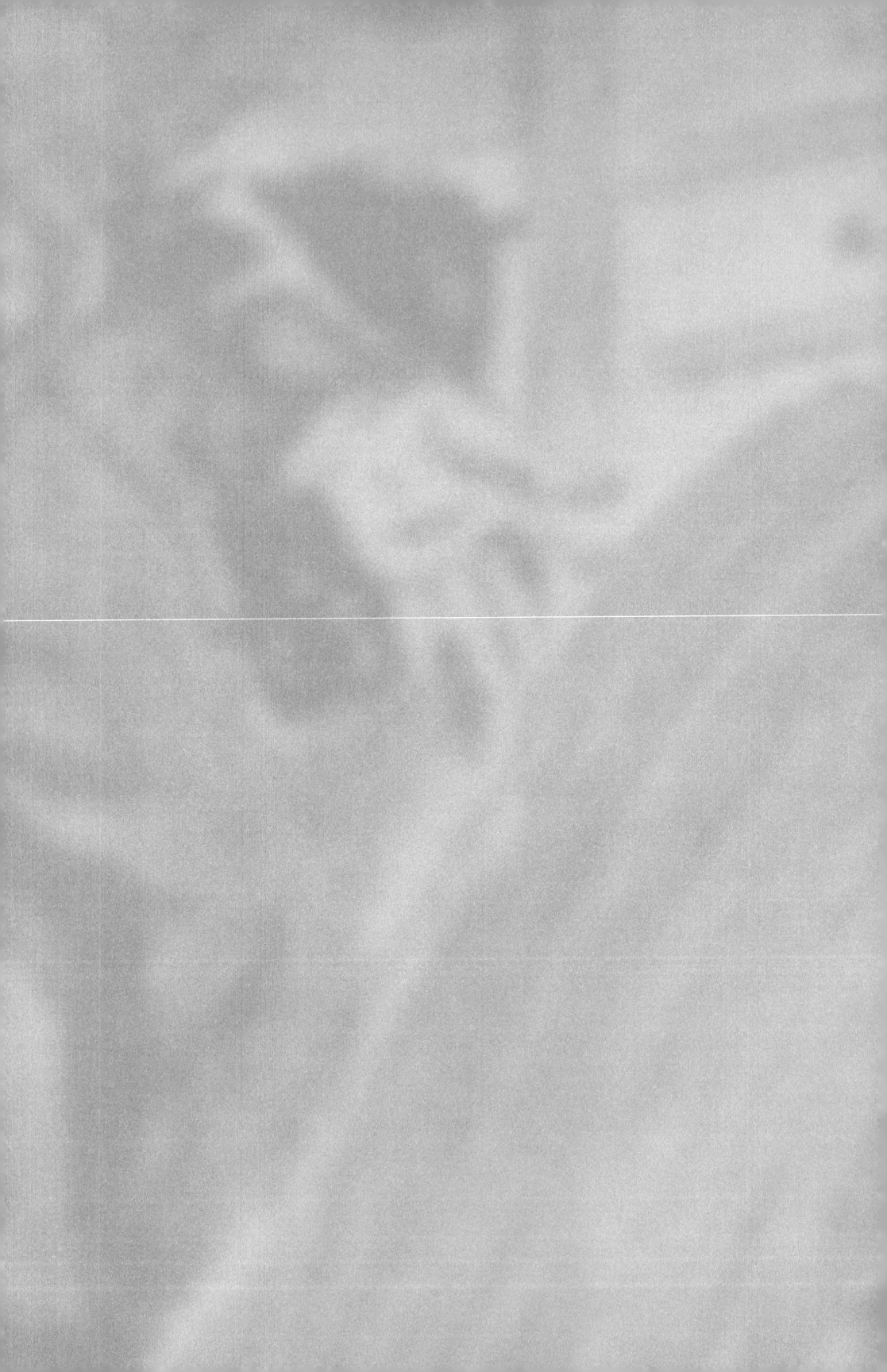

TELL IT TO HOMICIDE

LIFE BECAME BLEAK FOR
ALLHOFF'S TWO ASSISTANTS
WHEN THEY ALLOWED A MURDER
TO BE COMMITTED RIGHT IN HIS
OFFICE WHILE HE LAY HELPLESS
WITH AN ATTACK OF SHINGLES.
BUT WHEN THEY FELT THE FULL
FURY OF THE LEGLESS COFFEE-
TIPPLER, THEY WISHED THEY'D
NEVER BEEN BORN AT ALL.

CHAPTER ONE
HOMICIDE WHILE
YOU WAIT

I **WAS** a half hour late. A domestic difference concerning the purchase of new furniture had held me up. From eight thirty until nine o'clock I had argued an unsteady and futile negative. At 9:01 I had capitulated, written out a check which my wife had borne triumphantly, like a captured pennon, to the department store.

Hence, I arrived at Allhoff's chronologically late, spiritually low, and filled with wonder at how those ancient potentates who kept whole harems ever retained their sanity, or, for that matter, their hearing.

I plodded up the rickety stairs that led to Allhoff's slum apartment. The dim hallway smelled of age and dampness. Beyond that a remote unpleasant obligato odor informed me that another rat had died somewhere within the building without benefit of either clergy or incineration. This fragrance, however, was normal enough. The fact that the acrid aroma of vitriolic coffee did not prevail, was not.

At the stair-head I pushed open the door and the hinges creaked like the bones of a rheumatic skeleton. I entered the room and looked about. A gray rug of dust covered the floor. At the side of the window, through whose dirty pane light struggled ineffectually, Allhoff's laundry formed a pallid weary hill. Dishes, equally unwashed, were pyramided in the sink. Beneath, a lidless garbage can erupted

Allhoff reeled into the
room in a gray nightshirt
like a half-pint ghost.

miasma. A cockroach waddled away from it, replete with
breakfast.

Battersly, tall, youthful and rather handsome in his
patrolman's uniform sat at his desk. His eyes, dark and
vastly too old for a man under forty, stared dully at the
comic strip held before him. He looked up, saw me, and
sighed heavily.

I glanced over at Allhoff's desk. The swivel chair before it was empty. The electric plate which held the percolator was unlit. This, at nine thirty in the morning, was phenomenon indeed. I caught Battersly's eye and lifted my brows inquiringly.

Battersly jerked a thumb in the direction of the bedroom. He said in a low whisper: "He's in bed. He's sick."

The frown which corrugated my brow, the sigh which escaped my lips were engendered by no sympathy for Allhoff. Rather, a deep and abiding concern for Battersly and myself. Allhoff, glowing with ruddy health, was bad enough; Allhoff, querulous and dictatorial in a sickbed was something to strain the endurance of Gibraltar and the patience of Job.

I said very softly, very hopefully: "Is it serious?"

Battersly shook his head sadly. "Shingles."

I crossed the room to my desk, removed my hat and coat. A heavy depression was upon me. I disapproved of Allhoff's shingles for two reasons. First, it wasn't serious, second, it was damned painful. Allhoff's sadistic temper without the stimulus of pain was maddening. With the agonizing spur of shingles to drive him to bitter epithet, similar profanity—I contemplated the situation and trembled.

I said, still in a whisper: "When did it happen?"

"Sometime early this morning. The doc left a few minutes ago. I think he's asleep now. He swore he was awake all night. Say, Sergeant, what *are* shingles?"

"I'm no expert," I said. "But I know they're not critical. However, they're damned painful. Sores that break out on the body, usually caused by an upset nervous system. No one, I'm sure, ever died from them. That's what you wanted to know, isn't it?"

HE DIDN'T answer. He had no opportunity. From the half-open door of the bedroom came a roar vaguely imitative of a lion with its tail caught in a mangle. Allhoff's voice filled the room like laryngitic thunder. For the first minute he called upon several deities to witness his sorry plight. Then, from the sewers of his vocabulary he dug up several choice adjectives and applied them impartially to Battersly and myself. Toward the end of the paragraph he reverted to simpler and printable English.

"Am I to die in agony, unattended and without coffee?" he shrieked. "A quarter to ten in the morning and I've had no coffee. Battersly, you idiot, bring me my coffee."

Battersly stood up and approached the bedroom door with all the confidence of Marshal Petain signing the armistice. He thrust his head through the jamb and said: "Inspector, the doctor said you weren't to have coffee."

Allhoff cleared his throat so savagely that I am willing to wager it was recorded on the Fordham seismograph. It seemed, in several hundred words, that the doctor's mother had not only been unclean and immoral, but that she had also indulged in several practices which would have raised the eyebrows of Krafft-Ebing.

There was an epilogue, too, which stated flatly that Battersly's intelligence would have received no homage from some of the lower primates. Then came a ringing line in conclusion which shook the rafters and announced categorically that Inspector Allhoff would have his coffee in spite of hell, high water, the stupidity of subordinates or the injunctions of any jerk medico who doubtless had taken the veterinarian's course by mistake.

I got up and switched on the electric plate. Battersly filled the percolator. Allhoff muttered to himself. I, with no success whatever, tried to convince myself that coffee in the stomach of a shingles sufferer would prove fatal.

I carried the coffee pot and the thick chipped cup of cafeteria gray into the bedroom. The chaotic disorder in there surpassed the disarray of the other room. A cracked green shade covered the top half of a grimy window pane. A rickety chair stood at the side of the bed, Allhoff's trousers draped drunkenly over its back. His shirt, which never would have been used in a soap ad, lay on the seat. His coat had been deposited neatly upon the floor.

The counterpane, which at the time of the Civil War, had been a pale blue, was now torn and black. The pillow on which lay Allhoff's tousled head looked like crumpled soot. His hot agate eyes stared up at me from the bed. Pain gave added bitterness to his gaze. His lips were parted, revealing yellowish teeth. He looked very much like a man about to snarl. He did.

He snatched the coffee from my hand. He drank it like a Death Valley prospector stumbling upon an oasis, when his canteen has been empty for a week come Tuesday. He made a horrible noise with his mouth which sounded like something between the hissing of a snake and a death rattle broadcast through static from a gallows.

He slammed the cup down on the chair bottom. He said, as if he held me personally responsible: "These damned shingles. They hurt like hell. They itch like hell. They're driving me mad. I shall be damned short tempered today."

"No," I said, with all the irony I could summon, "not really?"

Allhoff's announcing that he would be short tempered was as startling a piece of information as Hitler announcing he would have a hostage shot. However, he didn't answer me. He closed his eyes and emitted a groan. I tried my utmost to register sympathy. The only thing I achieved was a grin.

ALLHOFF OPENED his eyes, saw me and his face twisted with wrath.

"Don't think," he shouted, "that because I'm ill the work of this office will be neglected. We're still functioning—and better than any other bureau in the department. Only now, I expect you guys to do a little work for a change. Is there anything due this morning?"

He groaned again and twisted around in the bed as if to adjust his body in a more comfortable position. I went outside to the other room and picked up my desk pad. Battersly, sitting at his desk, like a school boy afraid of the master's anger, looked at me inquiringly. I shook my head.

I returned to the bedside. I consulted my pad and said: "There's this guy Wayne in the Westerly case. He's supposed to be here in about fifteen minutes."

Allhoff nodded. "All right," he said. "Give me the details."

I thumbed the pages of my book. "Westerly," I told him, "was killed three days ago. Homicide seems to think the case is open and shut."

Allhoff summoned up some energy through his pain. He snorted contemptuously, "Homicide!"

I hurried on before he could formulate several thousand words on the subject of the Homicide squad. "This Westerly," I said, "had a brawl with a guy called Robinson. Arthur Robinson. Overheard by two of Westerly's servants. Threatened to kill him unless he did something Robinson demanded he do within three hours. Robinson returned three hours later. The maid entered Westerly's study, found him dead. Robinson in the room."

Allhoff groaned again. I paused and looked at him. He signalled me to continue.

"There was a gun on Westerly's desk. His own gun. One round missing, found by ballistics in Westerly's brain. Robinson says he'd just entered the room and found the body. He refuses to talk about the subject of the quarrel between the pair of them. Personally, I agree with Homicide. I—"

"In the prime of my health," snapped Allhoff, "I am not interested in your opinions. Now what about this guy, Wayne?"

"Wayne got in touch with the Commissioner through a mutual friend. Says he's got something that indicates Robinson is innocent. Commissioner told him to see you at ten today. It's ten now. What'll I do when he arrives? Bring him into your delicate pink and French ivory boudoir?"

He glared at me. He bit his lip and his fists clenched. "Well," I said, "what are you considering? Where we shall receive our customer?"

"I'm considering," he said bitterly, "how I can frame you, get you kicked out of the department with the loss of your pension. By God, I swear, I'll do it someday. Now listen to me. I'm too damned sick to see anyone. You and Battersly can listen to Wayne's tale. Leave the door ajar. I can overhear whatever's said in the other room. You do whatever questioning is necessary. I'll listen."

"All right." I cocked an ear as I heard creaking footfalls on the stairs. "I guess that's him now. I'll attend to it."

He snorted again as I left the room. I gathered it was derision at the idea that Battersly or I could attend to anything without his assistance.

I sat down at Allhoff's desk as two men came into the room. One of them stood uncertainly before me and announced, "I'm Gregory Wayne. This is a friend of mine who came along. Mr. Timmons."

I bowed. Wayne was short and rather pudgy. He had a round, chubby face and a pair of immensely naive blue eyes behind a pair of thick glasses. Timmons was tall and gaunt. He wore his right arm in a black sling and a suit cut as if it had been tailored in Times Square by a cutter who knew several actors making less than forty dollars a week.

I GESTURED toward two chairs. "Sit down, gentlemen. Inspector Allhoff is lying down. He's not feeling well. However he can overhear us. Now, Mr. Wayne, what's on your mind?"

The pair of them sat down. Timmons on Wayne's right. Wayne licked his lips and glanced about. It seemed to me he was a trifle nervous. His blue eyes blinked rapidly.

"Well," I said, as he didn't speak, "you have some evidence, I believe, which indicates that Arthur Robinson did not kill Wallace Westerly. Is that correct?"

Wayne looked at me, transferred his gaze to Timmons, and said: "Well, no, as a matter of fact, I haven't."

I looked at Battersly and blinked. "But," I said, "I understood that the Commissioner said—"

"Wayne made a mistake," said Timmons. "He found out that his information was incorrect. Didn't you, pal?"

Wayne nodded with what looked like eagerness. "That's right," he said. "A mistake."

I shrugged my shoulders. On the face of it, it had seemed to me that Homicide had a cold case against Robinson anyway. "All right," I said, "then, I guess there's nothing more to be said. Is there?"

"Why, no," said Timmons, rising, "we just dropped in since we had the appointment. We—"

Allhoff's voice came through the bedroom door like a blast of a battleship's guns.

"You fool, Simmonds. You idiot. Ask him what evidence he had and how he found out he'd made a mistake."

I gestured apologetically to the pair of them. Timmons sat down again.

"Well," said Wayne hesitantly, "I heard only yesterday that Westerly had another enemy. A man who'd tried to kill him once before. Then only this morning I learned that the fellow who told me all this was kidding. See?"

"Then," roared Allhoff, from the bedroom, "what the devil did you come down here for?"

Wayne glanced nervously at Timmons. "Well," he said and it seemed to me there was an odd note in his voice, "I really hadn't intended to. But early this morning, I was driving downtown. Driving west on 54th Street, when I saw a police officer I happen to know. I stopped to speak to him. Told him I had an appointment here but I'd decided not to keep it. He advised me that I should."

That I could appreciate. Every officer on the force knew better than to cross Allhoff. Probably the copper had figured that if someone stood Allhoff up on a date the whole department would be hearing about it directly or indirectly for days.

"So," went on Wayne, "I left the officer, kept my appointment at the Putnam Building, then picked up my friend Timmons and came down here, just to tell you I was wrong. I didn't want to keep you expecting me and not show up."

That sounded all right to me, save, perhaps, for Wayne's garrulity in the matter. I stood up. "All right, gentlemen," I said. "I guess that satisfies the Inspector. I suppose you may go now."

Allhoff screamed from the bedroom that he was satisfied only in respect to a certain portion of porcine anatomy. He added: "Let them wait a minute. I want to think."

We all sat in stupid silence while Allhoff's brain functioned. I sighed heavily. I had known he was going to be more trying than usual today and he certainly was starting out right. I was positive that there was nothing more in his head at the moment than a well phrased curse. This little byplay went under the general heading of impressing the customers.

"HEY," CAME the voice from the bedroom, "that guy there with Wayne—has he got his hands in his pockets?"

I glanced over at Timmons. His left hand rested on his knee. His right, of course, was in the sling.

"No," I said. "Neither has he got his feet on the chandelier. However, he is wearing black shoes and his right arm is in a sling. And what, Mr. Holmes, do you deduce from that?"

There was a moment's silence. Then Allhoff erupted like Mount Vesuvius to the accompaniment of all the jungle drums in Africa.

"Cretins!" he bellowed. "Dolts. Drooling idiots. Grab him. Grab that Timmons guy. Arrest him. Grab him quick!"

Neither Battersly nor I moved. We looked at each other, agreed tacitly that Allhoff's pain was driving him across that last borderline of insanity where he had dwelt so long. Then I turned my head again in the direction of our visitors.

Timmons was standing up. He was looking at Wayne with black eyes, cold and relentless as the Arctic Sea. Wayne blinked bluely back at him. The color receded from his chubby face. He said: "Timmons, for God's sake—"

"You," said Timmons, spitting out each word as if it were a metallic watermelon seed, "are a low-down double-crosser!"

There were two sudden explosions. Smoke flowed oddly through the fabric of Timmons' black sling. Wayne slid gently from the chair to the floor. His own blood preceded him there. For an instant I sat stunned.

I heard a thud from the bedroom as Allhoff rolled out and hit the floor. A moment later he reeled into the room in a gray nightshirt, looking like a half-pint ghost. Timmons sped to the doorway, tearing his arm from his sling as he did so and revealing the automatic that the bandage had concealed. I, at last, broke the amazed paralysis which was upon me and started after him.

I had moved less than a foot when my shoe cracked against the leg of Allhoff's desk and I fell heavily to my knees. Now, Battersly dragging his gun from its holster, sprang to his feet and raced after Timmons. Allhoff waddled across the room and crossed Battersly's path almost at the doorway. Sweat stood out on his brow indicative of the pain he underwent. He staggered for a moment, groaned, clapped a hand to his head, and toppled over in slow motion. He lay on his back breathing heavily at the side of Wayne's corpse.

Battersly charging along behind him was moving too speedily to check his pace. His moving foot came into sharp contact with Allhoff's body and threw him off balance. He tried desperately to hold himself up, then failed. He fell heavily over Allhoff's body.

He got up clumsily, looked down the empty stairwell and then at me. I shook my head. Pursuit was futile now. Timmons was already in a taxicab and a good eight blocks away. Battersly reholstered his gun. Together we bent down and picked up Allhoff. We carried him into the bedroom and laid him on top of the dreary bedspread.

His face was wracked with pain. His breath came in short gasps. Sweat gleaming on his face gave it an odd expression. His flesh looked like glazed citrus fruit. He clenched his fists for a moment and bit his lower lip. He took a deep breath and I knew it cost him an effort to speak. "A corpse," he said bitterly.

"A corpse in my own office! A man murdered in my apartment." He propped himself up on one elbow and suffered a moment's Gethsemane before he could continue. "Troglodytes!" he said. "No, by God, you can't be such half-witted fools." His little eyes grew narrower. He fixed us with them. "Did you do it on purpose to embarrass me?"

I gaped at him. "Do what on purpose?"

"Let that murderer kill Wayne in my office? You did it to make a fool of me. Me! With a corpse in my office!"

I sighed and shook my head. "Allhoff," I said with remarkable patience, "why don't you get some rest? If you'll think it over you'll realize it was impossible for anyone to know that Timmons had a gun in his sling."

Allhoff rolled his eyes, made a horrendous noise in his throat and for a moment I thought he was going to foam at the mouth.

"*I* knew it!" he screamed. "You lunatic. *I* knew it. Why couldn't you?"

"How on earth could you know it?"

"I knew it the instant I heard Timmons was wearing a sling. Hell, it was obvious. Wayne's suddenly changed story. His nervousness. Plus the fact that he threw us two clues dealt off the cuff. God, he was asking for our help! And you let him be killed. And in my office!"

BY NOW I had reached the conclusion that Allhoff's concern was much greater regarding the geography of the killing than the killing itself. The fact that Wayne was dead didn't touch him much. The fact that Wayne had been killed in his office was a direct blow at his prestige.

Battersly scratched his head. "Inspector," he said, "what do you mean that Wayne was asking for help. He never said anything like that."

"The hell he didn't," snapped Allhoff. "He said he was driving west on Fifty-fourth Street, didn't he? Said he stopped and spoke to a copper whom he knew."

"Well," I said, "so what? It's quite conceivable he *did* know the copper on that beat."

"It's not conceivable he knew any copper who'd let him drive west on Fifty-fourth Street," yelled Allhoff. "It's a one-way street, east-bound. The even numbered streets are east-bound. The odd, west. My God, a police sergeant who doesn't know that! Then what about his date in the Putnam Building. Do you know where the Putnam Building is?"

"No," I said. "I can't quite place it."

"Of course not. Because it isn't there."

"It isn't where?"

"It isn't anywhere, you fool! It was torn down fifteen years ago when they put up the Paramount Theatre. Wayne was saying those things to draw our attention to the fact that something was screwy. Expecting to find a modicum of intelligence in my office, he took that way of informing us that Timmons was forcing him to change his story."

I thought that over carefully. I came to the reluctant conclusion that Allhoff was right.

"Is that why you asked if Timmons' hands were in his pockets? You figured he may have been holding a gun on Wayne?"

"Of course. The instant I heard about the sling I knew the answer. Now, we've got a corpse and a mystery on our hands. And there's something else."

Groaning, he swung his body around and faced Battersly. I grew apprehensive. If there had to be an immediate target for Allhoff's savagery, I preferred to be that bull's-eye myself. At me, he became only insanely angry at Battersly, he went berserk. I steeled myself. From the wild expression in his eyes I knew it was coming.

"You!" he said and it sounded worse than the foulest oath. Battersly's face was suddenly drawn and white. A shadow came over his eyes and he took an involuntary step backwards. "You," said Allhoff again, "you and your clumsy legs. You don't deserve a pair of legs. You could've got that guy. But you fall over me! You filthy cowardly oaf!"

He paused and drew a deep breath. I wracked my brains for something with which to divert him. Battersly stood with his back against the wall in both a literal and figurative sense. Then like a bomb on an open city came the blast. Allhoff, trembling like a man with fever, rattled all his vocal cords, and hurled mouthfuls of slime at Battersly. He cursed, raved, ranted. He invented catchwords that would have stunned a philologist.

He beat his fists against the side of the bed until the mattress rocked like a cradle. Protruding from the bottom of his nightshirt where his thighs should have begun, were two leather tipped stumps. These flailed frantically against the soiled counterpane, beating a frenzied tattoo of hysterical hatred.

I caught Battersly's eye and signaled him out of the room. He fled, Allhoff's blasting vocabulary pursuing him, like a pack of hounds in full cry. I stood there, bearing the brunt of it, until at last Allhoff, utterly exhausted fell back upon the grimy pillow. I pulled the covers over him. I left the room, the sound of his stertorous breathing sounding in my ears.

Battersly sat at his desk. His face was buried in his arms. I sighed heavily as I filled my pipe. I found myself wishing I could afford the luxury of a nervous breakdown.

CHAPTER TWO
A WILLING WITNESS

THE SITUATION which was driving me quietly mad, had its genesis several years ago when Battersly was a raw recruit and Allhoff an inspector with two legs. We had learned that a couple of thugs for whom we were searching were hiding out in a rooming house on upper West End Avenue. We had learned further that a Tommy gun on the stairway commanded the door in the event of a raid.

Battersly's assignment had been to effect a rear entrance and disable the gun's operator at zero hour—when Allhoff came clattering in the front door with the raiding party. Battersly had carried out the first part of his assignment all right. Then, becoming suddenly panicky, had run up the stairs and waited too long before attempting to engage the man at the machine gun.

The net result of this maneuver was that when Allhoff came charging in the front door he was greeted by a hail of bullets, at least a dozen of which lodged in his legs. Gangrene followed that and amputation was next.

Although the Civil Service code proscribed such odd characters as legless inspectors in the department, the Commissioner was of no mind to lose his best man. Through some devious bookkeeping device, he arranged that Allhoff still draw his full pay, that he live in this slum because of its proximity to headquarters, and that he still devote his talents to the solution of those cases which taxed the brains of the rest of the department.

Allhoff, for his part, had made a single grim demand— that Battersly be appointed as his assistant. The Commissioner had agreed. From that day Allhoff, who had lost a little of his mind along with his legs, had exacted a full and bitter revenge. Battersly had never been permitted to forget that error of years ago. Allhoff's hatred for the younger man made the heart of Hitler seem a soft and yielding organ.

I was the innocent bystander that had been hit by the truck aimed at someone else. Since I had come up with Allhoff, since I was reputed to know him better than anyone else, I had been sent over here with Battersly. In theory I was supposed to look after the paperwork. Actually, I was supposed to pour cans of oil on the troubled waters whenever Allhoff went berserk. Every night, I prayed for a transfer as a Pole prays for freedom. With precisely the same result.

The boys from the morgue came up and took the Wayne corpse out in the meat wagon. Battersly and I sat in complete silence. In the bedroom Allhoff poured caffeine into his system and brooded. The simple fact of his being silent was boon enough for me. The morning passed slowly and without development. Allhoff didn't speak to us and we certainly weren't suckers enough to talk to him.

Battersly and I returned to the tenement after lunch perusing a copy of the afternoon paper which contained the story of Wayne's death. It was publicity I was positive Allhoff wasn't going to relish. Figuring that, I discarded the paper before I entered the flat.

I peeped into the bedroom to find Allhoff staring at the ceiling. His brow was wrinkled as if he were in deep thought. He still did not speak.

Then, a little before two o'clock Alicia Dorman came in. She was tall, blonde and beautiful. She looked as out of place in Allhoff's drawing room as an ermine wrap in a sewer. Her eyes were blue and deep as a bucket of turquoise. Her lips, full red and provocative. She glanced around the room, wrinkled a tiny nose and said, in a voice that tinkled like an ecstatic bell: "Is Inspector Allhoff in?"

"To no one," yelled Allhoff from the bedroom. "I'm thinking about a murder case."

I MADE an apologetic gesture to the blonde. Battersly stared at her like a farm boy at the *Police Gazette*. Her full red lips parted in a smile. She said, in a voice which carried into the bedroom: "Which murder, Inspector? Westerly's or Wayne's?"

There was a moment's startled silence. Then Allhoff's voice rose like an explosion.

"You fools!" he yelled. "Bring that woman in here."

That nettled me. I escorted the blonde into the bedroom. I said: "You will excuse the condition of the room. The Inspector has shingles. He's been unable to wash the bedspread this year. However, you needn't worry. Germs are afraid of the Inspector. They—"

A feminine presence did not stay Allhoff's tongue. In three words he insulted both my mother and myself. He showed his teeth at the blonde. If you knew him you were aware that this was his politest smile; if you didn't, you would have received the distinct impression that he was rehearsing the alter ego of Dr. Jekyll. He indicated a chair with his hand. The blonde drawing her skirts gingerly about a pair of magnificent thighs, sat down.

"I am Alicia Dorman," she said. She opened her bag and took from it a cigarette which had been clinched. She lit and blew a cloud of smoke in Allhoff's face.

He propped himself up in bed and poured himself a cup of coffee. He said: "What do you know of the Wayne murder?"

She looked at him archly. "Oh," she said, "I know who killed him."

For the first time in his life Allhoff put down a filled coffee cup without tasting the brew. He said, excitedly, "Who?"

I watched his eager little eyes and reflected that he was shot with luck. Without any effort on his part a clue to the ignominious corpse that had fallen on his own floor was about to drop into his nonexistent lap.

"Timmons," she said. "Harry Timmons."

Allhoff nodded his head excitedly. "Yes, yes, what else do you know?"

"Why that's all," said Alicia Dorman. "That's everything I know about it, Inspector."

Allhoff's brow clouded. "Then how do you know that?"

"Why, Inspector, I just read it in the afternoon papers."

I chuckled. Allhoff glared at her. She returned his gaze with ingenuous blandness. She took the last puff of her cigarette, smoking it down so fine that it almost singed the rouge on her voluptuous lips and before Allhoff could speak, she said calmly: "I also know who killed Wallace Westerly."

Allhoff's eyes narrowed again. "All right," he said, "I suppose you mean Arthur Robinson and you read that in the papers, too."

She shook her head. "This man, what's his name? Robinson? He didn't kill Westerly."

Allhoff still suspicious of another gag, asked warily: "Who did?"

She stamped a high heel down on the cigarette butt she'd dropped on the floor. The smile and the softness went out of her face. The sweetness had gone from her voice as she said with ineffable bitterness, "My husband."

I could see Allhoff's muscles tense. He came to the point like a setter. "Why?" he snapped.

"Jealousy," said the blonde. "He was jealous of him."

"Who," said Allhoff, "was jealous of whom?"

"My husband was jealous of Westerly. I loved Westerly. I hate my husband. My husband found out that I'd been seeing a lot of Westerly and he killed him."

Allhoff looked at her for a long time and appraisingly. "You're sure of this?"

"Positive."

"What's your motive in coming here?"

"I'll tell you," said Alicia Dorman and her voice rippled with hatred, "I want my husband to die for killing my lover. I want him to be killed in turn."

"Proof," said Allhoff. "Can you prove it?"

"That's your job. I know my husband killed him. I tell that to you. It's your job to find the evidence."

ALLHOFF TOOK a deep breath. His brow was wrinkled. "Do you merely *think* your husband killed Westerly or do you know?"

"I know," said Alicia Dorman vehemently. "I *know*. I *know*."

"How?"

"Because he told me he knew what was going on between Wallace Westerly and myself. He told me he would revenge himself on Westerly. Then a day later Westerly is killed. Of course, my husband killed him."

"All you're giving me," said Allhoff, "is motive. There's an equally good motive for Robinson. Moreover, Robinson was at the scene of the crime."

"I know that. But I'm telling you my husband killed Westerly. You're a detective, aren't you? Knowing who the murderer is, you should be able to find the evidence to convict."

Allhoff nodded. "All right. I'll send my men out to your house to look around. I'll grill your husband. If Homicide thinks Robinson killed Westerly the chances are it was someone else anyway."

Alicia Dorman's eyes narrowed. "Wait," she said. "Don't send your men out until tomorrow night. It's my husband's lodge night. He won't be in. It'll be easier if he doesn't know you suspect him. Besides, I'm afraid of him. I think he tried to follow me here tonight."

"Why?"

"He doesn't trust me. He often follows me. I changed subways three times to shake him off."

"Taxis are easier if you're being tailed," said Allhoff."

"I don't use taxis."

Allhoff looked at her expensive outfit. "Why not? I gather you can afford it."

"I watch pennies," said Alicia Dorman. "I didn't always have an easy life. I don't mind spending money on clothes and jewelry for myself. But I won't throw it away. Subways are good enough for me. I smoke cigarettes down to the end. I'd sooner have cash in the bank than the memory of the good time it bought me."

I lifted my eyebrows.

"If my husband knew I came here, that I've told you these things, he might even kill me. He's jealous and crazy when aroused. He might even kill you, Inspector."

"Better men have tried," said Allhoff. He lifted his voice to make sure Battersly overhead him. "Only one has even partly succeeded."

Alicia Dorman stood up. "Very well," she said, "you'll send your men out tomorrow night to look over the house?"

Allhoff nodded. "All right," he said. "I'll play it your way. If I fail to find anything I'll play it my own. I should be very happy if Robinson were innocent, since Homicide thinks he's not."

She nodded and walked to the doorway. Allhoff threw a sudden question at her. "Did you ever know Wayne?"

She shook her head. "Never heard of him until I saw that story in the paper."

She strode regally out of the room. Battersly's gaze followed her hungrily.

I went out of the room, leaving Allhoff to his shingles and his meditation. I didn't know what was going on in his head. But it seemed to me that he was eminently more interested in Wayne's death than Westerly's. Wayne's came under the head of a direct challenge.

It was a little after four o'clock when the phone rang. I answered it, listened and went into the bedroom to report.

"Hey," I said, "they've sprung Robinson. One hundred grand bail. Are you interested?"

Allhoff took his eyes off the ceiling. "Vitally," he said. "Who sprung him?"

"Honest John McLeod," I told him.

"Get him," said Allhoff. "Send Battersly for him. I crave an audience with that Scotsman. Leap!"

CHAPTER THREE
A COUPLE OF CLUES

THE ADJECTIVE preceding Honest John McLeod's name was no ironic sobriquet. He was a gaunt gangling Scotsman, dour as the highlands that gave him birth. He was an avid man where an honest dollar was concerned. He would not lift a finger for a tainted one.

He followed Battersly into Allhoff's bedroom. The constant air of melancholy peculiar to him hung over his head like a halo. He nodded mournfully to Allhoff. He said, with a distinct burr: "You sent for me, Inspector?"

"I did," said Allhoff. "What about this Robinson bail?"

"It was raised," said Honest John McLeod who saved words as carefully as he saved dollars.

"I know damned well it was raised," said Allhoff. "Who raised it?"

"I did," said McLeod as if he were paying full cable rates on the sentence.

"Don't be so damned garrulous," said Allhoff. "I mean who paid your fee?"

John McLeod looked about the room. He stared at Allhoff vacantly and said: "I'm sorry to hear you're ill."

"Listen, loose tongue," said Allhoff, "what can you tell me about Robinson's bail?"

John McLeod considered this for a moment. "This much I can tell you. Robinson sent me to his office to get one of his partners to pay the fee. It was a rather odd circumstance. One of the partners, Reddie, was away in a nursing home with a breakdown. Happened just before I got there. The other, a fellow called Williams, seems to be missing. No one's seen him for two or three days. Anyway, since the firm's checks need the signature of at least two partners, it was no dice. So we didn't get the fee from Robinson's office."

McLeod smiled faintly. He looked as if he had just let Allhoff in on the secret plans of the German High Command. He said, "I hope your health gets better soon, Inspector," and turned abruptly toward the door.

"Listen," said Allhoff, "I didn't ask you who failed to pay Robinson's bail fee. I asked you who did."

Honest John McLeod shook his head. "I have passed my word," he said.

"To whom?"

Honest John McLeod looked reproachful. "Inspector," he said, shaking his head, "what sort of a trap is that? I have promised my client that no names shall be mentioned."

I watched Allhoff closely. I fully expected him to lose his temper, to threaten McLeod with every rap in the book from spitting on the sidewalk to high treason. To my surprise Allhoff smiled blandly. He shrugged his shoulders.

"Well," he said, "if you won't talk, I guess there's no way to force you. By the way, Simmonds, will you put on another cup of coffee? Battersly, go along and help him."

I stared at him and suspicion welled up in me like heartburn. True, I'm not as young as I was once, nevertheless, I am quite capable of putting on a pot of coffee unassisted. Besides, there was something a trifle too smug in

Allhoff's smile, something too oddly acquiescent about him.

I left the room, followed by Battersly. I half-closed the door. I took up my position outside it and peered through the crack below the upper hinge.

ALLHOFF SAID, very softly: "Oh, McLeod, you know something about guns, don't you?"

McLeod nodded. Allhoff reached for his holster which was hanging over the back of the chair. He took his police special from it and handed it to Honest John McLeod. "The safety catch," he said, "there's something wrong with it. Take a look."

McLeod took the gun, held it by the butt, muzzle pointed to the floor and examined it. No sooner had he cast his first glance at the safety catch, than Allhoff let out a howl which could have been heard in Columbus, Ohio.

"Simmonds, Battersly! He's threatening me. With my own gun. Put that down, McLeod. You'll never get away with it. Merely because—"

Battersly charged into the room before I could move. He pounced on McLeod like Sam Rover recovering a fumble for dear Old Siwash. He wrenched the gun from the Scotsman's hand. He said to Allhoff: "Shall I arrest him, sir?"

He looked like such a beaming little hero, I could have kicked him. From where he had been standing it had been impossible for him to have heard Allhoff's remarks to McLeod. He was doing a first rate job of stooging for Allhoff and all the while feeling heroic about it.

McLeod frowned. He and Allhoff looked at each other with an air of complete understanding. McLeod said: "I suppose you're prepared to book me for everything up to attempted murder?"

"Everything," said Allhoff blandly.

McLeod sighed. Allhoff made his point crystal clear. "There are no witnesses," he said. "It's your word against mine. They usually believe coppers."

McLeod nodded. He seemed to bear no malice. Rather he appeared to be annoyed with himself for falling into such a simple trap. For a moment I was tempted to enter the room, announce I had observed the whole scene. The prospect of Allhoff's wrath dissuaded me.

"I passed my word not to mention it," said McLeod doggedly. "It's a nasty mess, Inspector."

"If it's your damned Scotch conscience that's bothering you," said Allhoff, "I'll let you satisfy it on a technicality. You promised not to *tell*. Write me your client's name on a piece of paper. That'll do."

McLeod wrestled silently with his conscience. Finally, he overcame it. He took a piece of paper and a pencil from his pocket. He wrote something down and handed the paper to Allhoff. He turned and strode to the bedroom door.

"Inspector," he said and his burr rippled through the room, "there are times when I consider you lacking in ethical qualities."

Which put him in complete accord with everyone else in the department.

I CAME down to work the following morning to find a convention in Allhoff's bedroom. Seated gravely at Allhoff's bedside was Doc Hennessy, the police surgeon. Standing at his side, registering annoyed concern, was the Commissioner himself, flanked by his aide and his secretary. Battersly, impressed and at attention, stood by the doorway.

Allhoff was propped up on the pillows. His ugly face still registered pain not unmixed with indignation.

"I tell you I'm all right, sir," he was saying. "Good God, sir, a man was killed in my own office. I can't let them get away with that. I've got to keep on the job."

The Commissioner took the cigar from his mouth and glanced at Hennessy. Hennessy shook his gray head. The Commissioner followed suit and shook his own.

"No," he said flatly. "I won't have it. You're a damned good man, Inspector, and I need you. I won't permit you to jeopardize your health. You're to stay there in bed, doing absolutely nothing until the doctor says you're fit for duty. Do you understand?"

Allhoff glared at him. He said, ungraciously, "Yes, sir."

"Moreover," went on the chief, "I know you, Inspector. I'm going to post a man on the door downstairs to see that you obey orders. He will be told to see that you don't leave the house. Further, I'm going to padlock those phones in the other room. I don't want you moving a brain cell until you're well. Haggerty—"

The aide stiffened to attention.

"Get some of those little padlocks. Put them on the Inspector's telephones. See that—"

Allhoff moved uneasily on his pillows. There was dissatisfaction in his gaze.

"But, sir," he protested, "I'm in the middle of a case. Not only the man who was killed here, but that Westerly business. I—"

"You've a staff, haven't you?" snapped the Commissioner, looking at Battersly and myself. "Let them handle it. You told me you're supposed to search that Dorman house for evidence. All right, let them do it. Sergeant Simmonds?"

"Sir?"

"You're in charge of this Dorman-Westerly case. See that the house is searched today. But keep the inspector out of it. Do you understand?"

"Perfectly, sir."

He nodded and marched out of the room. The aide and secretary followed him with the elan of a pair of storm troopers.

Allhoff glared after them. When the door slammed he turned on me savagely.

"That report," he snapped. "The one on Robinson and his partners that just came in. Battersly was reading it to me when the Commissioner arrived."

I grinned and shook my head. "No," I said, "I'm in charge. You heard the boss tell me so. You are to rest."

"You!" shrieked Allhoff. "You're not fit to be in charge of a privy. Damn you, I won't ask you to help me get out of here, or to help me use the phone. Those were specific orders. But he didn't say you couldn't talk to me. Read that report and tell me what's on it."

Our eyes met. I made no move toward my desk where the report lay. "Listen," said Allhoff, softly and menacingly, "you know what I could do to you if I wanted to?"

I knew all right. He could endanger my pension rights by swearing to a dozen things that had never happened. He could work me overtime every day. He could, under certain circumstances, send me into a nest of thugs with no chance in one hundred of my survival. I sighed and turned to the desk.

"All right," I said, "what is it you want to know?"

"Robinson," he said. "About his partners and that letter. It's on my desk."

I PICKED up the onionskin copy and read it quickly. I abridged it for him.

"Robinson," I said, "gets out of jail to find a registered letter notification in his mail box. He calls at the post office for his letter. It is from his missing partner Williams. Williams states that if anything happens to him the other partner Reddie, is at fault. He says he may be murdered or kidnapped. A friend was to mail the letter if Williams disappeared. Apparently he disappeared."

"Ah," said Allhoff, "it's getting clearer."

I looked at him with disbelief. "What's getting clearer?"

He ignored my question. "Anything else there?"

"Only that Robinson reported the letter to the cops at once. There's an alarm out for this guy Reddie."

"All right," said Allhoff. "So much for that. Give me that stuff on Westerly again."

I exhumed the clipped sheets of onionskin from the litter on my desk and took them into the bedroom. I gave him the details of the murder, all of which he already knew.

He interrupted me in the middle. "Never mind that. Did they find anything in the house? Papers, documents? Anything that might be at all significant."

"There was nothing significant to Homicide," I told him. "What papers they found pertained strictly to business."

"Get them for me," he snapped. "And another thing, find out who does the accounting work for us. Who's the best guy we have?"

I frowned at him. "An accountant? For what? Westerly ran his own business. A produce business. What the devil do you want an accountant for?"

"I love accountants," said Allhoff blandly. "Or if you don't like that explanation, consider it the whim of an ailing man." He lifted his voice and shouted at me. "Damn you, get me the name of the department's best accountant. Get me the stuff they dug up from Westerly's place."

He poured himself a cup of coffee from the percolator at his side. I went across the street to headquarters.

I returned with the name of an accountant and a sheaf of papers. Allhoff snatched the latter from my hand and perused them intently. He left Battersly and myself in peace for a good half hour.

"Hey," he called suddenly, "there's a wire here for Westerly from Frisco. Came a day before the killing."

"So?"

"It says: 'Have everything ready. Will ship when you say so.' It's signed 'Barkley and Greene.'"

"Well," I said with heavy irony. "That's just wonderful. It probably concerns a crate of cantaloupes."

"That is just what it doesn't concern," said Allhoff. "That's why it's significant."

That made about as much sense as the Japanese onslaught at Pearl Harbor and I said so. Allhoff sighed exaggeratedly.

"Leave me alone," he said, "I'm a sick man. Get the hell out of here and investigate Dorman. Now, right away."

"Not until tonight," I said. "Mrs. Dorman said her husband would be out then."

Allhoff lifted himself on the pillows. "Don't question me," he roared. "I said now. I want to be alone."

I smiled my sweetest smile at him. "I'm in charge of the investigation," I told him. "If you doubt me call the Commissioner."

A HALF-HOUR later a uniformed policeman with a face that had been fashioned in Kerry County marched into the room. He took something metallic from his pocket and announced importantly, "I'm under orders to padlock the dials on these phones. Then I am to stand guard outside. The inspector is confined to quarters."

I grinned at Battersly as I heard Allhoff swearing angrily in his pillow.

About nine o'clock that evening a maid admitted Battersly and myself to the Dorman residence. A moment later we were ushered into the presence of Alicia Dorman.

She shook hands with me. She said, nervously: "Go through the whole house. I don't know of anything specific that you might find. But there must be *something*. A criminal always leaves a clue, doesn't he?"

That was the beautiful theory of a layman. However, I didn't disillusion her. I shrugged my shoulders and walked out of the room toward the stairway. Battersly followed me. We went upstairs and began the frisk.

We began, reasonably enough, in Dorman's room. With little hope and no enthusiasm at all I went through Dorman's desk. Battersly gave his attention to the closet. I groped my way through piles of innocuous papers and was about to give up altogether, when Battersly's startled voice struck my ears.

"My God, Sergeant! Look!"

I swung my head around to see Battersly holding what seemed to be a soiled shirt at arm's length and staring at it in a sort of triumphant horror.

"It's a shirt," he said. "A shirt with blood on it. And here's a wallet bearing the initials *W.W.* They were stuck behind an old suitcase. There was a letter there, too."

I took the letter from his hand. It was typewritten and it stated quite plainly that the signer was going to see Dorman's wife whenever he felt like it, threat or no threat. It was signed Wallace Westerly.

"And the wallet," I said, "undoubtedly Westerly's. There must have been something in it Dorman wanted. He took the whole thing."

"Sure," said Battersly, "and the shirt. See, he didn't dare send it to the laundry. It's a cinch, now. And we solved it. Allhoff had nothing to do with it."

"Nothing at all," I said with grim satisfaction. I wrapped the exhibits in newspaper and we went downstairs.

I led the way into the library where we had left Alicia Dorman, then pulled up short. Alicia Dorman stood enveloped in the arms of a man. Their lips were together and they clung in passionate embrace. I was about to cough discreetly when the man released her.

He said: "I can't imagine who called me. But the moment I thought you were in trouble, I came. I—"

I gave out with my cough. The pair of them spun around and looked at me. The man, I observed, seemed apprehensive. Alicia Dorman's poise did not desert her.

"An old friend of the family," she said. "Haven't seen him for years. Did you find anything, Sergeant?"

I nodded. "Plenty," I said. "But I'd rather not discuss it now. What we've found we're taking back to the office."

She smiled sweetly. She summoned the maid who escorted us to the door.

The following morning Allhoff pretended to be unimpressed with our evidence. He heard our story in glum silence, gulping coffee the while.

"They picked up this guy, Reddie," he said. "A report came in this morning. A copper spotted him from the description at a bus station. Reddie pulled a gun when the cop tried to make the pinch. They shot it out with the result that Reddie's in the Larchmont nursing home."

I grinned. Obviously, he was breaking his neck to change the subject.

"Battersly," he said. "There's a letter on my desk in the other room. Take it at once to Larchmont. See this guy, Reddie. Give it to him and wait for the answer."

"Now listen," I said, "what do you care about Reddie? We're supposed to be working on that Westerly killing. Remember? Reddie is—"

Allhoff glared at me and drew a deep breath. "Battersly," he yelled, "get going. Run on those damned sound legs of yours. Pick up your muscular feet—"

Battersly snatched up the letter and ran.

"You," said Allhoff to me, "will round up Robinson and the Dormans. Get them here as quickly as possible.

"For what?"

"I'm going to solve a murder case."

I regarded him quizzically. I thought of the stuff Battersly had found in the Dorman closet. "*You're* going to solve it?" I said with heavy irony as I put my coat on and left the room.

CHAPTER FOUR
A DEMON'S REVENGE

A HALF hour later the Dormans arrived. Ten minutes after that Robinson came up the stairs. I started as he came in the room. For Robinson was the same man I had seen holding Alicia Dorman in his arms last night. For a moment I thought of communicating that information to Allhoff. However, he seemed so cocksure that I held my tongue.

Allhoff's tiny bedroom resembled Grand Central Terminal at the rush hour. Arthur Robinson sat on the edge of the sagging bed looking as if he fully expected a bedbug to climb up on his lap any moment. Alicia Dorman occupied a rickety chair. Her husband, frowning and ill at ease, perched precariously on the top of a battered steamer trunk.

Allhoff, himself, was propped up on two pillows. His hands were beneath the sheets and as he looked around the room he did not move.

He looked at me and said: "There are at least a couple of murders I'd like to explain to the assembled citizenry. Pour me a cup of coffee, Sergeant."

I poured some coffee from the chipped percolator which had been placed at the side of the bed. Allhoff withdrew his left hand slowly from the covers and took the proffered cup. He gulped the liquid with a sound which would have made Mrs. Post swoon. I watched him appraisingly. If he intended pinning Dorman's guilt upon him publicly, then taking credit for the evidence which Battersly had dug up, he was, to my glee, going to make an egregious idiot of himself.

Everyone in the department from the Commissioner down knew quite well that Allhoff had been officially confined to quarters, that his phone had been padlocked. It was impossible for him to claim he had discovered any evidence himself.

Allhoff handed me his empty cup. He thrust his hand back under the sheets as if it were cold. He said with mock humility : "Of course, in this case my movements have been circumscribed. However, I have done what little I can from my mattress which is more than any other copper can do with the whole damned town as his playground." He paused.

"Naturally, the first thing I did was to get in touch with Barkley and Greene of San Francisco. I—"

"Wait a minute," I said, "how could you get in touch with anyone? How—"

"It occurred to me," he interrupted calmly, "that Westerly, a produce merchant, would not be getting any produce shipments from San Francisco in the wintertime. Hence that wire did not seem to refer to Westerly's business. So I got in touch with Barkley and Greene and discovered they were private detectives."

I glanced around the room. Arthur Robinson studied his nails as if they held the secret of the universe. Mrs. Dorman stared intently at Allhoff. Her husband said querulously: "What the devil does it matter who Barkley and Greene are?"

"Barkley and Greene," went on Allhoff, "were working on an assignment for Westerly. They were checking a Mary Gooddale, a former habitué of Frisco's underworld. They checked very successfully. Didn't they, Mrs. Dorman?"

Alicia Dorman met his gaze steadily. She said: "I don't know what you're talking about."

Dorman was sitting bolt upright. "My God," he said suddenly, "you mean Westerly was right all the time. He was—"

"He was so right, it killed him," said Allhoff. He took his left hand out of the bed and signaled for more coffee.

"From the description which Westerly gave his private detectives, it wasn't difficult for me to realize that Mary Gooddale and Alicia Dorman were the same person. You see, Westerly who never approved his pal Dorman marrying Alicia had often tried to tell him that Alicia was a tramp. Like most lovers, Dorman wouldn't believe it. Westerly set out to prove it for him."

I took the pipe from my mouth. "In view of the fact that Westerly and Alicia Dorman loved each other, that's palpably ridiculous."

"You are consummately gullible," he said. "That is a high class phrase meaning sucker."

Again I took the pipe from my mouth.

"Put it back in again," said Allhoff. "With your mouth shut these lovely people might think you intelligent. Now listen: Westerly hated Alicia Dorman. So much so he was about to expose her to her husband. He got the dope, or was just about to get it. He sent for Alicia. He told her about it. He told her to tell Dorman the truth or he would. So she killed him. There you are. Motive and everything."

I blinked. Motive? Maybe. Everything? Not by a long shot. I said as much. I added: "Primarily you can't get behind the evidence we have against Dorman. Or even the fact that Robinson was on the scene of the murder."

"Robinson is easy," said Allhoff. "When he heard of what Westerly was about to do he threatened to kill him. Later when he went back to see him he found Alicia had already done it."

"Why?" I yelled exasperated. "Why should Robinson stick his nose in? What the devil did he care what happened to Alicia Dorman—"Then I remembered last night's scene and shut my mouth.

"Hell, man," said Allhoff grimly, "he was in *love* with her."

Dorman's face was very white. His wife stared at Allhoff.

"How on earth can you know that?" I asked.

"Several reasons. The principal one is that Alicia denied knowing Robinson. Yet when I got in touch with him last night, told him she was in grave danger, he was most concerned. So much so that he called on her immediately."

I almost bit the stem of my pipe through. "*You* got in touch with him? How? How the devil—"

"Besides she put up his bail. And she isn't very free with money by her own admission. Moreover—"

BATTERSLY'S ENTRANCE interrupted him. He came, breathless and excited into the room.

"Inspector," he said, "Inspector, what do you think? I went up there and—"

Allhoff gave him a look which would have frozen mercury. "Shut up."

Battersly swallowed. "But this is important. I saw that guy, Reddie. I—"

"Now," Allhoff interrupted, "we have a pretty good case. A motive, coupled with the fact that Dorman will admit Westerly constantly stated that Alicia Dorman was a tramp and said that he would prove it. Too, we have her lie about not knowing Robinson. It's a good circumstantial case that should convince a jury. Unfortunately, juries being sentimental idiots rarely send a woman to the chair—"

He broke off as Alicia Dorman dropped a cigarette to the floor and ground it out with her heel. She flicked open the catch of her bag and stood up, and suddenly there was an automatic in her hand. She said in a voice like breaking glass: "If I've killed one man, Inspector, I can kill two. I'm leaving here when you're dead. No private detectives will ever catch up with me this time."

As I thought it over, it occurred to me it was a fool-proof situation. If I saved his life he was in my debt. If I grappled with the woman too late he was dead. Either way I won. I hesitated no longer. I dove down into my shoulder-holster and moved toward Alicia Dorman. I had my gun in my hand when the shots rang out.

There were two of them. One sped over my head and ate into the plaster of the wall. The target of the second I did not immediately recognize. The baffling fact of which I was at once cognizant was that neither shot had been fired by Alicia Dorman nor myself.

Alicia's automatic was on the floor. Blood dripped from her wrist down upon her shoe. There was a black hole in the counterpane of Allhoff's bed. He withdrew his right hand from beneath the sheets and there was a smoking Police Special in it.

He fixed the Dorman woman with triumphant eyes. He said, brutally: "Sit down, tramp."

She sat down. Her upper teeth were sunk deep into her lower lip. Yet she made no outcry. Futilely she essayed to stem the flow of blood from her wrist with a fragile handkerchief.

"A doctor," yelled Robinson. "I demand you call a doctor."

"That wound won't kill her," said Allhoff. "It would be stealing money from my friend the State Executioner." He looked over at me and added conversationally, "I got this little idea from our friend Timmons and his sling. Neat, eh?"

"But the evidence," I said. "That stuff Battersly found."

"Battersly is an oaf," snapped Allhoff. "Mrs. Dorman played us all for oafs. She planted that stuff herself. You see, she killed Westerly. Then she discovered her lover was being charged with a crime she had committed. That wouldn't do. So she hit on the device of killing two birds with one stone."

"Go on."

"By planting the crime on her husband, she automatically got rid of him, collected his dough and sprung her lover, Robinson, at the same time."

A single look at the faces of Alicia Dorman and Arthur Robinson convinced me that Allhoff was talking true. But how the devil he had done it was utterly beyond me. After all, he had been confined to his rooms as effectively as if he'd been in jail. As for the telephone—

I walked into the living-room and examined the padlock on the dial. It was intact. Allhoff was clumsy with his fingers. If he had picked it there would be signs, I came back into the bedroom unhappy and bewildered. Allhoff lifted his coffee and tossed it off like champagne.

"If you'll call that idiot downstairs who's supposed to be guarding me," he said, "you can deliver these two prisoners to him. Then send Dorman home. He needs aspirin."

The downstairs copper took Alicia Dorman and Robinson across the street to book them. I put Dorman in a taxicab. I returned to Allhoff's bedroom. Allhoff stretched his hand out to Battersly.

"You have my signed document."

Battersly nodded. He took a long envelope from his pocket and handed it to Allhoff. Allhoff opened the envelope and read what was inside.

"Good," he said. "I thought he'd do it. That cleans up everything."

"Listen, Inspector," said Battersly desperately. "I've just got to tell you, sir."

"That Reddie is Timmons?" said Allhoff. "Is that what you've been trying to tell me?"

Battersly's jaw fell down. I sighed and sat down on the edge of the bed.

"My brain reels," I announced. "Why is Reddie Timmons?"

"It's quite elementary," said Allhoff. "Reddie is Robinson's partner. So was Williams. Williams has disappeared. Reddie visits Robinson in his cell. Robinson has already seen Alicia Dorman so he knows that this guy Wayne is coming to see me. Robinson tells Reddie that Wayne is the one man who has evidence to save him from the chair."

"All right," I said, "Who's Wayne?"

"A stooge of Alicia Dorman's. She didn't intend seeing me personally. She sent Wayne to spur us to digging up evidence against her husband. When Wayne got killed she had to take over herself."

"What about Reddie?" I said.

"Reddie is a crook. I thought he might be when Robinson couldn't get bail from his own office. That's why I sent an accountant over there. Reddie has been robbing the firm for some time."

"So?"

"So," said Allhoff impatiently, "it stands to reason that Williams found out about it. Possibly gave him a chance to make restitution. Realizing Reddie was desperate, he wrote a registered letter to Robinson, telling him Reddie was responsible if anything happened to him—Williams. Doubtless gave it to a friend to mail if Williams disappeared."

I NODDED my head. "Now I get it. Reddie killed Williams. He knew of the letter. Figured with Robinson in jail he would have time to get hold of the letter himself and destroy it."

"At last," said Allhoff, reaching for the coffee cup, "your limited intelligence functions. When Reddie hears this man Wayne is going to spring Robinson, he finds out where Wayne lives and goes to see him, forces him at the point of a gun in his sling to tell me that cock and bull story."

"There's still a hole," I told him. "Why doesn't he kill Wayne at once? Why let him come here?"

"My God," said Allhoff, "are you a complete moron? If Wayne never showed up, I'd investigate, wouldn't I? It was much better to let him come here, disarm us with his story and then kill him. That's what Reddie planned. If Robinson gets that letter, the exposure would have brought Williams' death right down on Reddie's shoulders, he figured he might as well burn for two murders as one."

"So," said Battersly, "when you knew Reddie had been picked up you figured he was Timmons."

"That I did," said Allhoff, basking in his triumph. "I sent you up with a confession that he'd killed Williams for him to sign. I called his attention to the fact that since there were no witnesses to that murder, he might claim self-defense, or, anyway, have a better chance of beating it than the murder of Wayne. I promised him I wouldn't testify against him for killing Wayne."

I knitted my brow. "What the devil did you care about the confession on Williams? If Reddie burned for Wayne, wasn't that enough?"

Allhoff grinned maliciously. "Those monkeys across the street will swoon when they know I already have that confession. They're worrying about the case."

"But you can't do that," I protested. "You can't let him get away clean with the Wayne murder. He might beat the rap on the other one."

Allhoff grinned horribly.

"I only promised *I* wouldn't testify. I said nothing about you and Battersly. You saw it, didn't you?"

I said: "I didn't think of that."

"Neither," said Allhoff, "did Reddie." He looked at us over the edge of his cup.

"Suppose I'd really taken a rest as the Commissioner suggested. You and Battersly would have felt like a couple of red-faced idiots when you burned Dorman, wouldn't you?"

We didn't answer. Then something occurred to me that I had forgotten.

"You couldn't have possibly done all these things," I said, "while you were lying in that bed. You spoke of getting in touch with people. Yet, obviously, you didn't leave the house or use the phone."

He sat up in bed and grinned maliciously. "Who says I didn't use the phone?"

"Stop clowning," I said testily.

ALLHOFF NARROWED his eyes thoughtfully for a moment. Then he said: "I can get numbers on that phone without touching either the padlock or the dial. What do you think of that?"

Battersly stared at him for a moment and said: "I don't believe it."

Allhoff threw back the covers. He slid out of bed and stumped into the living-room. He pulled himself up into his swivel chair. He put his hand on the receiver. He turned to Battersly, his little eyes hot with hateful malice. He said: "How much don't you believe it?"

Battersly looked scared before Allhoff's gaze. But he stood his ground. "I don't believe it at all."

"Very well," said Allhoff. "If I call the Commissioner's office without touching either the padlock or the dial, will you speak to him? Will you tell him he's a fat-headed fool?"

I sensed a trap. "Allhoff," I said sharply as Battersly hesitated.

"Shut up," snarled Allhoff. "He called me a liar. Now I'm calling him. Will you do it, you yellow hound?"

Battersly flushed. He nodded his head and said, "Yes," in an almost inaudible voice. Allhoff grinned and took the receiver from its cradle.

He held his forefinger over the two contact points upon which the receiver had rested. He tapped one of them lightly and in perfect rhythm. Pausing between each series of taps, he repeated the process seven times.

He waited a moment and held up the receiver so that we could hear the ringing sound at the other end of the line. A moment later, a voice, which I recognized as that of Burns, the Commissioner's secretary, answered.

"This is Inspector Allhoff. I'd like to be connected with the Commissioner."

"Hello, Inspector," said Burns. "The Chief's tied up on another wire. Will you hold it a moment?"

"Delighted," said Allhoff. He turned a grinning triumphant face to us.

"For God's sake," I said amazed, "how do you do that?"

"Your knowledge of the workings of a dial phone," said Allhoff, "is equalled only by your knowledge of anything else. You don't need to touch the dial to get a number. You can do it with the hook. There are ten contacts on a dial phone, one for each finger hole. If the hook is pressed and released once for each number you want to call, if the manipulation is spaced absolutely evenly, you'll get the number. The hook makes and breaks the same ten contacts as the moving dial."

I heard a familiar voice come over the wire. "Yes, Inspector, this is the Commissioner."

"Good afternoon, sir," said Allhoff sweetly. "Patrolman Battersly asked me to call you. He wants to speak to you."

He swung around and handed the receiver to Battersly. Battersly's face was deathly white. He took the phone in nerveless fingers. He stood there in complete silence for a moment. Then as Allhoff's yellow eyes bored mercilessly into him, he said in a thick strained voice: "Sir, you are a fat-headed fool."

He hung up as Allhoff rocked with laughter. That laughter echoed about the room like something mad and evil as we waited for the return call which was going to bring a departmental trial to Patrolman Battersly.

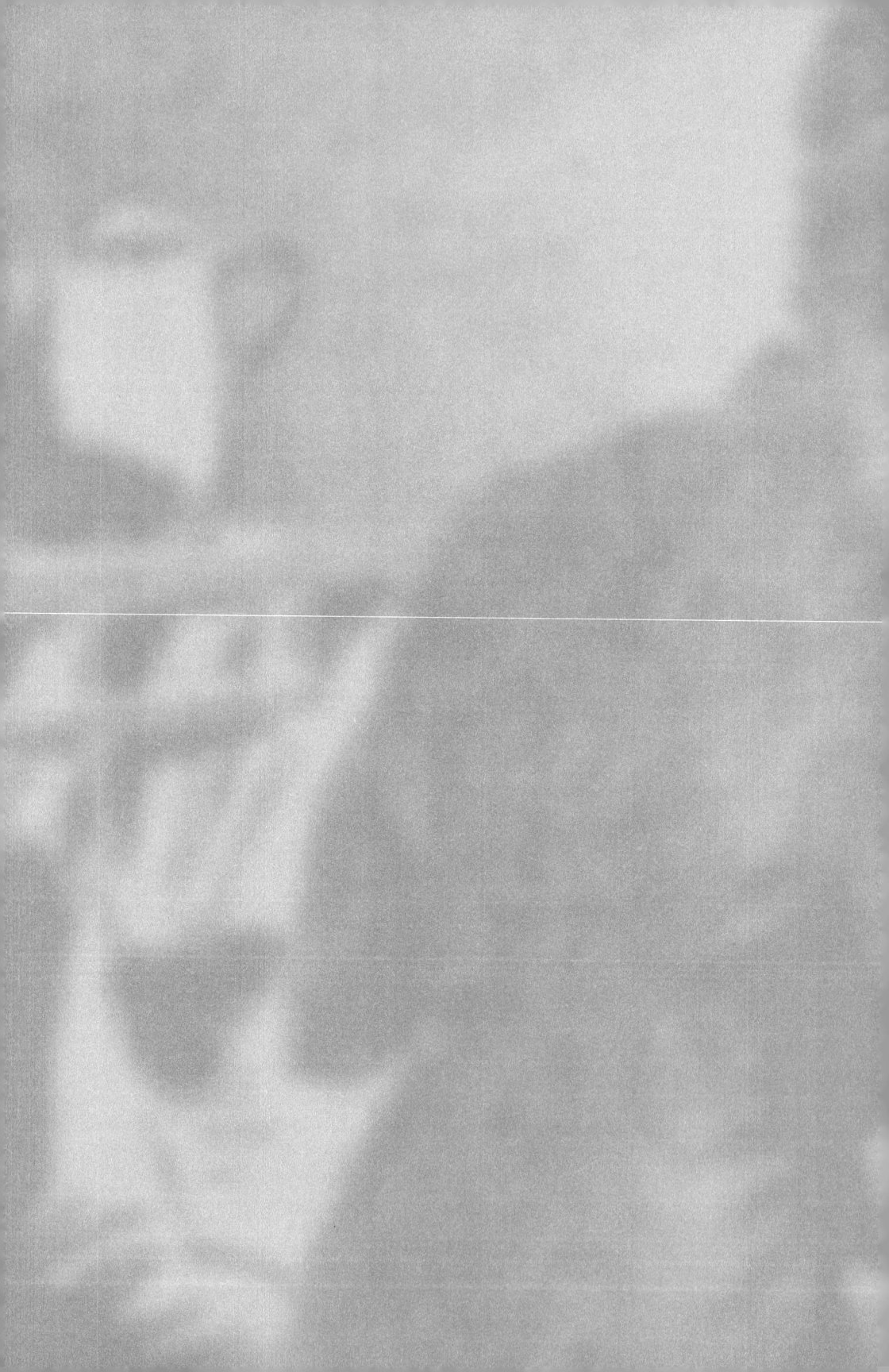

MURDER IN THE MIRROR

ONLY CUPID'S CUNNING COULD HAVE NERVED BATTERSLY, THE BROW-BEATEN COP, INTO BRINGING IN A MURDER CASE FOR HIS LEGLESS, COFFEE-TIPPLING CHIEF TO SOLVE. ALLHOFF'S SOLUTION HAD ALL THE COLD-BLOODED SKILL OF A SURGEON— ONLY IT WAS BATTERSLY'S HEART THAT FELT THE SHARP EDGE OF THE BLADE.

CHAPTER ONE
BATTERSLY HAS A CASE

OUTSIDE IT was August. Within Allhoff's tenement apartment the atmosphere was that of an untidy tank, afire on the Libyan desert. Heat poured across the dusty window sill and oozed through the tin of the roof. Across the street the red bricks of police head-quarters shimmered in the morning sun. It was a New York summer day—humid, enervating, stifling.

I sighed and looked around the room. Its appearance would have caused the stomach of the hardiest interior decorator to turn slowly over. The floor was dusty, the walls begrimed. Dishes, unwashed, had been piled in the sink until it looked like the city dump. Allhoff's laundry was stacked up against the south wall, a gray slumping moun-tain.

Two sounds afflicted my ears and annoyed me. An English sparrow chirped inanely on the window ledge; Allhoff's percolator gurgled dispiritedly upon the electric base at his desk. He had already poured two pints of the black liquid into his system, but the caffeine coursing through his veins had, apparently, little effect on the uplift of his disposition.

He sat with his squat torso hunched up closely against the edge of his desk. Once he turned his head around and glared savagely at an empty chair in the corner of the room.

Then he elaborately consulted his watch. I sneaked a sur-
reptitious glance at mine. It was ten forty. Battersly was
not in yet.

That fact annoyed me. Not as much as it annoyed Allhoff,
certainly, and for entirely different reasons. Battersly doing
nothing at all could drive Allhoff to berserk rage; accom-
plishing something positive, like being an hour and a half
late might well result in a hysteria which would set a new
high in vocal decibels.

Allhoff drank more coffee with the sound of a herd of
thirsty cows stopping off at the pasture brook. He crashed
the heavy chipped cup down on the desktop and fastened
his angry eyes upon the door.

He was awaiting Battersly's arrival like a torpedo waits
for a tanker. His vocabulary was already fitting words into
neat and obscene epithet. He was storing the phrases in
the back of his brain, ready to shoot them from the malevolent torpedo tube of his mouth.

I fingered through the morning reports and trembled.
Repetition would never inure me to the scene of Allhoff
swinging his vengeful verbal hammers upon Battersly's
head.

The morning reports held nothing of any significance.
There were a few routine felonies which didn't affect us.
We got them only when they were either important or
when the best brains across the street at headquarters has
fallen down. Frankly, I preferred work to inactivity. Idleness
set the devils in Allhoff's brain into motion.

Outside, there sounded heavy footfalls on the rickety
stairway. Allhoff's eyes lighted up. He thrust his head
forward in the direction of the door like a bird dog coming
to point. The footfalls drew nearer. The doorknob turned
and Battersly stood upon the threshold.

With trembling fingers she detached the wooden ornament and gave it to him.

Allhoff glared at him and drew a deep breath with the sound of an asthmatic lion. A salvo trembled on his tongue but before he could speak, Battersly said, "Inspector, we have a case."

Allhoff stared at him, his mouth still open. I turned my head about and lifted my eyebrows. In our setup, Allhoff either got a case because he asked for it, or because it was assigned to him specifically by the commissioner. Never via Battersly.

Allhoff closed his mouth with a snap. Battersly came into the room and stood before Allhoff's desk. Allhoff eyed him balefully.

"Well," he said, expelling his breath with a hissing sound, "so we have a case, eh?"

He touched his temple with his hand and added, "Congratulations."

BATTERSLY LOOKED at him dumbly. I feared the worst.

"On what, sir?" asked Battersly.

"Your promotion," said Allhoff.

Battersly's face was blank. "My promotion?"

"Why, yes," said Allhoff, "to deputy commissioner, undoubtedly. Since I'm an inspector, since you've taken command of this office, I assume you outrank me. Are there any orders, sir?"

The mockery in his tone was thick as molasses and bitter as gall. Battersly's face grew pale. He stood shuffling his feet before Allhoff's desk. A dark shadow of apprehension was in his eyes, an anxious frown above them.

I unleashed a sigh that came from the soles of my boots. God knew the relationship in this tenement slum was bad enough without Battersly's tactlessness and stupidity to make it worse. I waited for Allhoff to explode. When he spoke in a gentle, smooth voice, I worried even more. He was building up to an eruption now.

"And, sir," he continued, "what is this case we are taking?"

"The Riordan murder, sir," said Battersly fearfully.

Automatically I shuffled through the reports. What little Homicide already had on the Riordan case was there, neatly typed on onionskin. It was an ordinary routine killing as I saw it. With neither the principals nor the circumstances worthy of Allhoff's talents.

Allhoff filled his coffee cup. He emptied it. He slammed the cup on the desktop and the room shook. He filled his lungs with air and turned his face to Battersly as if he were aiming a gun.

"If you're a deputy commissioner," he said, "I'll salute and investigate the Riordan case. If you're not you'll please tell me what the devil you mean by reporting almost two hours late? You'll also explain who you are to pick the cases for us? You're a presuming, incompetent idiot. I either choose a case myself or the commissioner assigns it to me. Now, answer my questions."

Battersly licked his lips. "I'm late," he said in a frightened whisper, "because I stopped off at the commissioner's office. I asked him to assign the Riordan case to us. He agreed. He told me to tell you to go to work on it."

Allhoff blinked. I was more than a trifle surprised myself. As a general rule Battersly did not hobnob with the commissioner, neither did he request cases for Allhoff to work on. Allhoff was so amazed, he didn't detonate.

"You went to the commissioner and asked him to assign the case to me?"

"Yes, sir."

"Why?"

Battersly was painfully ill at ease. He juggled his cap nervously with his hands.

"I—er—thought it looked like an interesting case, sir. Something that only you could handle, sir."

This servile flattery was a trifle sickening. Pointless, too. With Allhoff he'd never get away with it. Allhoff looked at the younger man oddly for a moment, then swung around in his swivel chair and addressed me.

"All right, Simmonds, what have you got on this intensely interesting Riordan case?"

I picked up the report. "Nothing much yet. It just broke. This Riordan was found dead in his workshop back of his cottage in Bay Ridge. Married, had one daughter. That's all they have. They'll give us what details they dig up if and when we ask for them."

Allhoff nodded and reached for the coffee pot. Battersly sat down. There was a silence in the room—it was not a comfortable silence.

For once I was certain that Allhoff's mind and mine were flowing through the same channel. We both wondered what on earth had prompted Battersly to take an interest in a murder case. Ordinarily, he did as he was told and kept his thoughts and outside interests to himself. I was still puzzling over it when I heard light feminine footsteps on the stairs outside.

ALLHOFF GROWLED, "Come in," in response to the knock on the door. When it swung open two women appeared. One was fat, clad in flowered silk. There was too much makeup on her face and it was badly applied. Her hair was yellow and the color seemed as artificial as the short wave radio from Nippon. The second woman, to put it briefly, was a knockout.

She was young, with long legs and a sweet oval face. She ran across the room, seized Battersly's arm and said: "We thought we'd better come up and give you the details so you can go to work on the case right away."

Battersly stood up, flushed and swallowed something in his throat. Allhoff twisted his head about slowly and fixed his eyes on Battersly and the girl.

The elder woman, obviously the girl's mother, stood by the doorway as if she were on the threshold of a particularly fragrant pigsty. She wrinkled her nose and sniffed. Her housewife's eye examined the chaotic filth of the room and she shuddered perceptibly. The expression on her face was the expression of a duchess who has smelled a very bad smell.

"Marion," she said to the younger woman, "do be careful, dear. Don't touch anything. Germs, you know."

Allhoff brought his neck back to the normal position and looked at her. "Better to die from germs, madam, than bullets. I'm sure your husband would agree with me."

She gasped. Her eyes were suddenly moist. She took her handkerchief from her bag and dabbed at her eyes. The younger girl set her jaw firmly. She said to Allhoff, "What a horrible thing to say." She turned to Battersly. "Reprimand him."

I blinked at that. The idea of Battersly reprimanding Allhoff was something to be assimilated slowly, not gulped all at once. Allhoff filled his coffee cup. Doubtless, he knew more of what this was all about than did I. There was a ghastly grin on his face, and unholy light in his eye.

Battersly, the girl still clinging to his arm, had turned pale. He looked as if he expected a battalion of dragons to attack him at any moment. Allhoff emptied his coffee cup with the sound of a catarrhal whale.

"It seems to me, Miss Riordan," he said to the younger girl, "that your gentleman friend is a liar. He has, apparently, told you that he runs this office in an effort to gain your confidence which would undoubtedly lead to more lustful things."

The girl flushed. The mother bridled. She said, "How dare you?" Then, to her daughter, "I told you not to get mixed up with a policeman. Thugs, that's what they are. Terrible people."

Slowly, it all dawned on me. Battersly, obviously, had been making a pass at the Riordan girl. He had given the impression that he was the authority, the brains in Allhoff's slum office. Hence, when her father had been killed, she had turned to him for help. That explained his visit to the commissioner. That explained our assignment to the Riordan killing.

Allhoff was grinning like Satan gloating over a battle-field. He drew a deep breath and faced Battersly. Now, I knew, he was about to explode like a shelled ammunition dump. Nothing, on earth could stop him. Yet, to my amazement, something did.

The door opened suddenly. We all stared at the insane caricature standing upon the threshold. Doubtless, it was a man; it looked infinitely more like a scarecrow. His hat was a Texas Stetson, so large that it enveloped his ears. His shirt, open at the throat was filthy dirty. His coat was ill fitting and patched. His trousers hung as if they had weights suspended within them. His shoes were directly out of burlesque. They were tremendous, wide soled, and frayed.

Were it not for two other details, his appearance would have been screamingly funny. A black handkerchief was tied over his face and in his right hand he held a revolver. In a voice, squeaky and muffled, he said, "Put up your hands."

INCREDULOUS, MRS. RIORDAN lifted her arms. With the exception of Allhoff, the rest of us followed suit. Allhoff's face was a dark puce. He glared at the revolver as if he could intimidate it. The scarecrow with the gun took a step toward the desk and spoke to Allhoff with its eyes. The message was grim and unmistakable. Slowly Allhoff lifted his arms above his shoulders.

The weird figure held out his left hand, palm up to Allhoff. "Give me," he said, "your fountain pen."

Allhoff took the pen from his pocket and handed it over. The apparition glanced at me. "Your pipe," he said, "and that can of tobacco on the desk."

I said: "What the devil sort of a holdup is this anyway?"

He didn't answer, but his compelling eyes bored into mine. I handed over the pipe and tobacco. The scarecrow moved over to Marion Riordan. He eyed her speculatively for a moment.

"Now," he murmured musingly, "what can I take from you?" He looked her over examiningly. His gaze rested on a small wooden ornament pinned at the neck of her dress. "Ah," he said, "a nice piece of work. I'll take it."

Marion Riordan did not move. She said, with sudden emotion: "No, not that, please. It has a sentimental value. It has a—"

"Give it to me!"

The menace in his voice frightened her. With trembling fingers she detached the wooden ornament and gave it to him. The masked figure turned his attention to Battersly.

"Are you wearing a belt?"

Battersly, utterly bewildered, nodded his head.

"Give it to me."

Battersly hesitated for a moment. Then with scarlet face, unbuckled his belt and surrendered it. The weird holdup man moved toward the door. He took the key from the inside of the mortised lock and fitted it in the outside. He stared at the terrified Mrs. Riordan for a moment, then snatched her purse from her hand. He leaped out of the room with swift agility, slammed the door behind him. Stupefied we heard the key turn in the lock, heard the flapping of his ludicrous shoes pattering down the stairs.

For an instant we all stared paralyzed at the closed door. Allhoff whipped open a drawer of his desk and jerked out a Police Special. With accurate aim he blasted the lock.

"After him!" he shouted to Battersly. "Hurry, you yellow lying oaf."

Battersly raced to the doorway, handicapped by the fact that he reached for his gun with one hand while he held his trousers up with the other. I got up and followed him.

A moment later we returned to report that there was no sign of our scarecrow robber in the street below.

Allhoff grunted. "Had a car waiting, probably."

He drank coffee quickly, his brow wrinkled. I sat down and grappled with the problem of why an insanely dressed thug should risk a holdup in order to obtain a pen, a pipe, a belt, a wooden ornament and a purse. The purse contained some semblance of logic. Nothing else did.

CHAPTER TWO
THE SHATTERED MIRROR

ALLHOFF SET down his cup, turned his head about and faced his audience. "Now, listen," he said. "The commissioner has assigned me to find out who killed George Riordan. Those are my orders and I shall follow them. But let us, Mrs. and Miss Riordan, have it completely understood that I run things here. When this rat, Battersly, implied that *he* did, he lied. For the obvious purpose of making advances to your daughter, Mrs. Riordan."

Marion Riordan gasped. Battersly looked like a little boy who has caught his father in the commission of a felony. Mrs. Riordan elevated her nose three more degrees.

"Sir," she said, "your insinuations are vile. Heaven knows, I don't want my daughter a policeman's wife. But only a low mind would hint that there was anything wrong in their relationship. Everything is already arranged. Next month Mr. Battersly will march up the aisle with my daughter."

I winced at that last verb. It was most unfortunate diction. Battersly's face was the color of Devonshire cream. Allhoff's jaw set like concrete. His eyes were yellow slag.

"March up the aisle," he murmured in a voice like poisoned honey. "March up the aisle, eh?" He paused for a moment, gathered all his vocal strength and screamed, "On whose legs?"

The two women, taken completely unawares, stared at him as if he had suddenly gone mad. Which, in a sense, he certainly had. He put his hands on the edge of his desk. He pushed hard. The swivel chair rasped across the floor on rusted rollers. The movement revealed Allhoff's body. The torso was thick, muscular and squat, but where the torso ended so did Allhoff.

Where his legs should have begun there were a pair of leather tipped stumps. These flailed violently now against the edge of his chair. His mouth was open and a fleck of saliva dropped onto the lapel of his coat. His larynx rattled like a distant drum and the words erupted out of him like lava from Vesuvius.

"He'll march up the aisle on my legs! Mine, do you hear? The legs he stole from me. The legs that were burned in the incinerator at All Souls' Hospital. So, you're going to marry a cowardly rat who steals the very flesh from his comrades, eh? Take him, and welcome. He's—"

He uttered an epithet which would have stunned an elder and aroused the admiration of an etymologist. He attended to the moral dissection of Battersly's ancestor with vehemence, hatred and magnificent syntax. Then, suddenly and completely out of breath, he shut up. Panting hard, he pulled his chair back up to his desk and stretched forth his talon-like hand in the direction of the coffee pot. He drank like a man who has just walked in from the Sahara.

The two Riordan women were horrified. They stood dumbly looking at Allhoff as if he were the devil, himself. Battersly's head hung. He studied the dirty floor intently as if he would read the riddle of life there. I stood up.

I took the Riordans' arms and walked them over toward the door. "You'll excuse the inspector," I said. "He's not quite himself. If he wants any information about Mr. Riordan's death, I'll have him call you. Good-day."

They went, without reluctance, down the creaking stairway. Battersly ran trembling fingers through his hair and sat down, shaken. Allhoff continued drinking coffee as if it would drown the terrible demons that dwelt within him. I sank down in my chair and sighed. I wondered if I was too damned old to enlist in the Marines.

THE AWFUL conflict that held our disorderly office in thrall had its genesis several years ago. In those days, Allhoff had been a biped and Battersly a raw recruit. A stool-pigeon had tipped us off that a pair of notorious thugs, for whom six states were searching, had established a hideout in a rooming house on upper West End Avenue.

We had also been informed that they had a tommy-gun parked on the stairway, commanding the front door in the event of a surprise incursion of the police. Battersly's assignment had been to effect a rear entrance and, at zero hour, disable the operator of the machine-gun as Allhoff and his doughty squad came charging through the front door.

Battersly had carried out the first part of his orders well enough. He had breached the house all right. But at the last moment had contracted a sudden attack of buck fever. He was young, and it was his first important job. Quite understandably, he had become panicky.

His nerve cracked and, at zero, he fled up the stairway instead of closing with the thug at the gun. Allhoff leading his men through the broken front door had, as a result of Battersly's weak moment, walked directly into a hail of machine gun fire.

A score of bullets had smashed into his legs. Gangrene had set in and shortly afterwards amputation followed.

Naturally, the Civil Service code forbade the employment of a copper without two legs. But the commissioner, shrewd and of no mind to lose one of his best men, had formulated the plan under which we now functioned.

Through a devious bookkeeping device, Allhoff was still paid his full Inspector's salary by the city. He had rented this miserable slum in order to be near headquarters. As his price, he had demanded of the commissioner Battersly's services as his assistant. This demand the commissioner had met.

I had been included in this jolly little setup because I had known Allhoff for years—perhaps, been the closest thing to a friend that he had ever had. Ostensibly I was here to take care of the paperwork. Actually, I was supposed to act as peacemaker when Allhoff's savagery, his long and bitter revenge at Battersly, became too much for anyone to bear.

For Allhoff had lost something more than his legs when that amputation took place. A part of his mind had gone with them. He hated Battersly with terrible venom. He let no opportunity to harass the younger man escape. There were times when I was certain any psychiatrist would have certified him insane. And there were times when his crazed behavior brought me close to that condition myself.

Were it not for the fact that I was rapidly approaching a pension, I would have walked out years ago. I was tired of pouring oil on these troubled waters, of seeing Allhoff beat Battersly with his tongue as surely as any Gestapo agent beat his prisoner with a whip.

However, with a family, with no other resources save that imminent pension, here I was. And here I would be forced to stay until I reached the age limit, or until Allhoff suffered a lethal cerebral hemorrhage during one of his more flamboyant outbursts.

UNDER ALLHOFF'S orders Battersly and myself drove out to the Riordan home in Westchester County. A few more details on the killing had trickled into our office from Homicide which added a possible importance to the case and Allhoff had thrown himself wholeheartedly into the problem of its solution.

Riordan, it appeared had been a naval architect. He, according to his colleagues, was a man of unimpeachable integrity. Certainly, it seemed he was mixed up in no dealings in which he betrayed the trust reposed in him by the Navy Department.

At my side, Battersly, driving a police coupé, was morose. Doubtless he felt like a fool for misrepresenting his position to the Riordan girl. Moreover, to have suffered beneath Allhoff's attack in the presence of the girl he presumably loved, was, to say the least, humiliating.

The Riordan home was a neat white cottage set in a bright green landscape. The front door opened into a long, dimly lighted hallway. As we entered I observed an old-fashioned pier glass at the far end of the corridor. As we approached it, I observed something else. The center part of it had been shattered. I examined it curiously, Battersly looking over my shoulder.

"Looks like a bullet hit it," he said. "See. Right there in the middle."

I nodded. That was exactly what it looked like. Though why a potential killer should practice on a mirror before blasting his victim was something I could not, at the moment, fathom.

The maid who had admitted us ushered us into the living-room. Mrs. Riordan sat, freshly hennaed, in an armchair. She looked through Battersly with icy eyes and bowed to me. Marion Riordan smiled at me, then ran across the room to Battersly. She put her arms around him and kissed him chastely. She did not speak, but her eyes told him eloquently enough that whatever he had done, whatever had happened yesterday was over and done with, forgiven and forgotten.

We were introduced to the dapper little man standing by the mantelpiece. He was, it appeared, Ralph Saletan, an intimate friend of the family. He was a small man with remarkably delicate, almost feminine features. He was dressed in a tight fitting double-breasted suit, an elegant linen shirt, and his tiny shoes were polished to a dazzling degree.

I sat down, produced my pencil and notebook and asked routine questions. Marion Riordan answered the first one.

"Yes," she said, "I found father's body. I came home in the early evening. Apparently, there was no one in the house. It was the maid's day off. The first thing I saw was the broken mirror in the hall. I went out to the back of the house to dad's workshop. I found him—" Her lower lip quivered. "You know how I found him."

"What was this workshop?" I asked. "Some hobby, perhaps?"

Mrs. Riordan nodded. "Wood carving. It was more than a hobby. It was an obsession with my husband. He devoted all his spare time to it. For instance, that carving the holdup man took from Marion. He was very proud of that. It was a surprise gift for her. George refused to let any of us, anyone, see it until it was finished. It was the last carving he ever made. It—"

A sob strangled the words in her throat. Saletan, trying to ease the situation, said: "Yes, his carvings were remarkably good. Really magnificent stuff. That present of Marion's was to be his masterpiece. He kept it strictly undercover. I was very anxious to see it. But I guess I never shall now."

I WROTE this all down assiduously. The difficulty of working under Allhoff's instructions was that you never knew what you were supposed to find out. Allhoff invariably sent us out to pick up information at random, retail it to him. He would then dissect it, figure its significance. I concede it usually worked. However, I always felt stuck on precisely what questions to ask.

Thinking of nothing more I stood up. "I'd like to take a look at the workshop," I said.

Saletan volunteered as guide. He led me down the long hallway to the back of the house. There, out beyond the kitchen was a long room smelling cleanly of wood shavings.

A work bench ran along the back wall. A vise and a hundred saws and knives were arrayed at the back of the bench.

Even though my interest in wood carving was as intense as that of a glass manufacturer in the shortage of tin, the stuff was good. Deftly carved and damned imaginative. However good he may have been as a naval architect, George Riordan was first rate at his avocation.

Saletan was obviously interested. "Wonderful stuff, eh, Sergeant? I play around with it a bit myself. But my best isn't anywhere nearly as good as this. I was intensely interested in his work. We built up a fine friendship on that mutual interest."

He jabbered on, boring me. I made my excuses and left the workshop. I wandered through the house idly, wondering if anything faintly resembling a clue would turn up, when I suddenly heard voices from the dining-room.

It was a woman's voice, pitched high and querulous—the voice of a typical neighborhood scold. I stopped to listen.

"Yes, sir, officer," it said. "I wouldn't gossip for the world. I believe in strictly minding my own business. But in times like these, one must subordinate the interests of one's friends to the interests of one's country."

I stood behind the curtains which divided the dining-room from the serving pantry. I heard Battersly mumble disinterestedly.

"Yes," went on the woman. "I was visiting her last night. Just dropped in to see if I could help, when this Jap came with the money."

"What?" said Battersly, disinterested no longer.

"Yes, sir. This Jap came into the room. He said something to her in that outlandish language and handed her a big envelope. She opened it in front of me and took out a big roll of bills. I put two and two together. Her father killed and him connected with the Navy. Right after his death his daughter collecting a lot of money from the Japs."

"My God," said Battersly, horrified. "You're not saying Marion killed him, are you?"

"I'm not saying anything," said the rasping voice. "I'm leaving it to the police but you can't stop me from putting two and two together, can you? These young girls today. They'd do anything for money, you know."

I heard a soft footfall. I peeped out from behind the curtains to see Marion Riordan enter the room from the other door. The scold saw her, blushed, and hastily took her departure. I moved to come out of my cover, saw Battersly and the girl embrace and decided to stay where I was for a moment.

"Look," said Battersly, "did a Jap bring you any money yesterday?"

"A Jap," said Marion. "I thought he was Chinese."

BATTERSLY GROANED. "Then it's true."

"That this man brought me some money? Of course it's true. What of it?"

"Don't you understand? Your father, connected with the Navy, is killed. He's privy to a lot of information the enemy would like to get their hands on. Then, a few hours afterwards, a Jap appears and hands you some cash."

"But, dear," said the girl, "I can explain the money."

"For God's sake, do."

"About an hour before the money arrived I got a phone call from a Mr. Whitby. He said he owed my father some money, that he was sending it over with his house-boy who didn't speak English. I was too upset to discuss it. I just told him to go ahead."

"Who is this Whitby?"

She shrugged her slim shoulders. "I don't know. I never heard of him before. Probably some friend of father's."

"I hope we can find him," said Battersly fearfully.

"Why? Does it matter?"

"Matter?" shouted Battersly. "Do you think Allhoff's going to believe a tale like that if we can't get Whitby to corroborate it?"

There was a long silence. "Do you mean," said the girl slowly, "that you think I am mixed up in this? That I plotted to murder my own father?"

"I believe you," said Battersly miserably. "But Allhoff won't. And that, I assure you, is what counts."

Marion Riordan flared up at that. "Do you mean he'd dare—"

"He'd dare anything," said Battersly. He added bitterly, "Especially this, since it affects me."

They stood there for a long silent moment. Then Battersly said: "Listen, don't mention this at all. Leave it to me."

"You mean I shouldn't tell the inspector about that Chinese or Japanese or whatever he was?"

"No," said Battersly. "He'd crucify you. Me, too."

"All right. I suppose you know best."

She kissed him and left the room. I entered it. We looked at each other and both of us flushed.

"I'm sorry, son," I said. "But I'm afraid I just eavesdropped on a conversation of yours."

Battersly bit his lip. He didn't speak so I went on. "Allhoff or no Allhoff," I said, "we are coppers. We have a certain public trust. We can't very well withhold evidence."

We dwelt in another long silence. Battersly sighed heavily. "All right," he said. "We'll tell him. But you know damned well he'll tie Marion up with the killing if he possibly can. He knows it'll hit me."

He was dead right there. I regarded him miserably. It did look bad for the girl. If her story was true and Whitby could not be found, neither Allhoff, the D.A., nor the grand jury was going to believe her.

We went out of the house to the coupé and drove back to town.

CHAPTER THREE

"LALAPALOOZA"

ALLHOFF SAT hunched over his desk ingurgitating coffee with the sound of a quicksand clutching at a leg. He listened to my detailed recital of what information we had picked up out at the Riordan house. I concluded my story with the tale of the Japanese delivering the envelope of money to Marion Riordan.

I lapsed into silence. Both Battersly and I watched him, waiting for him to pounce on this evidence which implicated Battersly's girl. Rather to my surprise it wasn't that in which he seemed interested.

He put down his cup. He said, abruptly: "That mirror. Are you sure it had been broken by a bullet?"

"It looked that way."

He tapped an unwashed forefinger on the desktop. "About how many feet from the floor would you say the bullet had struck?"

Battersly and I consulted for a moment. We agreed about four and a half feet. Allhoff stared thoughtfully at the wall. It was difficult to say whether or not the mirror had any significance or if Allhoff's profound expression came under the general heading of impressing the help.

Battersly shuffled up to his desk. He looked scared and I knew that register reflected what was in his heart.

"About that money, sir," he said diffidently. "Do you think the cash delivered to Miss Riordan has anything to do with the case?"

Allhoff turned around slowly in his swivel chair. He looked at Battersly like a cat who is about to play a rollicking game of tag with a white mouse.

"Ah," he said softly, "the money, eh? The money brought by that Japanese spy."

"Yes, sir. Do you think Marion will get into any trouble?"

There was an evil calculating expression in Allhoff's eyes. He said softly, "You love her very much?"

Battersly nodded. "We're going to be married. I'd do anything to keep her out of trouble."

"All right," said Allhoff. "Find this Whitby. Then, if her story's true she's out of trouble. If you can't find him, whether her story's true or not she's in one hell of a mess. Find Whitby."

But we didn't find Whitby. Battersly and I devoted two days to tracking him down. No friend or acquaintance of George Riordan had ever heard of him. Mr. Whitby was very nonexistent.

Allhoff heard of our futile search, frowning over the chipped edge of his coffee cup.

"Battersly," he said, "you realize what this means? Whether or not your girl was connected in the killing of her father, I frankly don't know. But I can tell you what the newspapers will say, what a jury will probably do."

Battersly licked dry lips. I thought for a moment and considered it odd that Allhoff should speak in such a friendly tone to the younger man. It was the first time in their coupled careers that he had ever done so.

"We're at war," he went on. "Mob opinion isn't going to be logical. With a good D.A. making the right insinuations, it will appear that while perhaps the girl didn't kill her father, she was working hand in glove with someone who did. It will appear that she was paid for her part in the work and that some naval information was taken from the dead man."

OF COURSE what he said was true enough. A bright D.A. could have a field day on this particular setup. However, it still didn't seem that there was enough evidence against the girl—even circumstantial—to make a good case, legally. I said as much.

"True," said Allhoff. "Perhaps she won't be convicted. But she'll go through hell all the same. Her name'll be dragged in the mud, smeared blackly across the tops of a thousand newspapers. Socially, she'll be ruined. It'll wreck her life. Then, too, in times like these, it's barely possible she will be convicted. That'd mean a hell of a long time in jail."

What he said made sense—but his solicitude for Battersly was not only puzzling but downright suspicious. Battersly stared at him miserably.

He said desperately: "Isn't there any way we can clear her, sir? I know she's telling the truth."

Allhoff shrugged. "Maybe. I haven't any idea what the answer to the murder is. But—"

He eyed Battersly shrewdly. He drank a cup of coffee and spoke in a tone that dripped with oily good fellowship.

"You think I'm a hard man. You think I don't give a damn about anyone's feelings. Well, in certain respects I suppose that's true. But I'm not the sort of a guy who likes to see a young innocent girl ruin her life. No, sir. Not Inspector Allhoff."

I stared at him in amazement. This was so utterly out of character for Allhoff that I searched his face for a sarcastic sneer, but he appeared to be in earnest.

"Get her away," said Allhoff. "Get her out of the jurisdiction as quickly as possible, before this tale about that Jap gets around. Speak to her mother tonight."

Battersly looked stunned. I didn't blame him. My reaction to this kindly thoughtfulness of Allhoff's was somewhat similar to my reaction to a rattlesnake who'd offered to buy me a drink. Allhoff's lips were parted and he beamed on us horribly, revealing his yellow snag teeth. He looked like Medusa trying to be seductive.

Battersly, grasping at straws, was not suspicious. "But where could they go? Where?"

"Oh," said Allhoff. "How about Argentina? Get them aboard a plane before that news about the Oriental messenger leaks. After they've gone I doubt if anyone would bother about extradition. But get them off quickly."

Battersly shook his head. "It's a wonderful idea," he said. "But I don't know about Mrs. Riordan. She's rather stubborn, you know."

"She'll be easy," said Allhoff. "Bring her up here and I'll scare her to death. I'm good at that. Besides, I gather she doesn't approve of you as a son-in-law. She'll probably be happy to get her daughter away from such a low social character as a copper. Bring her up, I'll talk her into it."

Battersly thought it over for a long moment. It seemed to me that there was a flicker of anxiety in Allhoff's eyes as he waited for Battersly's answer.

"It's tough," said Battersly in a broken, jerky voice. "I'll go crazy without her. But it's for her own good. I couldn't stand seeing her dragged through a dirty courtroom. The papers printing cheesecake pictures of her."

"All right," said Allhoff decisively. "Send 'em up to see me. I'll handle it for you."

Battersly thanked him profusely. It was the first decent thing I had seen Allhoff do in our entire association. That is, on the face of it. In my brain suspicion still rankled.

AS ALLHOFF had anticipated, he had no trouble at all in convincing Mrs. Riordan of the soundness of his plan. She was in no wise averse to getting her daughter away from Battersly. Moreover she had no desire to go through the torture of an investigation and possibly a trial.

"Stay away," advised Allhoff. "Leave no forwarding address. Tell no one where you are in case the police look for you. Keep away for a couple of years at least. But before you go there's one question I'd like to ask your daughter—alone."

He slid out of his chair and led Marion Riordan to his shocking bedroom. He remained closeted there with her for a few minutes.

Later in the day Battersly reported that the Riordans had booked passage on the Clipper to Buenos Aires. They were to leave within the week.

It was a damned long week. Battersly lived in a morose world of his own. Allhoff gulped coffee down like a sewer absorbing melted snow. The oddest circumstance was the fact that he had apparently completely forgotten the Riordan murder. Usually when Allhoff got his unclean hands on a case he never let it go. This time he never mentioned it, made no move toward its solution.

For a wild moment I entertained the theory that he really believed the girl was guilty of murdering her own father, that as a favor to Battersly he was letting the whole thing slide. But I couldn't quite accept that. First, his being nice to Battersly to that degree was incredible; second, there was his own reputation to consider. He had never failed yet, a fact to which he constantly drew the attention of the Homicide Squad.

For a week, I smoked my pipe living between the silence of Battersly and the silence of Allhoff, pondering it. Then at last I sighed and gave it up.

Battersly returned from the dock on the day that the Riordans departed. He entered the apartment, downcast and miserable. God knew he didn't lead a very happy life, anyway. Losing his girl was going to make it worse.

As he removed his cap and sat down at his desk, Allhoff became animated for the first time in seven days. He banged his cup down on the desk and said: "I want to know two things."

I looked up from the evening paper.

"First," said Allhoff, "we've got a Chinese interpreter across the street, haven't we? A guy who should know Chinatown, a guy that speaks the language."

"Sure we have. Charlie Loo. Good man, too. Why?"

"I want to see him this afternoon. Get him over here. The second item is this: Do either of you guys know a man who's rather small. I mean small featured. Little hands and feet. Probably very neatly, if not expensively dressed. Small hat size, too. May be addicted to wearing a derby hat."

Battersly and I looked at each other in astonishment. Allhoff, who, to my knowledge, anyway, had never seen

Ralph Saletan in all his life, had given out with a precise description of him.

"It's a sketch of a guy called Saletan," I told him. "He was a friend of George Riordan's. Do you know him?"

Allhoff shook his head. "No. But I will and very soon, too."

THAT WAS all he said. As Battersly and I went out to lunch, Charlie Loo, the Chinese, came into the room. Allhoff greeted him eagerly, offered him a chair and cup of coffee. Charlie, no fool, took the chair.

Two days later Charlie came back into the office bringing another Oriental along with him. Battersly and I looked up with interest. Allhoff's eyes lit up over the edge of his coffee cup. Charlie Loo said: "I think this is the guy you want. He doesn't speak English, though. Or that's what he says anyway."

He looked like an ordinary coolie to me. He was short, yellow faced and slant eyed. He was dressed in a soiled blue blouse and an old pair of pants.

"Is he Chinese or Japanese?" asked Allhoff.

Charlie Loo shrugged. "Probably Chinese. He talks Cantonese. He was registered at the Chinese employment agency. Still who the hell can be certain? Even in Chungking Japanese spies pose as coolies and get away with it."

I got up and lit my pipe. "What's it all about?" I asked. "Are we working for the F.B.I. now?"

Allhoff looked up at me and his eyes glinted. "You may be interested to know that this is the man who delivered the money to Marion Riordan."

Battersly sprang out of his seat as if a coil had suddenly released itself in the seat of his pants.

"Good," he said. "If we can get him to talk it'll clear Marion. I—we—"

He broke off miserably as he remembered where Marion was, as he considered the chances of seeing her again.

"Precisely," said Allhoff. "Charlie, what's his story?"

Charlie Loo rattled off several liquid syllables. The other man listened and answered at great length.

"He says," translated Charlie Loo, "he knows nothing about it. The agency was called for a man. He went along. He met his employer in Grand Central Station. There were two men there. One of them spoke Chinese. He was given an envelope, told to deliver it. He got five bucks for his end."

"And he's not Japanese?" said Allhoff. "You're sure of that?"

Charlie Loo shrugged. "Who can be sure? I think not."

"Well," said Allhoff, "let's prove it."

"How?" I said. "If Charlie Loo can't be certain, how the devil can you prove it?"

Allhoff ignored me. He spoke again to Charlie. "Ask him if he speaks Japanese, if he's ever lived in Japan?"

Charlie put the question. Without understanding the language I knew the answer before Charlie had translated it. The Oriental jabbered indignantly.

"All right," said Allhoff. "Let's make sure. Tell him to take off his right shoe."

Charlie looked puzzled but complied. Allhoff bent down and studied the coolie's right foot with interested eyes.

"Tell him he can put the shoe on again," he said. "Now, ask him to say 'lalapalooza.'"

This made as much sense to me as Albert Einstein in Sanskrit. I said to Allhoff, "How about a rousing game of consequences. Charlie can translate for our friend here."

"You are very funny," said Allhoff loudly. "Charlie, tell him to say 'lalapalooza.'"

Bewildered, Charlie did so. The other man came through with flying colors. He said lalapalooza three times.

"Let's ensure it," said Allhoff. "Tell him to go over to the window and look out at the view."

"A rare privilege," I said. "Nothing is too good for our visitors. Perhaps he's never seen a dirty brick wall before."

ALLHOFF IGNORED me. In response to Charlie's instructions the coolie walked over to the window and stared through the dirty pane.

Allhoff whipped a piece of paper from his pocket. Apparently he was reading from it. His lips moved and some unintelligible gibberish emanated from it. The coolie still looked out the window.

Allhoff nodded and returned the paper to his pocket. "O.K.," he said, "take him back where you got him, Charlie."

Completely incurious, Charlie Loo took his little pal and left the room, closing the door behind him. I stared at Battersly, then at Allhoff.

"I am not Chinese," I said, "hence, I possess none of the traditional inscrutability of Charlie Loo. I am aching to know what the hell you were doing. Optimistically, I hope it is an indication of the complete breakdown of the brain cells. I'm afraid, however, I am wrong."

"You are an idiot," said Allhoff, pouring coffee. "I told you what I was doing. I was demonstrating that the man was a Chinese, not Japanese."

"Which you accomplished," I said ironically, "by an examination of his foot, by listening to his utterance of the word lalapalooza three times and by muttering some jargon as he looked out the window."

"Right," said Allhoff. "I didn't think you'd figure it out?'

"Damn it," I yelled. "I haven't figured it out. Are you crazy or am I?"

"You are," said Allhoff blandly. "Japanese wear sandals with a strap between the big and second toes. Chinese don't. Therefore a Jap will have quite a space between those two toes. Our little friend didn't."

"All right," I said, annoyed that once again I was wrong and he was right. "What about lalapalooza?"

"Chinese can pronounce the letter L," said Allhoff. "Japs can't."

"And the gibberish and the window?"

"That," said Allhoff, "shall, for the time being, remain my secret. I may need to use it again."

Battersly shuffled forward. His question was far more to the point than mine.

"And what about Mr. Riordan, sir?" he asked. "Does this have anything to do with the killing?"

"Indeed it does," said Allhoff. "Tomorrow, I want you to bring this Saletan guy here. And on your way home tonight, stop in Herman's delicatessen down the block and tell him to drop in. I'd like a word with him."

"My God," I said, "you don't think Herman killed George Riordan, do you?"

"Sure," said Allhoff imperturbably. "He's serving him up instead of turkey sandwiches."

He returned his nose to his coffee cup without a worry in the world.

CHAPTER FOUR
A SNAPPY DRESSER

RALPH SALETAN sat in one of Allhoff's rickety chairs looking as if he wished for nothing more than a bottle of germicide. His fastidious nose was wrinkled. The polish of his tiny shoes gleamed bravely against the dirt of the floor. The crease in his suit was like a blue sword blade. He held a pair of champagne colored gloves and a well brushed derby hat in his lap.

Allhoff removed his lips from the chipped section of his coffee cup and said: "You give the impression of a very neat dresser, Saletan."

"I do my best to keep neat," said Saletan and added pointedly, "and clean."

Allhoff flushed. "You should apply the same axiom to your morals."

Saletan's face tightened. Obviously he was controlling himself. "Your insults," he said, "are not subtle."

"Your disguises," retorted Allhoff, "are as subtle as a neon sign."

The significance of this shaft evaded Battersly and myself. It hit Saletan. He bit his lower lip and blinked his eyes.

"Now," he said in his precise accent, "I do not understand you."

"You made the mistake of an amateur," said Allhoff. "An error which I'm sure your superiors will never forgive."

A dull flush crawled up from the edge of Saletan's collar. Allhoff's eyes held the light of a vulture who has spotted a corpse some hundred feet below.

"You thought," went on Allhoff, "that the best disguise was contrast. When you were forced to appear before those who knew you well as another personality, it occurred to you that it was more efficient to be as unlike your normal self as possible."

Battersly and I nodded at each other. A little light had permeated the brains of each of us.

"You mean that crazy stick-up?" I asked. "If so, I want my pipe back. What the devil did he want with it anyway?"

"And my belt," said Battersly. "Why should he want that?"

"He wanted neither," said Allhoff. "Nor my pen, nor Mrs. Riordan's bag. Did you, Saletan?"

The only expression on Saletan's face was the effort of keeping it expressionless.

"You didn't have much time," went on Allhoff. "You visited the Riordan home the day after the killing. You found that Miss Riordan was already out, that she planned to meet her mother here at my office. It didn't give you much time for makeup.

"Being in a hurry you decided on contrast. You who never wear filthy clothes, donned them. You who wear tiny shoes and the smallest size derby, obtained a huge ten gallon hat and a pair of comedy shoes. Instead of your immaculate suit you put on a patched coat and a pair of pants that seemed to have a bomb concealed in the seat. You wanted to look as different as possible from Ralph Saletan. You succeeded—too well."

Saletan said nothing. I said, "I don't get it."

"Naturally," said Allhoff, witheringly. "The trouble, Saletan, was that you looked like nothing in this world. You were so damned grotesque that I couldn't believe anyone would ever dress like that. Hence, I reasoned you had dressed like that for some reason. The contrast disguise theory, common among amateurs, came to me at once.

Your efforts served only to give me a pretty good picture of what you actually looked like."

"I remain baffled," I said. "If Saletan was the hold-up man why did he collect all that junk from us?"

"To cover up the thing he really wanted," said Allhoff. "He came for that wooden ornament Marion Riordan was wearing. He didn't want me to know that. So he tried to confuse me by taking the pen, the belt, the pipe and Mrs. Riordan's purse."

"**WHY SHOULD** he risk a hold-up for that piece of wood? Don't tell me naval plans were concealed in it?"

"Nothing quite that melodramatic," said Allhoff. "It was the last wood carving George Riordan ever did. He made it for his daughter. It was on his work bench when he was killed. Marion found it there, picked up it and wore it the next day—that's what I asked her about in my bedroom. So it wasn't in the workshop when Saletan came back to look for it."

"Why in the name of God, if he did kill Riordan, should he come back to look for it?"

"That's simple," said Allhoff, "when you consider all the circumstances. Saletan was a great admirer of Riordan's carving. After he had killed him he saw the ornament. He picked it up, as he had done a hundred times before with Riordan's work and looked at it. He went home. Later he recalled what he had done. He realized his fingerprints were on it. He recalled, too, that Riordan had sworn never to show that carving to anyone until it was finished."

"So?" I said.

"So," said Allhoff impatiently, "suppose Marion told me she'd got the thing from the workshop. Suppose, I, being a thorough guy, examined it for prints, where does that leave Saletan? He had to make sure he wasn't suspected for more reasons than the average killer."

"Since the average killer burns," I said, "why? Are there better reasons than saving one's life?"

"The manner of dying is important," said Allhoff quietly.

Saletan's cheeks were deathly white now. His lips were bloodless, drawn into a thin line.

"Yes," repeated Allhoff, "the manner of dying is very important. Ask a Pole, or a Dutchman or a German Jew. Saletan had to cover up. That's why he went to such lengths to incriminate Marion. He called her up, said he was Whitby. He wanted to make it look logical that the Japs had something to do with it. That would make an excellent cover-up. At short notice, however, he couldn't get a Jap. Under present conditions Japs are very careful. So he got a Cantonese coolie who looked rather like a Jap and couldn't speak English."

I lit my pipe. "How do you know these things?"

"I thought them out. This last one I checked through Charlie Loo at all the Chinese employment agencies in town. Saletan had no time to get his Oriental. The agencies provided the quickest means. His trick definitely tied up the Japs and Marion in the murder. That was what he wanted."

"Why?" said Battersly. "Why? I don't understand why he should want to make it look as if the Japanese had anything to do with it."

"Because," said Allhoff, "he was terrified someone might think that the Germans had something to do with Riordan's murder."

I saw part of it now. Not all and I said so.

"Apparently no plans were missing from Riordan's office. Doubtless, he was an honest man. Why should he have been killed?"

Allhoff's sigh indicated that he could save several tons of words if I were as intelligent as he was.

"I shall draw you a blueprint," he said. "Listen: Saletan, in the pay of the Germans, became friendly with Riordan in order to buy naval plans. When he thought the time was ripe he made his proposition. That was probably on the afternoon of the murder. However, he had gauged his man wrongly. Riordan wasn't having any. Moreover he said he would expose Saletan as a German agent. Saletan returned home and got his gun. If Riordan spoke he knew he was in more danger from the Gestapo than the F.B.I. They wouldn't run any risk of Saletan living to give away their secret."

ALLHOFF POURED himself a cup of coffee and drained it. It seemed to me that Saletan needed the stimulant more than Allhoff.

"Saletan returns to Riordan's house. He opens the front door stealthily. The corridor is dim. In the distant pier glass at the other end of the hall he sees his own reflection. In his highly nervous state he thinks that reflection is Riordan. He shoots and shatters the glass. He discovers his mistake. He goes to the workshop where Riordan actually is and kills him. He pauses for a moment to admire the carving Riordan has just completed and goes home."

Saletan stood up. With a slow deliberate gesture he flicked an invisible mote of dust from the well brushed top of his derby. He took a silver cigarette case from his pocket. The match shook in his fingers as he lighted it.

"Conjecture," he said in a husky voice. "All conjecture. No evidence. None at all. I deny everything. I know no Germans. I've never been in Germany. I can't even speak German. It's a tissue of lies."

Allhoff put down his coffee cup. He said, with rare courtesy for him: "Quite possibly, Mr. Saletan. I've made mistakes before, you know."

Battersly and I stared at him. Undoubtedly he had made mistakes before, but, God would witness the fact that he'd never admitted it.

Saletan looked at him uncertainly. Allhoff turned his head around and stared out toward Centre Street. He said: "Have you seen our view, Mr. Saletan? It's really quite impressive. I'd suggest you look out our window."

So we were going through this again. He'd sent the coolie over to admire the drab red bricks of police headquarters. Now he was offering the same rare scenic treat to Saletan. Saletan approached the window warily, like a mouse sniffing at a piece of cheese in a trap.

He stood at the sill and looked out into the shimmering heat, the old brick building, the crawling traffic below. Allhoff whipped a piece of paper from his pocket. He said slowly and evenly: *"Scheiss ihn in den Rucken, Feldwebel, wir werden niemals irgend etwas beweisen konnen."*

The words must have detonated in Saletan's ear like an exploding shell. He uttered a sharp cry. He spun around from the window like a frightened top. His right hand moved like a magician's. Miraculously there was a gun in it.

Two shots cracked through the room. Both of them from the Police Special in Allhoff's hand. Saletan dropped to the floor, his unfired weapon thudding softly in the thickness of the dust.

"That," said Allhoff, putting his gun back in the desk drawer, "is that. If he lives we have a good enough case. If he doesn't we don't need one. Battersly, get a copper and an ambulance. Get him off my floor. The blood will stain the wood."

The little housekeeping touch slew me. Four dead elephants would hardly be conspicuous among the chaos of Allhoff's floor.

Battersly went below. A few moments later, a uniformed policeman and an interne removed the groaning Saletan from the apartment.

Battersly sat down at his desk. His eyes were fixed on Allhoff. Yet I knew he didn't see him. He was thinking, deeply and profoundly. It was an alien process for Battersly, yet I understood it. I knew what was going on in his mind.

It was something else, however, that bothered me. I waited until Allhoff had gulped his cup empty. Then I said: "What was this scenic business? You did it twice. You had both the coolie and Saletan admire the view across our window sill. Will you tell me why?"

"The circumstances were exactly similar," said Allhoff. "You recall the coolie denied speaking Japanese. Saletan denied speaking German. To make sure I tested them both."

"With that jargon you spoke?" I inquired.

"Right. A friend of mine at Columbia University told me the Japanese words for, 'Shoot him in the back, Sergeant, we'll never be able to prove anything anyway.' From the coolie that crack got no response at all."

I nodded slowly. "And from Saletan it did."

"Sure. I got that German from Herman of the delicatessen. Saletan reacted quickly enough. I rather thought he would. I was ready for him."

I looked across the room at Battersly, He was still bowed down with heavy thought. I knew what he wanted to ask Allhoff. I decided to ask the question myself.

"Allhoff," I said, "you owe us an explanation on one thing. Battersly, come here."

Battersly stood up. He came over to Allhoff's desk, his brow still wrinkled. Allhoff filled his coffee cup and looked up at me, a peculiar glint in his eyes.

"Well," he said. "Go ahead and ask. I thought I'd cleared it all up so that even you and Battersly could understand it thoroughly."

"You have. It's something else I want to ask you about."

Allhoff became suddenly and suspiciously expansive. "Go ahead," he said, "anything at all."

"Did you know that Saletan was guilty when you cooked up that scheme to send Marion Riordan away?"

"You want an honest answer?"

"I want an honest answer."

We stood there tensely for a moment I could hear the intake of Battersly's breath in my ear.

"No," said Allhoff.

"Your word?" I said.

"The inspector's right," said Battersly. "I've been thinking about it. He couldn't have known. He didn't go to work on anything until after they had left. Do you remember?"

Difficult as it was to believe, it seemed that Allhoff had not deliberately wrecked Battersly's romance. Considering the chronology of the case, it seemed that Allhoff had not yet reached the theory which involved Saletan until after the *American Legion* had sailed.

"All right," I said. "Incredible as it seems, it's not your fault. I concede you did not know of Saletan's guilt until after the Riordans had left. Your motives were all right. Maybe you're not such a louse as I thought."

HE GLARED at me as if the last phrase was insult. He breathed deeply and banged the coffee cup on the table.

"You fools!" he screamed. "You blatant, stupid idiots. What the hell would I care whether or not Battersly's girl was dragged through the courts? Why the hell should I care if his paramour is smeared in the newspapers? Do you think I'm a doltish altruist?"

"But," I said bewildered, "you gave us your word you didn't know of Saletan's guilt at sailing time."

"I didn't, you cretin. But I knew Marion Riordan was innocent."

Battersly stretched forth a hand and gripped the back of a chair until his knuckles showed white.

I asked in an icy voice: "How could you know she was innocent if you didn't know who was guilty?"

"You are an obtuse zany," said Allhoff. "Any fool would have known she was innocent. Battersly can go to his grave reflecting that if he had one single ounce of intelligence he'd still have his girl."

I kept my temper. "Very well," I said, "explain it to me."

"The mirror," he said. "The broken mirror. A high school boy could figure it."

I thought it over for a moment. "I am a high school boy," I said. "I can't figure it."

"I told you," said Allhoff, "that the killer opened the door, saw his own reflection in the mirror and thinking it was Riordan blazed away."

"So?"

"So, you crazy Kallikak, the murderer had to be a *man*. It couldn't have been a woman. The killer came to murder a man. Hence if he saw a woman's reflection in the mirror, he wouldn't shoot. In order to mistake the reflection for Riordan that reflection had to be that of a man. So a woman couldn't have killed him. That's why I knew Marion Riordan was innocent."

He glared at us, triumphant, his lips red and wet, his eyes aglow with an evil light. He looked like a cross between Lucifer and the Hunchback of Notre Dame.

Battersly uttered a weird sound half sob, half oath. He turned around and ran blindly from the room.

Allhoff's laughter, Gargantuan and horrible, pursued him down the stairs.

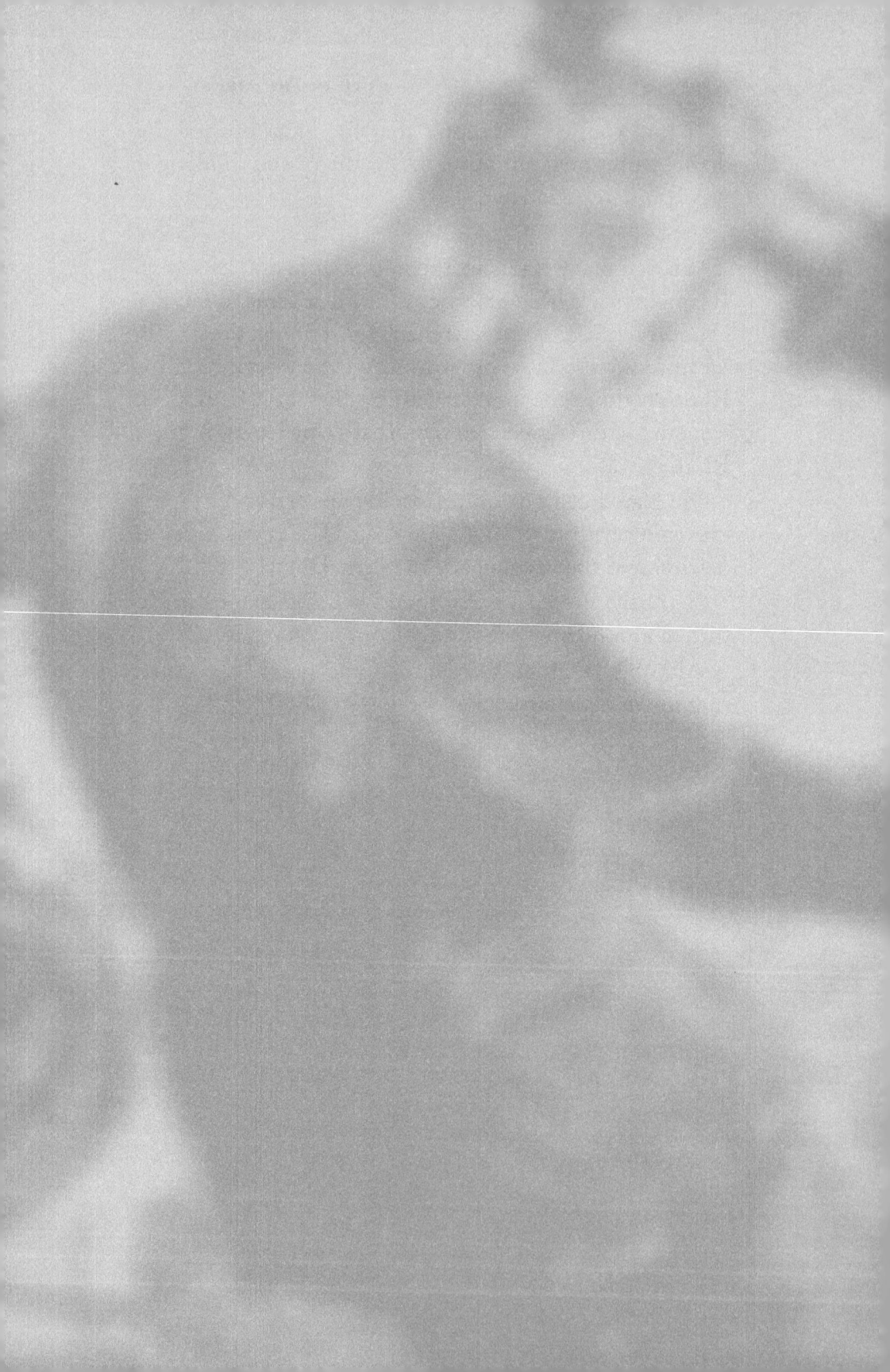

A LEG ON MURDER

TO THE LEGLESS COFFEE-
TIPPLER OF CENTRE STREET, THE
WILTERN CASE LOOKED LIKE THE
SWEETEST SLAYING HE'D EVER
ATTEMPTED TO SOLVE BETWEEN
CUPS OF HIS BITTER BREW. FOR
HADN'T SERGEANT SIMMONDS
BEEN FOOLHARDY ENOUGH
TO WAGER THREE MONTHS'
SUGAR RATIONS THAT ALLHOFF
COULDN'T PUT HIS GREEDY
FINGER ON THE PLAYBOY'S
KILLER?

CHAPTER ONE
MURDER IN A SICK-BED

DINNER WAS a meal I invariably enjoyed. The day's work, arduous and performed in an unwholesome and venomous environment, was thrust completely from my mind. I munched good well-cooked food in a domestic atmosphere of affection which acted as an antitoxin for the hatred I had rubbed shoulders with at the office.

I was engaged in the pleasant demolition of a huge steak under the approving eye of my wife when the doorbell rang. I ate on blissfully as she rose to answer the bell. A moment later I looked up, surprised almost to the point of being shocked, and beheld Battersly.

Embarrassment was stamped upon his youthful face as he stood over the kitchen table. He was clad in his patrolman's uniform, his cap in his hand, and an apologetic expression in his eyes. I waved him to a chair and continued eating. In all the years that I had known him he had never before paid me a personal call.

I was not, however, flattered. Rather, I was annoyed. Battersly, perforce, was part of my professional life, and my professional life was most unpleasant. To be reminded of it as I ate my dinner was a damned nuisance. Only Battersly's humble and abashed air prevented my saying so.

"Excuse me, Sergeant," he said, "for busting in like this. But I had to see you. There was a murder this afternoon. I want to talk to you about it."

For a single instant hope glowed within me. I suspended a forkful of meat in midair and asked with the breathless interest of a politician inquiring as to the health of a constituent's baby: "Was it Allhoff?"

Battersly looked at me blankly and my hope receded.

"I mean was Allhoff killed?"

"Oh, no. It wasn't Inspector Allhoff. It was Wiltern. Maxwell Wiltern. You know of him, don't you?"

I pursued a pool of gravy with a chunk of bread and nodded. If one were literate enough to follow the flawless sixth grade prose of a tabloid newspaper, he knew of Maxwell Wiltern. In his prime, Wiltern was a man possessed of tremendous appetites. Moreover, he was possessed of the money with which to satisfy them.

He had been written up all over the front pages of the more sensational journals. In recent years, however, age, stomach ulcers, and it was rumored cancer had improved Wiltern morally, if not physically. Anyway, his publicity and carnality had ceased simultaneously.

I PUSHED my plate away and accepted a cup of coffee from my wife. I offered one to Battersly but he refused. He seemed rather upset though I could not guess why. I was as indifferent as the Sphinx to the death of Wiltern. I saw no reason for Battersly's concern in the matter.

"Wiltern," went on Battersly, "was killed sometime early this evening. Homicide arrested a fellow named Arthur Coller. They've got him now."

I munched a slab of apple pie and said: "So what?"

"Don't try to stop me, Simmonds," he said harshly, and brought his gun down on my skull.

"Well," said Battersly, "I can hardly believe he did it and my mother's certain he didn't."

I lifted my eyebrows. Battersly was an indifferent detective, himself. I could hardly imagine his mother taking the trail of a criminal with any better success.

I said, incredulously: "Did you say your mother?"

"Yes. You see, this Coller is a distant cousin of mine. His mother and mine were brought up together. They're very close. So naturally—"

I saw the pattern now. "So," I said, "Mrs. Coller, hysterically, called your mother, like all coppers' mothers, believed you had more influence than you have and you were charged with getting cousin Arthur out of the toils. Is that it?"

Battersly nodded briskly. I sighed.

"So you, having no influence at all, come to me to handle the job for you. Is that it?"

"That's it, Sergeant. I called Homicide and they won't even tell me what it is they have on Arthur Coller. I don't know if it's a tight case or not. I thought, perhaps, they'd tell you."

I shook my head. "They're not particularly fond of anyone connected with Allhoff. If they've broken a case themselves they won't want Allhoff to have any part of it. However, I'll do what I can."

Battersly stood up and shook my hand. "Thanks," he said. "My mother made me come to see you. In the meantime I'll do what checking I can."

"All right. But I promise you nothing. It's quite probable Homicide's right, too. Distant cousins have committed murders before."

Battersly shook his head as he stood in the doorway. "My mother seems certain—" he began, but I waved him out of the doorway. When it comes to crime no one is more naive than mothers.

I thought it over for a while as I digested dinner. I knew Homicide would give me no information, so I decided to call Turner. Turner was a newspaperman who knew more inside stuff about town than the Mayor.

I lit my pipe, donned my hat and went out of the house. A few moments later I sat across a littered desk looking into the cold gray eyes of a middle-aged man with a surprisingly young face.

"I want a favor," I said coming to the point at once. "Homicide has a guy in the can for killing Maxwell Wiltern. Do you know what they've got on him?"

Turner shook his head and I thought I detected irritation in his manner, probably at being caught without knowledge of something important.

"I know nothing," he said. "I just heard of the killing. Homicide isn't talking to the press. This guy, Coller, that they have, I never heard of. However—"

A far-away thoughtful expression came into his eyes. "Wait," he said. "There's a pal of mine, an insurance agent, who was telling me a few weeks back that he'd sold a huge policy to Wiltern. The beneficiary was Dick Hurlbut, the bookmaker. That fact struck me as odd at the time."

I looked at him keenly. "Are you suggesting Hurlbut killed Wiltern?"

He shrugged his shoulders. "I'm suggesting nothing. But it would please me if Homicide were wrong on this case. They've been rather short with me. See what you can see about Hurlbut. He's got a motive, all right. Find out if he has an alibi as well."

"All right," I said, "thanks." Then as I stood up I thought of something else. "Wiltern had a nephew, didn't he? Some cruising kid who figured to inherit? Maybe I ought to check him as well."

Turner waved this suggestion aside with an airy hand. "Save your time and energy," he said. "That kid had everything he wanted. Wiltern liked the way he played the nightclubs. Whatever he asked his uncle for, he got. There'd be little point in that kid knocking him off when he could draw on his inheritance just as easily."

"O.K.," I said, "I'll check Hurlbut at once."

"If you get anything—"

"Don't worry. I'll give it to you for the paper as soon as I have it myself."

I HIED myself off to Dick Hurlbut's apartment hotel feeling rather like a fool. After all, Homicide might well have a cast iron case. I was dabbling about in the dark. I thought of Allhoff's comment if he had known and I shuddered. However, I was in this deep, so I figured I might as well see it through.

I rang the bell of Hurlbut's apartment and waited an unusually long time before the door was opened by a stiff-shirted valet. I pushed into the room to find Hurlbut standing between two closed suitcases.

He stared at me with startled eyes and his face was paler than usual. "Simmonds," he said. "Good God, it's started already."

I said with notable naïveté: "What's started?" and as I uttered the last word of the sentence, Hurlbut's hand dropped to his coat pocket and emerged again holding an automatic.

He spoke desperately, harshly: "Simmonds, you're a nice guy. I want you to live to collect your pension. But don't try to stop me. I don't know who's pulling this frame or why. But I'm damned if I'm going to stand for it. I'm taking a powder. I'm desperate and I'm tough. I assure you my next move is as much of a favor to you as anything else."

I stared at him bewildered, not having much idea of what he was talking about. He moved a step toward me and suddenly lifted his gun. He brought it down thuddingly upon my skull.

I fell with slow dignity to the floor. My eyes closed and I could not open them. I remained in that condition for some time.

I recovered to find the valet who had admitted me swabbing my head with a damp cloth and solicitously offering me a shot of brandy. I waved the former aside, gulped the latter, and stood up. I blinked and said: "Where's Hurlbut?"

"On the lam, sir," said the valet with punctilious politeness, "I gathered from his remarks that he faced a murder charge."

I nodded my head. That last remark was encouraging enough for me to forget the aching in my head.

"Do you know where he was tonight?" I asked. "Say, between five and seven?"

"Well, he came home about four o'clock. He made a telephone call. To a Mr. Wiltern, I believe. I think he went out to meet him."

My pulse picked up a beat. It actually began to look as if I was going to break a case, alone, personally, and unaided.

"What makes you think that?"

"I heard him make the appointment over the phone, sir. He said he'd see Mr. Wiltern without fail and at once."

Without daring to hope for another right answer to drop in my lap: "Was there any trouble between him and Wiltern, do you know? Any argument at any time? Were they enemies?"

He hesitated. I dragged out my shield. "This is murder," I reminded him. "A clean answer may save your being held in the can as a material witness."

He sighed and nodded his head. "I've heard him talk to Mr. Wiltern before over the phone. I've heard him use abusive language to him. Something about Mr. Wiltern's welching on a bet."

I mopped my brow and beamed like a searchlight. I'd often read of those coppers into whose laps fell completely solved mysteries. I had never believed it might happen to me.

Rather to the valet's surprise I wrung his hand fervently. I went to the phone and called Homicide. I told them with a degree of condescension that they had the wrong man in the Wiltern case. I gave them the name of the right one and hung up before they plied me with questions. Then I put my hat on and went home feeling as smug and righteous as Allhoff ever had. I slept that night like a happy corpse who has died pleasantly from rich living.

CHAPTER TWO
SQUALID MISSION

I **CLIMBED** the rickety staircase to Allhoff's tenement apartment. I pushed the door open, entered, and as I threw up the window wondered how it was that Allhoff had never heard of the benefits of fresh air.

A crisp breeze came reluctantly over the sill into the disorderly living room. The floor-boards held a veneer of dust and the sink was weighted with dirty dishes. The lid had fallen from the garbage pail and the atmosphere was redolent of ancient food about which cockroaches scurried happily

The door of the bedroom was ajar, revealing a disarrayed bed and a pile of laundry that crawled up the wall like amounting heaps of soiled snow. The master of this untidy realm sat at his desk, his chest against its edge and his nose buried deep in a cup of coffee.

On the left side of the desk a blackened coffee-pot gurgled dispiritedly on its electric base. Allhoff sucked the black liquid from his cup with the sound of a lost soul disappearing in a quicksand, then put his chipped cup down with a banging sound which was the key to the mood he was in this morning.

Battersly was already at his place as I sat down. He winked at me and appeared very pleased with himself. Feeling precisely the same way I winked back. Neither of us, however, spoke. It was tradition that nothing was ever said in this slum until Allhoff had ingurgitated at least one quart of the steaming octopus ink which he was pleased to call coffee.

A uniformed copper entered suddenly, saluted and handed Allhoff a sealed envelope. He spun around and got out quickly before Allhoff had a chance to speak, a tactic, for which I gave him a great deal of credit.

Allhoff refilled his cup and slit the envelope open. He glanced at the sheets of typewritten paper inside and grunted.

"It seems Maxwell Wiltern is dead," he announced. "The Commissioner wants me to look into it. It seems Homicide is holding someone but as usual they're not sure. Since the papers are bound to plaster anything about Wiltern all over the front page the Department needs a good case. So I draw it."

He grunted with satisfaction. Any opportunity to prove Homicide, or for that matter, anyone else wrong, was meat and drink to him. He scanned the reports carefully. I stood up, beaming like the lad in the advertisements who, by a judicious use of Baxbum's toothpaste, has at last managed to land the contract, and tapped Allhoff gently on the shoulder.

He swung his head around in his chair and regarded me as if I had just disembarked from a German submarine and landed on Ponte Vedra Beach. I returned his gaze blandly. I was about to hit him on the head with a figurative hammer by announcing that I had already turned up the killer in the Wiltern case.

Then, before I could speak Battersly had risen, slithered excitedly across the room and was speaking volubly.

"Inspector," he said," I already turned in the guy in the Wiltern case. I did a little snooping around last night. I nailed a guy with motive, who gains financially by Wiltern's death and who, apparently, was at Wiltern's house around the time of the murder."

ALLHOFF BLINKED and looked at Battersly rather like a man observing an unpleasant miracle. I remained silent, surprised and aware of a mild annoyance that, Battersly, too, had found out about Hurlbut.

"Now, this guy," went on Battersly, "was the beneficiary of a big insurance policy on Wiltern's life. Besides that, there was bad blood between them. Further, this guy phoned Wiltern a few hours before the murder and made an appointment to see him last night around six o'clock."

I nodded my head in happy corroboration as I watched Allhoff's expression of utter bewilderment not unmixed with rage that Battersly should dare take it upon himself to embark upon the solution of a murder case.

Allhoff glanced down at the typewritten report in his hand. Then he looked up at us again. He said in an odd repressed tone which should have warned me: "And what is this murderer's name?"

Again I opened my mouth to answer and again Battersly spoke before me.

"Waverly," said Battersly. "Harry Waverly. He's a newspaper man on the Herald."

"Wait a minute," I said. "You've got that wrong. It's Hurlbut. Dick Hurlbut, the bookmaker. He slugged me last night when I went to question him."

Allhoff looked from Battersly to me and the color was crawling slowly into his face like live steam into a red hot boiler.

"Well," he said, "make up your minds. Which one do we electrocute?"

Battersly and I exchanged confused glances. "He's made a mistake," I said, "on the name. I checked last night. I went to see Hurlbut. He slugged me making his getaway. The facts are the same. Battersly merely has the name wrong."

"Well?" said Allhoff, his hot little eyes on Battersly, who registered complete bewilderment.

"Why, Inspector, I know I'm right. I saw Wiltern's butler last night. He told me that Waverly had this insurance policy on Wiltern's life, that Wiltern was sore at him about something he wrote in the papers about him and that he had an appointment to see Wiltern last night. I tipped Homicide about it."

"And you," said Allhoff to me, "tipped Homicide about Hurlbut. Is that it?"

"Why sure I did. Naturally—"

Allhoff's hissing intake of breath interrupted me. His subsequent roar would have interrupted a barrage.

"Naturally," he bellowed. "Naturally, as a punishment for my more unmentionable iniquities I have been endowed with two of the stupidest assistants ever to exist. The Commissioner wants to know if this office has gone mad. It's turned in two killers of Wiltern. Battersly unearthed one, Simmonds has apprehended the other. Who told either of you to conduct private investigations? Why did you do it?"

I didn't answer. Battersly, not so tactful, said: "My mother was sure Homicide had the wrong man in Coller."

Allhoff achieved an expression which was a nice admixture of Vesuvius about to erupt and a munition dump about to explode. His voice hit a falsetto like a Stradivarius suffering a nervous breakdown.

"Your mother?" he shrieked. "Your mother thought he was innocent. Do I hear aright? Your mother?"

I came in desperately trying to empty drums of oil upon the raging waters.

"Coller's mother and Battersly's were old friends. Battersly wanted to look into the case. He asked my help, too. I got certain dope on Hurlbut. He got some more on Waverly. So we have two suspects instead of one. But we certainly ought to have enough to clear Coller."

Allhoff gulped a cup of coffee like a man who has come upon an oasis. As he slammed the cup down again he had regained a measure of control.

"On the contrary," he said. "Coller's in the same spot as your two suspects. No better, no worse."

I blinked and thought that over. "It doesn't seem possible," I ventured mildly. "It doesn't seem that Homicide has as good a case against Coller as we have against our two men, Waverly and Hurlbut."

"It has," said Allhoff. "Just as good. Precisely as good. To the penny. Coller was the beneficiary of a life insurance policy of Wiltern's. To the amount of fifty thousand dollars. So were the other two. Coller once had an affair with a girl of Wiltern's. They had harsh words. That's motive as well as the policy. Moreover, Coller phoned Wiltern last night, promised to meet him about the time of the murder. He has no one to attest to an alibi."

HIS VOICE died away and the only sound in the room was the monotonous drumming of Allhoff's dirty forefinger on the desktop. Battersly and I stared at each other. On the face of it the whole damned setup was absurd.

Battersly, Homicide and myself had all solved the Wiltern murder. We had three different prisoners. All with the same motives, the same amount of dough involved, apparently, and all of whom had planned to be at the scene of the killing at the time of the murder.

I scratched my head and sat down. I was now quite willing to let Allhoff take over.

"For God's sake," I said, "how do you figure it?"

"Yeah," echoed Battersly. "How?"

"Eh," snarled Allhoff with feral satisfaction. "Now you two Sherlocks come to me. So, for that matter, does Homicide. Well, I don't know who killed Wiltern. But I promise you, I will. And knowing the records of you two and Homicide to be wrong, I'll bet none of those three guys you've pinned it on, did it at all."

His cocksure manner settled me. "You've got a bet," I said. "How much?"

He looked at me for a moment and then his gaze fell on his depleted sugar-bowl. To Allhoff who used pounds of sugar a week rationing had come hard.

"Your sugar-book," he said. "For three months. Mine against yours."

"Done," I said. "You have a bet. Now what's the first move in the Wiltern murder case as you're handling it?"

Allhoff scanned once again over the report on his desk. "Wiltern's nephew, a tramp, I gather, Bob Newhall, is being sent over here by headquarters. We have a few questions to ask him. I'm also expecting a girl. Alice Darnell. It seems she was Wiltern's last fling. Anyway it appears she was the only woman he's been seeing since the doctors ordered him to lead a Christian life."

"When are they due?"

"Any minute. In the meantime, it seems, that Hurlbut hasn't been picked up yet. Waverly is held on suspicion and Coller's in the can."

Battersly shook his head. "I'm sure he's innocent, Inspector."

"I hope he is," growled Allhoff. "I hope he's so innocent that he can sue every copper on Homicide for ten grand and collect it."

He turned his head around, picked up his chipped coffee cup and thrust his corvine nose into its depths. Peace and quiet descended upon the office. They remained there for a quarter-hour, until the advent of Alice Darnell, Bob Newhall, and a fat pompous gentlemen named Weatherby, who it was announced was the attorney for Wiltern, the nephew and Miss Darnell.

MISS DARNELL, in a word, was terrific. Even Allhoff, who as a rule was as indifferent to sex as a harem guard, took his nose from his cup and stared at her. She was tall, blonde and startling. She possessed a pair of deep blue eyes which at times reminded you of a nun, at times of a madam. Her legs were so proportioned that they led one's thoughts directly to the gutter and her lips were a crimson invitation to deeds I am certain Battersly had never dreamed of.

He leaned forward in his chair and stared at her as she sat down, adjusted her skirt and crossed her legs. Newhall, thin, of middle height and about thirty, seated himself beside her. The lawyer fluttered over them both. He rubbed a pair of hands together and said oleaginously: "Anything my clients or myself can do, Inspector, we shall be glad to—"

"You can shut up," said Allhoff. Weatherby registered indignant pain. Allhoff, paying no attention to him, turned to the others.

"First," he said, "you, Newhall. You were on good terms with your uncle?"

Newhall nodded. "The best. We were pals. Never a hard word between us. He gave me everything I wanted. And more."

Allhoff filled his coffee cup. Battersly stared at Alice Darnell's legs. She smiled at him as if acknowledging his tribute. "Of course," continued Allhoff, "we can check that easily enough."

"Certainly," put in the lawyer. "The cancelled checks will prove it. Mr. Wiltern allowed his nephew twenty-five hundred dollars a month and wrote checks freely for anything else required. The bank statements will bear that out."

Allhoff grunted as if he didn't like it. For the life of me I couldn't see why he was hunting for another suspect when he already had two too many.

"All right," he said sullenly. "Now what about you, Miss Darnell?"

La Darnell took her eyes away from Battersly who by no means took his away from her legs, and met Allhoff's gaze reluctantly. It was obvious that she didn't like him, which, of course, wasn't stop press news. No one else did, either. However, Darnell did not dissemble. Her expression said quite plainly that Allhoff, to her, was a horrible little man.

"Well," she said ungraciously, "what about me?"

"You were Wiltern's last mistress, weren't you?"

The insult was gratuitous, but Darnell took it in her stride.

"That I don't know," she said. "I wasn't with him when he died."

Allhoff grunted again. "I suppose you're down for a hunk in his will?"

"I suppose I am," said Alice Darnell. "I might mention in that connection that I have a very lovely alibi."

"Besides," put in Weatherby, "Miss Darnell's position was much the same as Mr. Newhall's. Mr. Wiltern begrudged her nothing. She could have had many times the amount the will will give her for the asking."

Allhoff drained his coffee cup. From the murky expression of his eyes I knew he was annoyed. Apparently, he didn't like the way the interview was going.

Darnell looked over at Battersly again and generously lifted her skirts another two inches. Battersly blinked happily. Allhoff slammed his cup down on the desk and glared like a beacon.

"Miss Darnell," he said, his lips twisting angrily, "this is a murder investigation, not a shack in Cocoanut Grove, Panama. Battersly is a policeman, not a potential customer. Will you cover up your legs?"

Battersly jerked himself back to reality with a face as red as a cardinal's hat. Darnell stared at Allhoff coolly.

"I'll take care of my own morals, Inspector," she said evenly. "Besides, they are quite decent-looking legs. And even if they were thick and gnarled and ugly, I'll bet you wish you had them."

THE SILENCE in the room was clammy. I heard Battersly's sharp intake of breath. Weatherby fluttered his hands ineffectually and Newhall looked with a degree of admiration at Darnell. She had picked up the gauntlet flung by Allhoff and thrown it back full in his crimson face.

However, I felt no admiration. I was aware of a queasy sickening sensation at the pit of my stomach. I knew what was coming and the fact that I had witnessed the scene a hundred times before made it no easier to bear.

CHAPTER THREE
THE HATER

A LLHOFF OPENED his mouth and uttered an animal bark of rage. He put his hands on the edge of his desk and pushed so hard that his chair traveled halfway across the room on its rollers. As his torso moved away from the concealment of the desk it was seen that the torso was the better part of Allhoff.

Where his thighs should have begun were a pair of wooden stumps which now wriggled, beating furiously against the air. His hands hammered hard on the arms of his chair. His voice lifted up, crescendo, crashed against the roof and fell obscenely about our ears.

Harlot," he shrieked at Darnell. "Butcher," he howled at Battersly. "You yellow coward. You steal my legs then spend the rest of your life lustfully contemplating those of an immoral hussy. Insulted and mocked in my own home! Curse you both! I'll send you to the chair. I'll pin something on both of you. I'll—"

His mouth was like a machine-gun which had been loaded with pellets of mud. Panting and beating his chair with his clenched fists he screamed malediction down upon La Darnell and Battersly.

Battersly had risen. He stood with his back to the wall, figuratively and literally. His face was pale and a pitiful haunted expression shadowed his eyes. He avoided All-hoff's gaze. He epitomized guilt, conscience and misery.

Alice Darnell, on the other hand, was unmoved by Allhoff's frenzy. She regarded him with eyes that held a little of amusement, a little of contempt. A faint smile flickered over her full lips. Allhoff in the midst of a par-ticularly biological interlude, turned his head and saw her.

He broke off abruptly. "Get out, Jezebel! Get out, all of you! Now, at once! Scram!"

I hastened across the room and aimed the three of them at the door. Allhoff went on.

"You will pay for this insult, Madam. I swear it. There are black days ahead of you. There are—"

Darnell turned in the doorway. She stared at him coolly. "Black days?" she said. "You're a weather prophet, too, eh, Inspector? How do you do it? By the rheumatism in your legs? Or the tingling of your corns? I knew an old farmer once who—"

Allhoff's shriek of rage was an insane tremolo. Hastily, I thrust Darnell from the room, slammed the door behind her. Allhoff had swung around in his chair. Without missing a curse he had transferred his attention from Darnell to Battersly who stood up beneath the storm of epithet like a swaying, young sapling.

I poured a cup of coffee from the percolator. I waited until Allhoff was out of breath, then I thrust it swiftly into his hand. Gasping he held it to his lips, drained it. Then, panting and almost exhausted he drew his chair back to the desk and sat there, still, and staring bitterly at the scarred unpainted wall.

THE CHAINS of misery that held the three of us here had been forged several years ago when Allhoff was the youngest inspector on the force. He had led a squad, directed by a stool-pigeon, upon a raid on upper West End Avenue.

Battersly, a raw recruit at the time had drawn the assignment of effecting an entrance through the rear and closing with the thug who, we had been informed, operated a Tommy gun upon the staircase which commanded the front door.

Battersly had got in the house all right, but then with zero hour upon him he had developed a sudden, and not surprising case of nerves. Instead of leaping upon his man he had gone to pieces and sought refuge in the upper stories of the house.

The result of that moment's lapse was that Allhoff came charging in the front door at the head of his men to be greeted by a hail of machine gun bullets, most of which bit savagely into his legs.

Gangrene set in and of necessity amputation followed. In the normal departmental sequence of events, he would have been pensioned and that would have been the end of Allhoff. As it happened, it was but the beginning.

The Commissioner was of no mind to lose his best man, legs or no. Devious departmental bookkeeping devices arranged it so that Allhoff still drew his full salary. He had taken up his abode in this miserable slum primarily because it was just across the street from headquarters.

And the price of his acceding to the Commissioner's demands was that Battersly be given him as assistant. With too nice a sense of poetic justice the Commissioner had granted this request. And beginning at that point Allhoff had begun to extract his insane vengeance.

I always thought that when Allhoff lost his legs he lost part of his mind along with them. He was as forgiving as Genghis Khan. He lost no opportunity to needle Battersly, to remind him of that moment's cowardice of several years ago.

The situation was horrible and incessant. I had been detached from an idyllic desk job and sent over here, ostensibly to take care of the paperwork, actually, to act as oil-poured-on-troubled-waters when Allhoff's frenzy reached exploding point. It was a task I detested and would have quit long ago had it not been for the two vital facts of my family and my forthcoming pension.

THE FOLLOWING morning the coppers picked up Dick Hurlbut in Peekskill. They already had Waverly. And Coller, of course, was already in the can. Each of them told exactly the same story. That they had at one time or another quarreled with Wiltern. That the fact of his taking out insurance and naming them as beneficiaries was an absolute surprise to them.

That much I, and the rest of the force, was prepared to swallow. However, the last part of their story was too far-fetched for the police department. Each of them claimed that upon the day of the killing, they had received a message to call Wiltern, that when they had done so he had made an appointment with each of them for six o'clock, announcing that he might be late, and to wait, as it were of vital importance.

I related these facts to Allhoff as I culled them from a report which had been sent over from across the street. He seemed strangely uninterested.

"So what?" he asked. "It's all quite possible, isn't it?"

"Possible," I said. "But highly improbable. Do you know where those guys claim their appointments were?"

"I'll bet somewhere where alibis were entirely out of order."

I looked at him oddly. "That's right. Hurlbut was waiting alone in a hotel room, Coller on a subway station and Waverly at a remote corner in the Bronx."

"Well, said Allhoff. "It's all very interesting. But suppose we get to work and find out who killed Wiltern."

"You've got three suspects to work on," I told him. "Do you want some more?"

"Three hell," snapped Allhoff. "I have two. You get Battersly and go uptown. That Darnell broad lives at the Regal Hotel. I want you to get her out of the way and go through her apartment with a fine-toothed comb. When you've done that go over to Wiltern's joint. Look it over. Question the servants. Then come back here and tell me what you've found."

"And then," I said ironically. "You'll tell us who killed Wiltern?"

Characteristically, he took me quite seriously. "Quite probably," he said, "I shall."

Entering Darnell's apartment was simple enough. We waited behind a dispirited potted palm in the lobby until we saw Darnell go out, then we flashed a badge on an impressed maid and got ushered into the apartment via the skeleton-key route.

One glimpse of the flat and no doubt remained that old man Wiltern indulged Darnell to any extravagant limit. The furniture was magnificent. There were more furs around the palace than in an igloo. With splendid carelessness Darnell had left thousands of dollars in jewelry lying around on the bureau.

With one single and apparently unimportant exception there was nothing of any significance in the apartment. It was Battersly who found the yellow pawn ticket. He took it from a writing desk and brought it over to me.

"Sarge," he said. "This is sort of queer. That dame seems to have all the money in the world. Why would she be hocking a ring?"

I looked at the ticket he handed me. It stated that Alice Darnell had pawned a solitaire diamond for twenty-five hundred bucks yesterday afternoon. I thought it over for a moment then came to what I figured a simple solution.

"Probably Wiltern's death caught her short of dough. She hocked this to carry her over until the will's probated."

"Shall we take it down to the Inspector?"

"No. It doesn't mean anything."

We left Darnell's and journeyed in a taxi across town to Wiltern's triplex apartment. A butler, ancient, wavering and decayed admitted us. He was properly awed by our credentials and naturally garrulous. We pumped him dry, stopped off for a beer and returned empty-handed to Allhoff's slum.

ALLHOFF SIGHED his God-what-I-have-to-put-up-with sigh. "Look," he said, "suppose you're outside the emperor's palace in Tokyo and you suddenly hear that an

American has just assassinated Hirohito, would you take a powder?"

"What's that to do with it? I—"

"You shut up," said Allhoff. "First tell me about Wiltern's. Did you hear anything there?"

"Thousands of words," I told him. "All uttered by a senile and prolix butler and all about nothing."

"Tell me," said Allhoff. "Everything you can recall."

I shrugged my shoulders and quit. He invariably treated me as if I were a retarded half-wit who wouldn't notice a bloody knife at the scene of a murder.

Battersly carried on. "Oh, the butler told us a lot of stuff," he said. "All about how sick Wiltern was. How he—"

"What precisely was the matter with him?"

"Stomach ulcers," I said, "and cancer, which, of course, explains why he was killed. Some medical student wanting to look at an interesting stomach dashed in with a gun and shot him in the head. He was about to open him up with a razor blade when interrupted by—"

"Shut up, you fool! Go on, Battersly."

"Well, he was sick, see? But it seemed he must've been getting better because for the past few years he'd been living on Graham crackers and milk and stuff, but this night—the night he was killed, he ordered a big feed. Steak, potatoes, pie. So the butler figured he was getting better, see? So—"

Allhoff scribbled furiously on his desk pad. I watched him and seethed. He was impressing us. Pretending he saw mighty clues where we saw nothing. Where, as I figured it, there *was* nothing.

"Who was his doctor?" asked Allhoff. "Did you get his name?"

Battersly shook his head. Allhoff frowned, opened his mouth to call us several profane brands of idiots. But I spoke quickly, before his words were uttered.

"You can get that easily enough by phone." I told him.

He grunted, made another note, and signaled Battersly to continue. Battersly took up his rambling tale. Allhoff did not scribble or interrupt again until the story of the dog was reached.

TO ABRIDGE the butler's version considerably, it went like this: A long time ago the dog of a friend had bitten Wiltern. Three years later, Wiltern saw the dog again, remembered the bite and kicked the animal severely, breaking two of its ribs. The tale was calculated to impress us with Wiltern's relentlessness. I found it merely dull but Allhoff's eyes lit up and he scribbled furiously again. I decided on a slight needling process.

"So that's it," I said. "This dog had a sweetheart, a brooding bitch who never forgot the harm done her mate. She waited for years until she saved up enough dog biscuit to exchange for a gun. Then she sneaked up on Wiltern and blasted him. She—"

Allhoff's voice roared through the room like thunder. Even though I was prepared for it, I flushed at the term he used. However, I kept my mouth shut. After all, I'd asked for it.

"All right," he said at last. "That'll do on Wiltern. Now what about Darnell?"

"This time nothing at all," I said. "Not even the gabble of a butler. We went through the joint. We found nothing that even you could find significant."

Allhoff scowled. Battersly broke the silence saying, "Well, Sergeant, there was that pawn ticket."

Allhoff's eyes narrowed and he inhaled swiftly. "What pawn ticket?"

"For a ring," said Battersly. "I kinda thought it funny. She seemed to have so much dough, why should she hock a ring?"

"What sort of a ring?" barked Allhoff. "When did she hock it and for how much?"

"A diamond," I said. "Solitaire. For twenty-five hundred bucks and she hocked it yesterday, which, of course, explains how Wiltern was killed. The pawnshop keeper—"

Allhoff glared at me. "Give me one more theory," he said, "and I'll have you brought up on charges. Insubordination." I shut up. The Commissioner had a very bad habit of believing Allhoff.

Allhoff poured himself another cup of coffee. I noted that the hand which held the percolator trembled slightly. "A solitaire," he muttered. "Hocked yesterday. Steak and potatoes. Stomach ulcers. Good God."

I looked at him with distaste. If he got anything out of those three items I was prepared to eat them. Now, my case against Hurlbut—

"You mugs," said Allhoff suddenly. "Go back to Wiltern's. Look around again."

"What are we looking for?" I asked. "A written confession?"

"Look in the bathroom," said Allhoff. "Look around for anything poisonous. Look in the room where he was found shot. See if there's any weapon there. Anything that might be used to kill a man."

Both Battersly and I stared at him. "Have you gone completely wacky?" I inquired. "In the first place, Wiltern was shot, so why are we looking for poison? Second, why should the murder-weapon be hidden in the house if—"

"Third," yelled Allhoff, "why should they butcher steers and let you live? Get out. Do as I tell you!"

So we went back to Wiltern's. There was, I am happy to relate, no poison in the bathroom. There was no weapon in the study where Wiltern's body had been found, and short of the meat-cleaver in the kitchen there wasn't a lethal instrument in all the house.

I used Wiltern's phone to call Allhoff and tell him so. There was a long pause on his end of the wire. Then at last: "Are you sure, Simmonds? Have you looked everywhere?"

"Sure. We've looked everywhere."

"But there must be something. You must have missed somewhere. You—"

"We've missed nothing," I told him angrily. "The only weapon is a chair and he didn't die from being hit over the head with a piece of Chippendale. We've been through the house thoroughly. Even looked in the fireplace."

"Fireplace?" said Allhoff electrically.

"Yes, fireplace."

"My God, why didn't you tell me there was a fireplace? Look up the chimney. I'll hold the wire."

I put down the receiver and with Battersly's eyes on me, walked across the room and stuck my head into the fireplace. I twisted my neck around and peered up the chimney.

Then, I blinked, reached up, and seized the gun. It was a thirty-eight and I had some trouble pulling it out of the flue. Around its trigger-guard was attached a thick length of rubber, the other end of which was fixed to a spike driven in the bricks of the chimney. Finally I detached and removed it.

I went unhappily back to the phone and reported. All-hoff's shout of triumph was discord to my ears. But then Battersly who was examining the gun said something and my spirits picked up.

"Hold the wire," I said to Allhoff. "You'll be discouraged to know that Battersly's just looked the gun over. It's completely loaded and apparently never been fired."

"Why should I be discouraged?"

"Because if it hasn't been fired it can't be the murder weapon!"

"Well," said Allhoff, and there was honest surprise in his tone, "who in the name of God *expected* it to be the murder weapon?"

That one I couldn't answer, or even encompass.

"Bring it down here right away," said Allhoff. "And incidentally, I hope you have your sugar book with you."

I hung up and back we went to Allhoff's.

CHAPTER FOUR
THE CHIEF IS
MYSTERIOUS

THE NEXT day Battersly and I arrived simultaneously at the tenement. Allhoff, apparently, had been up for some time. I could tell by his bland manner that he had already imbibed at least a pint of coffee.

However, there was something in his mien I definitely did not care for. He wore a cocky air. I was very much afraid that he had something important on the Wiltern killing. I was even more afraid that it didn't concern Hurlbut, Waverly or Coller. In which event my wife was going to make a lot of trouble regarding the loss of several pounds of sugar.

Allhoff drained his coffee cup with the poise of an Army dredge draining a swamp and said too casually: "Well, I expect to clean up this mess today."

Battersly blinked. He said, hopefully: "Was it Waverly, maybe, Inspector?"

Allhoff shook his head.

"Hurlbut?" I asked.

Allhoff shook his head again. "Nor Coller," he said. "I just ordered Coller released. And Homicide is laying off those other two suckers as well."

I sighed and looked around the unkempt room. I noted, somewhat to my surprise that the bedroom door was shut. This was a most unusual circumstance. I wrinkled my brow and performed a simple feat of deduction.

I figured that he had arranged to interview Alice Darnell again. She had put him upon the defensive in their last engagement, so he wasn't leaving himself any wider open than necessary. Or perhaps there remained a vestige of shame in him insofar as he didn't want a woman to observe the chaotic filth of his boudoir.

When I heard footfalls on the stairs outside I was sure I was right, hence I was a little surprised when the door opened and Bob Newhall, accompanied by Weatherby, the lawyer, entered the room.

Weatherby said: "You sent for us?"

"I sent for Newhall," said Allhoff uncompromisingly. He emptied his cup, refilled it and looked around the room.

"In a case such as the killing of Maxwell Wiltern," he announced, "we must first consider the character of the victim. This Wiltern was something of a nut."

Weatherby frowned and Newhall bridled. "I resent that," he said.

"What you should resent," said Allhoff evenly, "is your own impatience. You should have waited another hour or so."

"Waited? For what?"

Allhoff ignored the question. He repeated: "Yes, Wiltern was a nut. Maybe he wasn't quite so screwy when he was painting Broadway red. But the fact of his leading a monk's life made him a bitter old man, brooding about his fancied wrongs. He hated certain people. He satisfied that hate in an odd manner.

"Take that story of the dog who once bit him. Wiltern remembered that for three years. Then he broke the animal's ribs. He was vindictive—patient, too. You didn't inherit that quality, did you, Mr. Newhall?"

Weatherby, Battersly and myself looked puzzled at this repetitious reference to Newhall's impatience. Newhall, it seemed to me, looked puzzled and worried.

"There were three men," said Allhoff, "whom Wiltern hated above all others. They were Coller, who once took a girl away from him, Hurlbut, the bookmaker who had won a lot of his money, and Waverly, the journalist who had held him up to ridicule in the press. Headed for the grave Wiltern was prepared to forgive everyone else he hated, but not those three. He cooked up a neat little plan not without overtones of ironic humor."

"Sure," I said sarcastically, "he left them all a pot full of money."

"Your perception is limited," said Allhoff icily. "Sure, he took out insurance in their favor—deliberately. The premiums meant nothing to him. It was all nicely diabolical. That gave each of them a financial motive for killing him.

In addition it could easily be established that they all disliked him. Moreover, he arranged it so that witnesses would testify that each of them had an appointment with him just before he died and that none of them had an alibi."

He paused and refilled his cup. All that he said was apparently true. But it wasn't enough. After all, Wiltern was dead, wasn't he? If my inkling of what Allhoff drove at was true, it implied that Wiltern had known he was going to die.

"So," said Allhoff, "Wiltern dies. Each of those three he hated is suspected of his murder. There is a good case against each of them. Moreover, each of the three insurance companies will fight like hell to see that the beneficiary on their policy is convicted so that they won't have to pay."

"Under the circumstances," put in Weatherby, "it is quite possible a court may rule that none of those policies are paid because each beneficiary is under suspicion of murdering Wiltern."

"Exactly," said Allhoff. "Wiltern figured that. He figured one or more of them might burn for killing him. They'd all have a damned unpleasant time, rendered even more so by the fight for all that dough, more dough than they ever dreamed of. Wiltern wanted to make those three guys miserable. It was foolproof."

"Wait a minute," I said. "It was wonderfully foolproof. But the fact remains that Wiltern is dead. Do you mean that he knew someone other than Coller, Waverly and Hurlbut was going to kill him? That's why he plotted so elaborately against them?"

"That's exactly what I mean."

"Then who did he figure was going to kill him?"

"Wiltern."

"Wiltern? You mean Wiltern was going to kill Wiltern?"

"Precisely," said Allhoff. He grinned.

Across the room Newhall exhaled loudly. "So that was it," he said. "My uncle killed himself. He *had* been quite despondent about his condition, you know."

"Easy," said Allhoff, "you're going a trifle too fast. Let us move on to that condemned man's meal Wiltern ate shortly before he died. His servant figured that Wiltern fell to upon a mess of rare steak and pie because he was getting better. I spoke, via phone, with Wiltern's doctor who assured me the contrary was true."

I reasoned that one out myself as Allhoff devoted a moment to gulping another pint of coffee.

"**YOU MEAN** that Wiltern's condition was hopeless? That eating a decent meal with his ulcers and cancer would cause him excruciating agony later? So he intended killing himself before the pain began?"

"Your perception improves," said Allhoff.

Newhall sighed again. "It's too bad," he said heavily. "He was a decent old guy-"

"But the gun," said Weatherby. "How could he commit suicide and dispose of the weapon in order that those three men would be suspected?"

"He had that worked out, too," said Allhoff. "He fastened a thick rubber band to the trigger guard of a revolver. It was his intention to blow his brains out. The rubber band would jerk the gun from his inert hand."

"Jerk it up the chimney," I said brightly. "The other end of the rubber was fastened to a spike driven into the bricks of the chimney. No one would think of looking up a chimney for a gun."

"Except me," said Allhoff.

"Those three men owe you a great debt, Inspector," said Weatherby. "You've cleared them. You've—"

"Wait a minute," said Battersly. "That gun in the chimney, Inspector. It hadn't been fired."

I felt like a congressman explaining why he voted as he did on the Conscription Bill. I am no Einstein, but never before had Battersly got in ahead of me. And it was seldom enough we had a chance to correct Allhoff.

Newhall frowned. "Then," said Weatherby, "Wiltern couldn't have killed himself. You're wrong, Inspector."

"I didn't say he killed himself," said Allhoff. "I said he intended to."

"Then, for the love of God," I said, "who *did* kill him?"

"Now," said Allhoff, "we come to the point of Mr. Newhall's impatience, his unfortunate impetuosity."

"Then *come* to the damned point," I said, irritated. "You've been evading it long enough."

Oddly enough he didn't even swear at me. "The point," he said. "The wonderful ironic point, is that Newhall killed his uncle just about half an hour before Wiltern intended to do the job himself."

THERE WAS momentary and complete silence in the room. Weatherby frowned and fluttered his hands. Battersly looked baffled. Newhall kept his eyes on Allhoff who returned his gaze with what I read as mockery.

"You're crazy," said Newhall suddenly. "Why should I kill him?"

Allhoff sipped coffee delicately like a shoat plunging its snout in a trough. "For money," he said between gulps.

"Ridiculous," said Weatherby. "Newhall had everything he asked his uncle for. That we can prove in any court."

"True," said Allhoff. "But he knew that Wiltern wouldn't live much longer and he wanted to ensure his getting all the money he wanted after his uncle was dead, too."

"That's even crazier," said Newhall, and I observed his voice was raised. "I was the sole heir."

"You were afraid you wouldn't be if your uncle had lived a few more days."

"Will you make yourself clear?" demanded Weatherby.

Newhall shook his head violently. "It's a lie," he yelled. "A frame. There must be a motive in a murder case. There is none here."

"Originally," said Allhoff, "the motive was known only to you and your victim. A little later, you realized that Alice Darnell would know it, too. So you told her. Now I know it. Miss Darnell responded to my questioning. So three of us know the motive now."

Newhall stared at Allhoff. "What are you talking about? What motive?"

"Why, the marriage motive. If Wiltern married Darnell, his money would go to her, his widow, not to you. You heard that he was about to marry her. So you fought with him about it. Then killed him before he could make an honest woman of her."

Newhall's chair scraped against the floor. He stood up and literally put his back against the wall.

"Damn you," he yelled. "She told you! She told you! She was the only one who knew. Well, she's in it with me. If she's sold me out I can sell her. She's an accessory after the fact. I'll drag her down with me. I'll—"

"Open the bedroom door," said Allhoff. "Bring her out."

BEWILDERED, I opened the bedroom door. I stood, astonished, on the threshold. Alice Darnell sat on Allhoff's bed. A dirty handkerchief was in her mouth. Handcuffs held her wrists to the bedstead and her ankles were tied to the radiator pipe that ran along the side wall. Her eyes were flecked with rage and hate as I released her.

But as she strode into the other room her glare was directed at Newhall, not Allhoff.

"You miserable stupid fool," she said. "You've talked yourself into the chair and me into prison."

"You told him," cried Newhall, almost hysterically. "You told him."

"I told him nothing."

Allhoff beamed complacently. Newhall, pale as carded wool, said: "You must have. How did he know?"

"He probably figured it out somehow. Everyone isn't as stupid as you."

"Indeed not," said Allhoff looking like a bear who has come upon a honey cache. "Yet it was partly your fault, Miss Darnell."

Darnell turned her eyes on him, and they glared like forest fires.

"Yes," said Allhoff. "If Newhall was impatient, I'm afraid your cupidity got the better of you."

She stared at him silently.

"Yes," said Allhoff. "You told Newhall that Wiltern had promised to marry you, had given you an engagement ring. Of course he only did it to shut you up. He had no intention of marrying. He intended merely to die. However, Newhall charged him with it, they fought and Newhall shot him. He realized, then, that though the motive would be unknown to anyone else, it would be transparent to you. Hence, he was forced to confide in you. What did he offer? Half the estate?"

"A third," said Darnell dully. "I'll talk. I want to see the D.A. I'll make a deal."

"You had to get rid of your engagement ring," said Allhoff as if she hadn't spoken. "You should have hidden it, or tossed it in the East River. But you like money too much. You wanted cash for it. You hocked it. I found the ticket. From there on it was easy figuring."

"How?" I asked.

"Obviously Darnell didn't need the cash. Wiltern was liberal with her. There was more valuable jewelry in her flat and she hocked it the day after he gave it to her. An odd thing to do with an engagement ring. There was only one answer and I arrived at it."

"I want the D.A.," said the girl. "I'll make a deal."

Allhoff looked at her and the hatred in his yellow eyes was hotter, more furious than the rage in hers.

"You're an accessory after the fact," he said. "You can burn as well as Newhall."

"If you were the D.A. and the jury I would. As it is he'll need a witness. I'm it. I'll take a prison rap, thank you."

Allhoff shook his head sadly as if the thought of Alice Darnell in prison rather than in the chair was a particularly gloomy thought.

"I suppose you're right," he said. "Battersly, take them both across the street and book them."

Battersly stood up. He took Darnell's arm reluctantly. They walked toward the door, where Battersly grabbed Newhall's coat sleeve.

THEY WERE almost at the stairhead, when Allhoff called: "Battersly."

The trio halted. Battersly said: "Sir?"

"When that woman climbs the steps to headquarters take a good look at her legs. It's probably the last time you'll ever see them. Certainly it's the last time you'll see them in silk and without calluses on the knees from washing prison floors. And when she comes out she'll be old, unable to attract men. She'll probably starve to death, take to drink and finish in the gutter. Take a last look at the body, Battersly. I'm glad she's going to live, after all! Glad! Glad!"

His horrible laughter followed them down the stairs. I said, more to distract him than anything else: "How did that girl get in your bedroom? You know you broke at least three laws holding her there by force."

"My emotions got the better of me for once. I had to break one of them down. I knew Newhall would be easier than the girl but I wanted the satisfaction of cracking her. Well, she wouldn't break. Newhall was due any minute and I didn't want her to talk to him first, stiffen him up. I had nothing to put her in the can for, so at the point of a gun I tied her up myself where she could hear Newhall break down."

I shook my head. "You hate everybody, don't you?"

"No more than they hate me," he said bitterly. For a moment he was silent, morose. He brightened suddenly. "You," he said, "bring me two pounds of sugar tomorrow. And on every ration day thereafter."

He was silent for another moment then became even more bright. "I'd like to see you explaining that to your wife," he said, and laughed uproariously.

I bit my lip. I would have sooner faced a hold-up gang than my wife's wrath when she discovered I'd gambled away the sugar for three months.